Outstanding Praise for the Novels of T. Greenwood

Undressing the Moon

"This beautiful story, eloquently told, demands attention."
—*Library Journal* (starred review)

"Greenwood has skillfully managed to create a novel with unforgettable characters, finely honed descriptions, and beautiful imagery."
—*Book Street USA*

"A lyrical, delicately affecting tale."
—*Publishers Weekly*

"Rarely has a writer rendered such highly charged topics . . . to so wrenching, yet so beautifully understated, an effect . . . T. Greenwood takes on risky subject matter, handling her volatile topics with admirable restraint. . . . Ultimately more about life than death, *Undressing the Moon* beautifully elucidates the human capacity to maintain grace under unrelenting fire."
—*The Los Angeles Times*

The Hungry Season

"This compelling study of a family in need of rescue is very effective, owing to Greenwood's eloquent, exquisite word artistry and her knack for developing subtle, suspenseful scenes. . . . Greenwood's sensitive and gripping examination of a family in crisis is real, complex, and anything but formulaic."
—*Library Journal* (starred review)

"A deeply psychological read."
—*Publishers Weekly*

"Can there be life after tragedy? How do you live with the loss of a child, let alone the separation emotionally from all your loved ones? T. Greenwood with beautiful prose poses this question while delving into the psyches of a successful man, his wife, and his son. . . . This is a wonderful story, engaging from the beginning that gets better with every chapter."
—*The Washington Times*

Turn the page for more outstanding
praise for the novels of T. Greenwood.

Two Rivers

"From the moment the train derails in the town of Two Rivers, I was hooked. Who is this mysterious young stranger named Maggie, and what is she running from? In *Two Rivers*, T. Greenwood weaves a haunting story in which the sins of the past threaten to destroy the fragile equilibrium of the present. Ripe with surprising twists and heart-breakingly real characters, *Two Rivers* is a remarkable and complex look at race and forgiveness in small-town America."

—Michelle Richmond, *New York Times* bestselling author of
   The Year of Fog and *No One You Know*

"*Two Rivers* is a convergence of tales, a reminder that the past never washes away, and yet, in T. Greenwood's delicate handling of time gone and time to come, love and forgiveness wait on the other side of what life does to us and what we do to it. This novel is a sensitive and suspenseful portrayal of family and the ties that bind."

—Lee Martin, author of *The Bright Forever* and *River of Heaven*

"The premise of *Two Rivers* is alluring: the very morning a deadly train derailment upsets the balance of a sleepy Vermont town, a mysterious girl shows up on Harper Montgomery's doorstep, forcing him to dredge up a lifetime of memories—from his blissful, indelible childhood to his lonely, contemporary existence. Most of all, he must look long and hard at that terrible night twelve years ago, when everything he held dear was taken from him, and he, in turn, took back. T. Greenwood's novel is full of love, betrayal, lost hopes, and a burning question: is it ever too late to find redemption?"

—Miranda Beverly-Whittemore, author of *The Effects of Light* and
   the Janet Heidinger Kafka Prize–winning *Set Me Free*

"Greenwood is a writer of subtle strength, evoking small-town life beautifully while spreading out the map of Harper's life, finding light in the darkest of stories."

—*Publishers Weekly*

"T. Greenwood's writing shimmers and sings as she braids together past, present, and the events of one desperate day. I ached for Harper in all of his longing, guilt, grief, and vast, abiding love, and I rejoiced at his final, hard-won shot at redemption."

—Marisa de los Santos, *New York Times* bestselling author of
   Belong to Me and *Love Walked In*

"*Two Rivers* is a stark, haunting story of redemption and salvation. T. Greenwood portrays a world of beauty and peace that, once disturbed, re-verberates with searing pain and inescapable consequences; this is a story of a man who struggles with the deepest, darkest parts of his soul, and is able to fight his way to the surface to breathe again. But also—maybe more so—it is the story of a man who learns the true meaning of family: *When I am with you, I am home.* A memorable, powerful work."
  —Garth Stein, *New York Times* bestselling author of
    The Art of Racing in the Rain

"A complex tale of guilt, remorse, revenge, and forgiveness . . . Con-vincing . . . Interesting . . ."
  —*Library Journal*

"In the tradition of *The Adventures of Huckleberry Finn* and *To Kill a Mockingbird*, T. Greenwood's *Two Rivers* is a wonderfully distinctive American novel, abounding with memorable characters, unusual lore and history, dark family secrets, and love of life. *Two Rivers* is the story that people want to read: the one they have never read before."
  —Howard Frank Mosher, author of *Walking to Gatlinburg*

"*Two Rivers* is a dark and lovely elegy, filled with heartbreak that turns itself into hope and forgiveness. I felt so moved by this luminous novel."
  —Luanne Rice, *New York Times* bestselling author

"*Two Rivers* is reminiscent of Thornton Wilder, with its quiet New England town shadowed by tragedy, and of Sherwood Anderson, with its sense of desperate loneliness and regret. . . . It's to Greenwood's credit that she answers her novel's mysteries in ways that are believable, that make you feel the sadness that informs her characters' lives."
  —*Bookpage*

BOOKS BY T. GREENWOOD

The Hungry Season

Two Rivers

Undressing the Moon

Nearer Than the Sky

Breathing Water

UNDRESSING
the MOON

T. Greenwood

KENSINGTON BOOKS
www.kensingtonbooks.com

KENSINGTON BOOKS are published by

Kensington Publishing Corp.
119 West 40th Street
New York, NY 10018

ISBN-13: 978-0-7582-3876-4
ISBN-10: 0-7582-3876-2

First Kensington Trade Paperback Printing: October 2010
10 9 8 7 6 5 4 3 2 1

Printed in the United States of America

For my grandmothers . . .
and for Janet

ACKNOWLEDGMENTS

Thank you (as always) to Christy Fletcher for really listening to my voice. To Ron and Bradi Ross for the necessary lyrics. To Samantha Ruckman, Beya Stewart, and Whitney Lee for pointing out the sour notes, and to Julia Pastore for fixing them. To my family, my best audience. And to Patrick, my breath.

Things break. I've come to terms with that in my own strange way. I realize that there are things that will hurt us and things that will keep us safe; that sometimes it's hard to discover the line between them, and that sometimes they are the same thing.

—Kevin Wilson
from "A World of Glass," *Oxford American,*
September/October 1999

S he was always at the edge of leaving.

Cattails stand guard along the banks of the Pond. I am six years old, and I cannot swim. The cattails keep me safe. The air is so thick with summer it's hard to swallow; it's even hard to breathe tonight. I lift my hair off my neck, twist it into a knot, and pray for a breeze. But the air is still, and I am alone, waiting for my mother to come back. I can hear the sucking sound of her bare feet in the mud as she circles the water's edge, but I can barely see her in the waning light of the moon. Besides, she is moving too quickly to hold on to for very long.

I try not to think of Daddy maybe waking. Maybe standing in his gray slippers on the back porch, peering out into the starless night, wondering where she has gone. It makes me sad, the way he stands with his hands in his pockets, staring after her, whenever she leaves. His face turns the color of gravel even if she is only going to the grocery store. He might not see the note she left, perched between two bananas in the fruit bowl, saying that we were only going to look for the moon. He might think that this is the last time. That this time it's for good.

There is supposed to be a lunar eclipse tonight, and my mother explains it the way she explains shadows and thunder—without science or words too big for me to repeat or understand. It will just disappear, she says. Slowly. Like pulling a dark dress over its pale face.

I look up at the sky and watch as this happens: I'm struggling to hold on to the vague outline that is my mother as she wades deeper into the water. Panic is thicker than heat. I look for her, thinking of

Daddy's pockets, as she and the sliver of moon both disappear. I know she will come out again, wet and slippery and shivering. Like last time, like every other time, but there is always this terrible moment when I am unsure, when everything bad is possible.

And even after she finds me waiting for her and we start walking quietly back to the house, I am still afraid. Because strangely, on this still night, what scares me almost as much as my mother's ability to disappear is the absence of light. And I wonder, without my mother, who would undress the moon.

ONE

When you know you are dying, things begin to make sense. In the surprising bright light moment of one more day (stolen or granted, you don't know which), there is suddenly coherence where chaos used to reside, clarity where there once was confusion. When you lift your arms, amazed that they still work, and see your familiar face reflected—remarkably—in your bathroom mirror, coincidence promptly becomes destiny. And when you open your mouth and your own voice comes out, *still here,* every chance meeting and every decision you've ever made now seem serendipitous. Because everything you've ever done or said has led you to this moment. Right here.

That is why I am not surprised that on the very day I decide to stop my chemotherapy, a letter arrives from my mother. It is fitting. Serendipity.

My best friend, Becca, who has been sleeping on my couch lately, looks forward to the mail's arrival. This isn't even her house, but when she hears the mail truck pull up every afternoon, she rushes first to the window and then down my steps to meet the mailman. She knows him by his first name, and today I watch them talking on the sidewalk. She takes the small bundle of mail directly from him before he has a chance to stuff it into my mailbox, and then I hear her skipping up the steps two at a time.

"Phone bill, gas bill, Spiegel flyer, and another letter from your mum." She lays each piece of mail on my kitchen table like a Tarot card, resting the letter from my mother across the phone bill. With her long red hair wrapped up in a precarious knot, she could be a carnival fortune-teller.

"Will you *read* this one?" she asks.

I wrap my robe and my arms around my waist and shake my head.

This is the twelfth letter I have received from my mother in the last three years, since I found out I was sick: one for each season. I keep them in the back of my closet, in a shoe box that used to hold a pair of shoes I don't even own anymore. All the envelopes are the same size, though her handwriting varies depending on the season. In springtime, it is thin like bare branches. In winter, the ink is heavy and thick, my name and address a blanket of words. In summertime, she uses colored ink, each return address the color of somewhere else's summer. Impermanent. Wandering. It is autumn now, and today her words are only veins running through the middle of a fallen leaf. Sometimes the envelopes are as thin as a single sheet of paper; other times they are thick with whatever is inside.

"I wish you'd at least open it," Becca says, sitting down at the table where she has put a pile of her students' papers. "It couldn't hurt to *open* it."

I look at Becca as she thumbs through the stack of essays, absently licking her thumb when the pages stick.

"Not today," I say.

But I keep thinking about the letter that night after Becca goes back to school for parent-teacher conferences. I even leave it lying on the table the way she arranged it with her gypsy hands, thinking now that it likely would reveal more about my past than my future. And later, after the streetlights come on outside and after I have fixed Bog's dinner, I sit with my feet curled under me on the couch and hold the letter to the light, wondering what would happen if I didn't put this one away, thinking about how my life might change.

I haven't seen my mother since I was fourteen years old. And after she left my world fell apart. Everything that happened from the moment I knew she was gone until this moment, until now, has made me who I am. And who I am now is a thirty-year-old girl, body ravaged by a woman's disease. But somehow everything about this is logical. It makes sense. Dying can be a comforting thing to someone accustomed to chaos.

Finally, I carefully tear the end of the envelope open and spill its contents onto my lap.

I should have known there wouldn't be a letter inside. No words, only slivers—that was always her way. With tentative fingers, I reach down and carefully pick up the scarlet piece of glass.

If summer here were made of colored glass, this is the way the light would shine through the summer I turned fourteen: new leaves the green of dreams, fat June bugs' metallic wings, and the color of breeze. *Not spring.* By early June, the mud of the dirt road leading from our house to the lake had dried up, leaving a path of quartz and mica under bare feet, shiny enough to make you imagine that diamonds instead of fool's gold were piercing your winter skin. I picked the rocks up in handfuls and let the sun pour through my fists.

The road to the lake from our house was a corridor of green and sunlight, and after the two-mile walk there was this: a yellow sail, the red hint of a lost kite, and the blue, blue of watery summer. Azure lake, white at the shore, and silvery fish. It was clean and bright here, not like at the murky Pond with its sawdust bottom near our house. Here the shores were made of grass instead of dirt, and you could swim for hours without getting an earache. The sepia colors of the dark woods where we lived became brilliant, alive here, and that summer I wore bits of purple in my newly pierced ears.

The clarity of that summer is striking to me now. It seems that it would be clouded by everything that happened afterward, but instead it hangs in my memory like a strand of colored glass beads: each bead a small gem, moments stolen and then strung together. Vivid. And intact. I keep it somewhere safe now, in a place where no one can find it, going over the beads like a rosary when I can't sleep. And in my hands are the fragile remnants of the last summer that I believed the world to be a kind place. The last summer that I could see promise in something as simple as the curve of the moon. The last summer that I believed I knew my mother.

My mother was an artist. That wasn't her word; it was mine. But she was. She told people she was a housewife, a stay-at-home mom. And who would question that? She had a convincing story, and proof: no job, two children, and weathered hands. She was reluctant to talk about what she really did with her time. To strangers, especially. But inside our home, we knew the magic she was capable of. To my brother, Quinn, and me, she was not only a mother but a sorceress. She made life incredible in a place that was otherwise unbearable. That is why my father loved her. And why I wanted to become her someday.

The shed behind our house was where she worked. There was only one bare bulb hanging down from a cord in the middle of the room, but sometimes she would stay in there until long past dark. I could see the shed light from my bedroom window, hear the music coming from the little radio she kept in there. It wasn't a proper place for an artist; there was no heat in the winter other than the small electric space heater, and no real way to keep cool in the summer. But she never complained. It was her place in the world, she said. She didn't even mind the dirt floor or the leaky roof. The smell of rotten wood or the one smudged window.

She was a collector of glass: fractured pieces she gathered from the shores of Lake Gormlaith, the town dump where Daddy worked, and other people's trash. And in her shed, she transformed the slivers into stained-glass panels that hung in every window of our house. She never bought the glass; there were so many things already broken here. Beer bottles break when thrown; so do glasses and vases and lamps. Windows shatter with angry fists. Debris is easy to come by in a place where people are sad.

We lived two miles up the road from Lake Gormlaith, away from the *Vermont Life* pictures of serenity and summer homes and ascending loons, deep in the woods where some people still managed without plumbing. We lived among people whose poverty could be seen in the length of their faces, in their tired speech, and in the heaviness of their eyes. Everyone here was hungry. Everyone here knew too much about pain.

There was a time before, when Daddy and most of our neighbors worked at the furniture factory in Quimby, turning trees into pulp and pulp into plywood desks and nightstands and entertainment centers. There was money enough then for Sunday breakfasts at the Miss Quimby Diner, new shoes from Payless, even a trip down to Boston or Atlantic City every couple of years. But when the furniture factory closed down, the men didn't have anywhere to go during the day anymore. There were no jobs to go to. Arguments exploded like gunshots in these woods, where there used to be only the silence of water. And when people weren't yelling at each other, you could still hear the hushed angry whispers rushing through the tops of the trees. Desperate anger. Anger made out of empty pockets and empty refrigerators and empty promises. And so my mother gathered our neighbors' destruction and made it into something good. She rearranged their fury into transparent miracles that needed only a little light to come alive. She kept the shards in an old card catalog in the shed, each wooden drawer labeled by hue. By degree. Each row was a different color, and the first row was red. *Poppy, ruby. Scarlet, crimson, maroon. Burgundy. Carmine* and *wine.* Who knew there were so many shades of anger?

Daddy was lucky. When he lost his job at the factory, he found a new one right away at the landfill in Quimby, collecting money from the summer people who brought tidy bags of coffee grounds and banana peels in from their rented camps at Lake Gormlaith. By July, every camp on Gormlaith would be full, and the summer people made enough garbage to keep Daddy busy ten hours a day: mildewed bathing suits, broken water skis, watermelon rinds. Corn husks and inner tubes. In the summer, he came home smelling like other people's garbage, but sometimes he would bring my mother some shimmering thing he'd found poking out of a trash bag, or buried under a pile of dirty diapers. He'd polish the pieces as if they were gems and offer them to her in the same way.

Of course, there was pain in our house, too. I would have had to be blind not to notice the sad way he extended his hand to her, and the reluctant way she accepted. I would have had to be deaf not to hear their careful arguments at night. My father's job at the dump was a seasonal one. We all knew that summer would eventually end, and as much as we despised the summer people, we relied on them. Soon enough they would return to their real homes in New York and Connecticut and Boston, taking their money and their trash with them. The end of summer was a desperate time, even for us. I knew that instead of shopping for new school clothes, I'd have to pick through the summer people's leftovers dropped off at my aunt Boo's thrift shop. I knew that Daddy's fingers would be blackened by newsprint, the classified ads preserved in piles all over the house. That my mother's words would become careful, that all of us would have to move gingerly, until he found a winter job.

The first couple of years after the furniture factory closed, he worked pumping gas at a friend's station, but it closed down when the big Shell station opened across the street. This year, he didn't know where he would be working. Quinn had taken a job at the Shop-N-Save as soon as he turned sixteen. But despite my mother's pleas to *please* let her help, to let her find a

job in town waiting tables or at one of the shops, Daddy insisted that she stay home, that he could do enough. He said
that he would give her the world he'd promised when she first
loved him. And this made her angry. In my room, I held a
heavy pillow over my head so their words couldn't find me.
The slivers here weren't made of glass but of her sighs and his
tears. But my mother was a magician, and she could mend
things.

What I choose to remember, the beads my fingers linger
on, are these: The days when Daddy and Quinn were at work
and my mother belonged to me. The days that we went hunting. We made picnic lunches (cream cheese and cucumber
sandwiches, bottles of Orange Crush or lemonade) and walked
for hours, waiting for the sun to catch in the blue or green of
something broken. Of course, sometimes we could walk all day
without finding anything; sometimes the beach held nothing
for us but tangled fishing lines, a soggy shoe, wet plastic bags.
But other times, we'd find piles of glass in the road, the glori-
ous remnants of an accident. Or a perfect piece of cobalt that
used to be a wineglass. Those days, we felt like explorers or pi-
rates, and we would sit down under a tree and eat our junk-
food picnic as if we had been journeying for days without
food, counting the shattered pieces like medallions of gold.

Sing for me? she would ask later as we lay, bellies full and
brown, on the blanket she had spread by the water.

And as I sang, she would close her eyes. Sometimes it
scared me, how far away she seemed, as if my own voice could
send her away. But when I stopped, when I swallowed the only
beautiful thing I knew how to make, her eyes would flicker
open again, and she would return to me.

She was already further away than any of us knew.

In the evenings, she would put together the pieces we had
found.

"Look," she said.

I had tiptoed outside, past my father snoring softly on the couch, and past our dog, Sleep, who was doing just that on the front porch, to the shed. It was July, and the air was loud with crickets and the distant sounds of fireworks. The Fourth of July wasn't for two more days, but the summer people were impatient.

It was so warm I didn't need the sweatshirt I had grabbed on my way out. The door to the shed was open and light spilled onto the wet grass. I could see my mother's shadow moving across the walls inside.

I knocked softly on the open door and peered in at her. She held up one of her stained-glass panes to the bare bulb. "Look."

The glass was indigo: not quite black, not blue. But beyond that confused color was the certainty of ruby and emerald and amber. The verity of red and green and yellow, an explosion of color, but still perfectly intact.

Outside, the air cracked and burned with Roman candles. And as I sat on the wobbly stool while my mother worked, I thought about the possibility of explosion. About calmness, and sudden detonation. Watching her hands work across the broken pieces, I felt almost sick with appreciation, but there was no way to tell her how much I needed her.

That night after I crept back into the house, nearly tripping over Sleep's long body in the kitchen, the sickness stayed with me. It settled in my stomach and shoulders all through the night. If I'd been able to articulate the feeling, I might have realized that I missed her. Already, and she wasn't even gone.

The next day was brilliant and we walked to the lake to lie in the sun. The grassy place near the boat-access area was littered with empty fireworks shells, burnt at the edges and quiet.

Mum spread a threadbare cotton sheet across the softest patch of grass at the shore, kicked off her flip-flops, and pulled her legs under her, Indian style. She shielded her eyes from the sun and looked across the impossible expanse of blue, unbroken by motorboats or sails that day.

A pair of loons had nested at the opposite shore earlier in the summer and we'd watched them after their child was born, teaching the brown downy adolescent how to fish. But today the couple swam and cackled at each other, and the child was nowhere to be found.

"Where's the baby?" I asked, concerned that some irate fisherman had felt threatened by the bird's ability to find fish in the depths of the lake when he, himself, went home empty-handed. It had happened so many times before that now signs all along the lake warned that the loons were a protected species.

"They've probably left him alone. That's how they teach him independence. He's probably at the other end of the lake."

"Alone?" I asked, horrified.

"They'll go get him in a little bit. He's okay, Piper. He's just growing up." She reached into the bag she'd packed and handed me a cold sandwich, wrapped in wax paper. "It's meatloaf, with mustard." She smiled. Only she knew that cold meatloaf sandwiches were my favorite. She had probably even saved the last piece, hiding it in the back of the refrigerator, safe from Daddy and Quinn.

I unwrapped the sandwich carefully, like a gift, and ate it slowly, trying not to think about the baby loon alone on the other side of the lake, protected by the law but not by his own parents.

In the summer, we didn't worry about what would happen when winter descended. In the summer we didn't worry about money. About food in the cupboards or that my feet were growing so fast I would need new boots again once snow fell. In the summer, it was just me and my mother, searching for broken treasures in the mud.

The clarity of that summer still surprises me. Sunlight

struggling through the green of new leaves. The marbled pink of a sunburn, and tumblers filled with lemonade. I suppose the sunshine might have blinded me a little. With the beads of sunlight in my fingers, even now, I skip over the ones made of milky glass, the gray beads that would not let the light come through.

These were the days when Daddy didn't go to work. The *migraine days*. The days when he closed his eyes and saw falling stars. On those days, Mum didn't seem to know what to do. Normally, we would have walked to the lake or through the woods to the Pond, where some of the best glass lay buried in dank mud. But with Daddy home, lying on the couch with a cool cloth pressed against his temples, she stood in doorways, looking lost. On the migraine days, the TV was always on: game shows, soaps, talk shows. She pretended to be absorbed in programs I knew she had never watched before. She jumped every time the phone rang, because once when someone tried to sell her life insurance, Daddy grabbed the phone out of her hand and demanded, *Who is this?* When Daddy was home, we didn't go hunting, because every time she walked near the door, Daddy would reach for her, asking, *Where are you off to?* And then she wouldn't go anywhere. Not to the lake for picnics. Not even to the shed to work. But then Daddy's migraine would disappear, as quickly as it came, and he would go back to work. When he was gone, the light returned, and I had my mother back again. I had the green of grass after rain, the soft orange of peaches in a basket, and the violet of the sky outside my night window. If summer here were made of colored glass, this one would be made of *emerald, topaz, amethyst*. I suppose the sunlight blinded me a little, to the dark days.

On these days, the gray days, I could see the worry in her face and in her hands. I could hear it just under the surface of her voice. At night I listened to their whispers, pretended that their voices belonged to crickets, to bullfrogs, to loons.

★   ★   ★

"We're going to Quimby today," she said one morning in early August.

"Hmmmm." I nodded. I was busy pushing scrambled eggs across my plate, thinking about how I might ask her for a new pair of jeans for school. I had grown five inches since last summer; I was almost as tall as Daddy, and my clothes didn't fit anymore. But today was the first day in two weeks that Daddy had gone to work. We didn't have any money for new jeans.

"Piper?"

I looked up from my plate.

She was standing in front of the sink in her nightgown, and the sun was shining through the sheer fabric. Inside the giant nightie, I could see how small she was. It embarrassed me. I looked back down at my plate.

"I think I'll bring some of my pictures to the artists' gallery," she said softly, like a question.

I looked up again. She was running her fingers across the counter. Nervous.

"You should!"

"You think?" she asked. "Maybe the summer people might buy them?"

I imagined my mother's glass pictures hanging in strangers' homes. Filling windows in high-rises, the way they might change the yellow glow of a street lamp into something cool and green.

That afternoon I helped her gather her stained-glass panes and we took them to the artists' gallery in Quimby. While she met with the owner in the back office, I wandered through a labyrinth of jewelry and sculptures, quilts and paintings. I was amazed by so much beauty in one place and wondered what it would feel like to be able to buy something. To reach into my pocket and pull out enough money for the velvet crazy quilt. How it might look spread across my old bed.

Mum was smiling when she emerged from the back room. The handsome owner of the shop had his hand on her back. When she saw me, she smiled shyly. She blushed when he wrote her a check for the pieces, and she squeezed my hand tightly as we walked back to the car. At the Miss Quimby Diner, she said, "Order anything you want. Anything!" We got hamburgers and French fries smothered in gravy. I'd never tasted anything more wonderful. On the way home, I could still taste the salt on my lips. We rolled the windows down and sang, together, at the tops of our lungs.

But when she told Daddy that night at dinner, when she handed him the check, he was silent. Quinn stared at his plate and disappeared into his room right after dinner. I didn't know what to do with myself in all that quiet, and finally, reluctantly, I left them alone. Later, the words that crept under my door (*trust* and *cheat* and *whore*) wound their way into my dreams. He asked her, in whispers like pins, *Do I have to watch you twenty-four hours a day?* And I squeezed my eyes shut and tried to imagine what would happen to us if he never left the house again. The next day he got a headache that didn't go away for a week.

A month later, my mother had stopped getting out of bed in the mornings. I knew she was awake, listening to hear Daddy either getting ready to leave or clicking on the TV and settling onto the couch for another headache day. In my own room, I was doing the same. Quinn was the only one of us who seemed real anymore. While the rest of us wandered about the house like ghosts, Quinn went to work every morning, and he came home every night with stolen milk from the Shop-N-Save, eggs, and packages of sliced cheese so that we would have something to eat besides the contents of the dusty cans that had been in our cupboards since last winter.

One morning, after Daddy hadn't gone to work in three days, I thankfully awoke to the familiar sounds of his work boots shuffling across the linoleum, and the sound of Quinn cracking his back, twisting first left and then right. And finally, the rattle of the truck disappearing down the road with the two of them inside. I waited until I couldn't hear his tires crushing gravel anymore and then I crawled out of bed.

Summer was almost over, but the air was still hot. Sticky and stifling. I had taken to sleeping in one of my mother's old slips to stay cool, and in the kitchen, in my mother's tattered lingerie, I poured the last of the coffee into a mug. I wasn't supposed to drink coffee, but today I didn't care. I kicked the screen door open and went outside. Sitting on the rusty porch swing in my mother's slip, drinking the forbidden coffee, I pretended things weren't falling apart. That it was just another summer day. But my mother would not get out of bed, and there were clouds caught in the tops of the trees.

Inside, I walked tentatively down the short hallway to the door to Mum's room and peeked in.

"Morning." She smiled, rolling over to look at the clock.

I sat down on the bed, and she reached for me with her little hands, motioning for me to lie down next to her. Sometimes lately I'd felt as if she were the child; she was so small. But when I lay down next to her and she put her fingers in my hair, I was the little one again.

"Is it nice out?" she asked. Her breath was musty. I knew what she meant was, *Is he gone?*

"It will be. It's cloudy, but it'll burn off."

"Promise?"

I nodded.

"What do you want to do today?" she asked.

I shrugged. She hadn't wanted to do anything for weeks, and I didn't want to get my hopes up.

"I told Gray's sister I'd help her clean out the rest of his house. She said we can take anything we want."

Gray Wilder had been our closest neighbor, about a quarter-mile down the road from us, near the Pond. He had died that spring. He was the first dead person I knew. I was curious, and the idea of spending the day on an adventure with my mother thrilled me.

"I was thinking we might be able to find some things to sell at Boo's," she said.

My heart thudded in my ears. I wondered what Daddy would say if she came to him with another check. My hands shook with the prospect of another night listening to those words. But she held me so tightly, I couldn't say no. She needed this. She needed me to agree. And I missed her.

We walked to Gray Wilder's house carrying suitcases, and the sky threatened rain. It felt as if we were running away, but the suitcases were empty, and I wasn't wearing any shoes. My mother walked slowly, noticing things: a late raspberry, the red almost brutal amid all that green. A hornet's nest in the top of a tree. A perfect silver feather in the middle of the road. With her gestures, she tried to make all of this beautiful, to distract me from the gutted-out car over the bank near Gray Wilder's house and the bag of trash somebody had dumped there. But my eyes lingered on the crushed Valentine's candy box, empty aspirin bottle, and single filthy sneaker.

Gray Wilder's house was a trailer on concrete blocks. It smelled like an outhouse when my mother finally found the key and let us in. I'd never been inside a dead person's house before, and suddenly, I didn't want to be there. We collected a few things from the living room: a clock made out of lac-quered wood, a wicker magazine rack, two candles made of layered wax that looked like a sunset. But the smell got to me soon, and while my mother scoured Gray Wilder's garage for something valuable, I waited for her outside on a rock, picking the dead skin off my feet. The sky rumbled angrily.

After a long time, she finally came out holding something

wrapped up in the pages of a dirty magazine. She unwrapped it quickly, tossing the crinkled pages on the ground. In her face I could see something like desperation, as if her very happiness depended on what was inside the glossy pictures of skin and hair and lipstick. I couldn't help but stare at the fragments of women's naked bodies, at their pubic hair, shaved into tiny triangles, and at their swollen breasts, their colorless nipples. They reminded me that my own body (though I was growing in height) had yet to go through the magical transformations that some girls in my class had gone through one or even two summers before. I made myself turn away, looking up instead at the red glass vase in her hands.

"That's pretty," I said. I wanted her to know she had found it: the perfect thing that would save this day.

She set the vase on the rock next to me and looked at it. Without sun, the glass was dull and dark red, almost brown. I could smell rain coming. I could hear thunder somewhere, not too far away.

"Boo will love it," I said. "She will. She has all of those vases, the Depression glass ones, remember? But she doesn't have any red ones. I bet we could get twenty dollars for it." My words were tumbling, eager and clumsy.

She picked it up again, smiling, and ran her fingers across the rim. But she hesitated halfway around, her smile fading.

"There's a chip in it."

"Where?" I asked, as if it couldn't be true. As if she could have mistaken this imperfection. I stood up, went to her, looked at the glass. The chip was small but certain. The vase wasn't worth anything.

She set it back down on the rock and walked away from me, disappearing into the garage. I picked the vase up and cradled it, briefly, like an infant in my arms. I set it back down, embarrassed, and felt the first cold drops of summer rain on my shoulder.

She was inside the garage for a long time. I could hear her feet shuffling across the dirt floor. When she came out again, she was carrying a hammer. My throat felt thick. She scooted me out of the way and contemplated the vase again.

I looked at her, and her face grew soft. In a glance, I asked her to please stop.

"It's ruined," she said, her eyes pleading with me. "Already."

I stared at my hands. When I looked up again, she was standing over the vase with her eyes closed. When she swung the hammer back, her shoulder blades were sharp, like a bird's wings at her back. And the vase made a sound like music when it shattered with one gentle blow.

Tears welled up in my eyes but did not fall. I blinked hard.

She sat down next to me and leaned her head on my shoulder without taking her eyes off the pile of crimson shards. There was no sun shining through the fragments. It was just a pile of glass.

And then she stood up and brushed the pieces into the palm of her hand. She looked at me sadly. "Sometimes things need to get broken," she said.

I suppose I should have known then that it wouldn't be much longer before she was gone. I should have seen the dull prisms in her eyes as we walked home in the rain with two suitcases filled with the dead man's things. I should have noticed that all the sunlight had disappeared.

The only thing that remained of my mother after she left was glass: in every room, her slivered pictures reminders that there was a time before. That there was a time when things were almost beautiful here. The pane that hung in the window over my bed was the last one she made before she left and never came back. She used every color in this one, and at the very center was a piece she kept in the *crimson* drawer in the shed: a bubble of red from the glass vase transformed into a small heart inside the chest of a bird without wings.

If summer here were made of colored glass, this is the way the light would shine through the summer my mother disappeared: the dull green of turning leaves and branches reaching to a somber sky. But that summer she made me understand that it was not the glass that was beautiful, but the quality of light behind it. It was the sun, not the shards, that mattered. And when I peered through the heart, the world looked different. This was the way she might have seen things. When I forgot the tilt of her head or the smell of her hair, I looked through the bird's heart to the world outside my window and imagined that I was she and that this was what she saw.

And that fall, when she was already gone, autumn sunlight shone through the crimson shard and made spots like blood on my sheets.

I don't know what happened to that girl. I think she became lost a long time ago. I picture her wandering through the damp, dark woods of my past, looking for home.

This morning, after Becca left for school, I went to my closet and crawled inside (over boxes and under clothes) and found the shoe box with the rest of my mother's envelopes. Not surprisingly, all of them were filled with glass. But even after the envelopes were unsealed, their contents strewn across the coffee table like transparent puzzle pieces, I went back inside the closet. Searching. I tore open lids and untied bags. I reached into pockets and unwrapped packages. I kept telling myself that I wasn't looking for him. That I was only cleaning house. Trying to make it easier and more manageable for my friends, just in case. But finding my mother inside that closet meant finding him, too.

Finally, after an hour of excavating, I found the poem inside a wooden music box, one of the few salvaged relics of my childhood. The box was in the back of my closet, wrapped in the folds of an old dress that used to belong to my mother. But despite my attempts to protect it, the wood was chipped and the découpage of the Austrian Alps on the lid had faded. It came from the Trapp Family Lodge gift shop: he'd bought it for me during a class trip, slipped it into my backpack while I was sleeping on the bus ride home. It used to play "Edelweiss," but the brass key to wind it up had broken off years ago.

I've been thinking a lot lately about what I will be leaving behind. I have lived in the same apartment for almost five years, and the walk-in closet is a virtual tomb, a catacomb of gathered things. Of *saved* things. But what to me are sentimental tokens, to other people would probably seem, at best, like prospective yard sale items and, at worst, like possible Goodwill donations. That's the way with sentimental things: it's the memory the junk conjures that's valuable, not the junk itself. The true past is manifested not in the broken baby doll, but in her missing arms. In the lost or stained pages of sheet music for your favorite songs, in the holes of your favorite dresses. My past is the song captured inside that wooden box, and the words the poem doesn't say.

Perhaps she is hungry, having used her only bread as a futile trail home.

The paper was fragile, like chalky wings, and I was worried that it might crumble in my hands when I unfolded it. But remarkably, more than fifteen years after they were written, the words were still intact.

Edelweiss, edelweiss, edelweiss.

I remember falling asleep on the long bus ride back from Stowe. It was while I was sleeping that he slipped the music box into my backpack and changed everything. I didn't hear him or feel him come or go, but when I awoke I knew that nothing would be the same again. Shivering, my head pressed against the cold window, I made a cloud with my breath on the glass and started to write his name with my finger. I stopped after the first letter, realizing that despite the gift, the admission, I could never write his name, not even in the clouds I made with my own breath.

He was my secret. He was everything I kept hidden and *inside*. Even at fourteen years old, I knew plenty about deceit: I had lied to (and been lied to by) everyone I had ever loved. I guess that's why I wasn't afraid. At least this secret belonged to me. But because I was only fourteen, I also lied to myself. I believed that he was the end of the world. He appeared after I'd already lost everything. He arrived just in time; I thought then that he was saving me.

I am aware of my body now, sixteen years and as many lovers later. I am ever conscious of skin and bones and marrow. The distant dankness of breath and the gentle yellowing of teeth. I am older than I seem. These creases run deeper than you'd think. I know who I am and what a body can and cannot do. But then, when I was a child, I knew only what he told me. And that was *love* and *music, music* and *love*. I only vaguely understood the power of one hand on my hip, defiant, or the potency of my braid swinging over my shoulder, loose hairs making me wrinkle my nose. I didn't know that a single careless gesture of mine could be the end of his world, too.

I don't know what happened to that girl.

He was already broken when I met him. I was wise enough to see right away that he was made of fragments too, that he was also comprised of slivers. He offered me his sorrow, not as an explanation, but as a gift. He gave me in whispers the names of his lost wife and then his lost child. *Felicity. Felicity.* Her name sounded like a constellation to me, like an imagined girl. But all that happened long before I knew him. When I met him, he was already broken. I know I'm not to blame for that, at least. And now, that is what comforts me.

I was not innocent. I am not innocent. But sometimes I look for ways to blame him for what is happening to my body now. I sometimes imagine that the decay began the moment I saw his face. That it infected me. That he started killing me all those years ago, and that now the dying is just finally settling in. I think that this must simply be the completion of our exchange: a life for a life.

After the birds descended, after the trail of bread was gone, where did she go? I imagine she spun on the tips of her toes, until dizzy, and the wet green of leaves could have been a kaleidoscope of tears.

After I reread the poem, I carefully folded it along its familiar creases and put it back inside the music box. I wrapped it up again in my mother's soft blue dress (whose pockets were filled with their own secrets) and wondered what would happen to it after I was gone. Becca has the best intentions. She has denied me my thrift store, pawnshop, yard sale pleas. She's told me that she'll take care of my belongings if she needs to, but for now I don't need to get rid of anything. That I should leave the door to my closet closed, keep the artifacts inside: my mausoleum of not-forgotten things. I'm grateful for her tenacity: I would never really be able to get rid of the closet's contents. Like my mother, I have unwittingly become a reluctant but proud curator of broken things.

Autumn, and everything was falling.

For the first few weeks after Mum left, we expected her to return. We all pretended that she'd only gone for a walk, that any moment she would walk back in the door with a handful of late-summer berries or a single fallen maple leaf, like a giant golden palm. We pretended that she'd only gotten lost in the colors of fall.

Sometimes I'd sit on the porch and squint my eyes, imagining that the red of a maple tree was the velour bathrobe Daddy had given her three Christmases earlier. That the wind was her hair. But inevitably, the trees remained trees and she didn't come home.

When she left, she didn't take much, just enough to let us know that she'd gone willingly. A suitcase, a fisherman's sweater. Her favorite jeans, her shoes and socks and toothbrush. When I ran away at six years old, I took the same sorts of things: my tattered sock monkey, six pairs of underwear, a hairbrush. Of course, I only got as far as Lake Gormlaith before I turned around and came home. But she wasn't a child; she wasn't afraid of leaving.

It wasn't until later that I found the other missing things. The good flashlight, the radio, the pocketknife I'd won at the state fair. Her best slip, a scarab bracelet from Boo, and the copy of *Alice in Wonderland* we bought at the library sale that reminded her of the one she had when she was little. The magnetic plastic pages of the photo album didn't lie right now that some of the photos were gone: my first cartwheel, Quinn learning to ski. I searched my drawers for other things she might have taken; I ran my fingers through my hair, wondering if she might have cut a lock of it while I was sleeping.

I think I was the first one to realize that she wasn't coming home. Daddy and Quinn didn't know her like I did. They believed she needed them, when I knew she didn't need any of us.

In September, I started high school, terrified by the maze of classrooms and the ease with which everyone seemed to move along the pale green hallways. I sat near windows. I spoke to no one. I thought my silence might make me invisible, as if a voice alone could make you real. Becca and I had opposite schedules. We passed each other in the hall, similarly scared, but reversed, like faces in a funhouse mirror. We had the same lunch period, thankfully, and we sat at the far end of the cafeteria, studying the gestures of the pretty girls and the way the boys walked. For twenty minutes each day we pretended that all of this would be all right, that some of the Quimby kids might befriend us, that we didn't come from a town without a name. But it was clear early on that the dividing lines were drawn long before we got there. We were the poor kids, the *Pond* kids—as if we'd come from the murky depths of the sawdust-bottomed Pond instead of from our mothers' wombs. And with my mother gone, it seemed this could be true.

Quinn was a senior that year. Sometimes I saw him emerging from the boys' bathroom in a halo of smoke, hands shoved into his pockets, laughing with the other guys. He would nod at me, but we didn't speak. I knew that he had worked too hard for this, and I wouldn't take it from him. He'd fought his way from the depths of the Pond, crawled out, *evolved*.

When school was over and we were outside the big brick building, he'd find Becca and me sitting under a tree by the football field and offer to drive us to Boo's on his way to work at the Shop-N-Save. Quinn drove our mother's car, another thing she had left behind. There were still candy wrappers from her Tootsie Rolls in the ashtray, and an empty paper coffee cup rimmed with her lipstick rolling on the floor. I would let Becca sit up front while I peered through the back window at everything falling away.

At Boo's shop, we played dress-up: Becca searching the discarded clothes for some hidden treasure, and I for clues about where my mother had gone.

"Look at this!" Becca said, pulling a paisley scarf from a plastic bag like a magician.

Someone had just dropped off ten Hefty bags full of clothes and ties and shoes.

Boo was sitting behind the makeshift counter, untangling a mountain of costume jewelry. "It's silk, I think," she said, looking up over the tops of her glasses. She and my mother didn't look related. She was Mum's little sister, but while my mother was miniature, like a doll, Boo was like me. Tall. Big hands, long legs. Boo had even played basketball for the UVM girls' team. Sometimes when the shop was quiet, she and I would shoot hoops outside the garage.

I tore open one bag, and a bunch of scuffed shoes fell out. They smelled like sweaty feet.

Becca stood in front of the full-length mirror, adjusting the scarf around her neck and head. The burgundy swirls clashed with her strawberry hair.

I reached for another bag. It was light. Inside were two pillows, lumpy and stained. "Ugh," I said and tossed it in the trash can.

"Someone dropped off some dresses. Nice ones," Boo said. "Why don't you look through those instead?" She motioned toward a rolling rack at the far end of the garage.

Becca let the scarf fall from her hair and rushed to the rack.

I sat down next to Boo on an orange leather hassock. The stitching was coming undone, and the stuffing inside was gray.

"How's school?" she asked.

"I hate it."

She nodded and worked on the chains in her fingers.

"How's your dad?" she asked.

I shrugged. For the first few weeks after Mum left, Daddy stayed at home, sitting on the front porch smoking cigarettes, staring into the trees. I think he saw the red of her ratty old bathrobe among them, too. But when it was clear she wasn't coming back to us, he didn't wait anymore. In the mornings, he'd get dressed as if he were going to work, and then he'd get in his truck and leave. Sometimes he didn't come home until midnight, and I knew he was looking for her. I imagined him driving all over the state, to Burlington and Rutland and Montpelier, searching for her, as if she would just be walking along the edge of the interstate or sitting in a restaurant somewhere and he would be able to take her hand and lead her home. He wasn't looking for a job, because he was too busy looking for her. I didn't tell Boo that, though. I only shrugged.

Becca had something pink in her hands. "Can I try this one on?" she asked shyly.

"Of course, honey. Use the bathroom inside."

Becca scurried into the house, and I watched Boo's fingers. Three silver chains, knotted and intertwined. A heart pendant, someone's class ring, a broken locket.

"Tell me about Gramma," I said.

Boo rolled her eyes.

"Please?"

"Which story?" she asked, loosening one of the reluctant necklaces.

"The one about when she finally left Grampa and took the train to California." In this story, which Boo and my mother told together, my grandmother wore a straight gray skirt and a hat with a peacock feather. She carried a plaid suitcase in one hand and a train case filled with makeup in the other. In this story, she smelled like Evening in Paris perfume. My mother once found one of the midnight-blue bottles, broken and buried in the mud near the Pond, and she held it in the palm of her hands like a wounded baby bird.

Boo set the jewelry down and looked at me sadly. "Your mum didn't go to California," she said softly.

My throat ached. I looked at her, but she wouldn't look at me. Her fingers worked the tangled necklaces, her eyes straining in concentration.

My throat was thick, my hands shaking. "Tell me," I said softly. "Please." And I waited for her to tell me where my mother had gone. She *knew.*

But instead she only recited the imagined life she and my mother had made for *their* mother after she was gone. The pink hotel from the four or so postcards she sent. Chandeliers and white sand. The smell of salty air and smog and the sound of waves that crashed into their uneasy sleep. I clung to the green of palm fronds and the taste of Italian ice eaten with a flat wooden spoon.

"Boo, where *is* she? You have to tell me."

Boo closed her eyes and offered me explanations, a thousand tangled necklaces I tried to separate in my mind. *Your daddy. For a long time. She couldn't breathe.* But I already knew *why.* What I didn't know was *where.* But just as I opened my mouth to demand that she tell, Becca opened the door and stood there in a hot-pink dress two sizes too big, waiting for compliments, and I felt sad and sorry that I'd even tried.

Later, after Boo had given us supper, Quinn pulled into the driveway and waited patiently for Becca to pick out the few things she wanted to keep before he took us back home. Sometimes Daddy was there, but that night he didn't get home until after I'd let myself slip off the edge of the wooden pier into the cold dream water where an undertow threatened and birds screamed.

My body mimics that girl's now. It has lost its softness, without the necessity of curves. There will be no babies, so there is no need for hips, and I am returning to the body I remember. In this way, nothing can hide underneath the skin's surface anymore; I have made certain of that. What was buried is now laid bare, each new malignancy revealing itself as soon as it is born. I am prepubescent in this remembered body. And I wonder if this is how he saw me then. As possibility. As *before* and *someday*. He would be sad to see me now, though. He would be sad to know that I am dying.

I remember his fingers more than I remember his face. I suppose that's because touching was always so much more important to me than anything a face could disclose. His fingers had a way of skipping over my skin like stones skipping across the lake. I remember lying facedown on his bed, the pills of a chenille spread beneath me, feeling like water.

The discovery of the first lump was accidental. I wasn't looking, having given up searching a long time ago. I found it the way you stumble across a dollar bill on the sidewalk. You know you should stop to pick it up, but it also means pausing, breaking your momentum. It was like this the first time.

In my terra-cotta-colored room, I was naked and alone, my hair wet and tangled from a shower. I was swollen, aware of my breasts and hips and the softness of down. Under covers, I pretended exploration, but it was too familiar. All of this. There were no surprises in my body to be found anymore. Nothing startled me the way it used to. But there was comfort in the predictable rhythms of blood and heart and breath. It was like sleepwalking, this touching. Smoothness of skin, interruption of navel, the edge where skin seemed to stop and then start again, warmth and wetness. My seamstress fingers always working, pushing and pulling at the fabric of my body, the needle moving up and down, precise tension and speed. But when I reached for myself, held onto myself, pretending my fingers were not my own, they stumbled. Remarkably, it wasn't fear the small knot evoked, but relief: My body could still surprise me. There were still secrets to be found. And I let my fingers linger there, the certainty of what it was no different from the certainty of a new gray hair, wiry and strong amid softness. But later, when the inevitable connections between the lump and the meaning of the lump engaged, I knew my mother had been wrong. Some things are best undiscovered.

It is for this reason that I made myself forget about what I'd found. I left it there. I dismissed it. But, like the ignored weeds in my rooftop garden, it grew. It grew and grew, until finally I couldn't ignore it anymore. Because of my neglect, it made itself prominent. It demanded attention. It became angry.

Now, in this child's body, nothing can hide anymore. But somehow, this remembered innocence (of bones and blood and breath) makes what is happening seem almost cruel.

Once, as we lay looking at the lake through his bedroom window, he told me that there was nothing more beautiful than dying. That violence and peace are companions, peace always preceding and following violence. I knew he was talking about his wife. About her skin and bones fractured by the windshield and dash. About the way the air was so quiet around them inside the car as she lay dying. About the absolute silence of glass after it's broken.

Daddy met Roxanne at the lodge in October, and she looked to me like a fallen leaf. Her skin was brown and weathered. She wore leather pants and scratchy sweaters. She hired him to bartend, even though he didn't know the difference between vermouth and vodka. When he gave up looking for my mother at the side of the road, he looked for her in the shadows, in places she would never have gone. He must have thought she was only hiding. And strangely, looking for my mother, he found work, something none of us expected. But he also found Roxanne. Autumn, and everything was falling.

I knew Roxanne, because her son, Jake, was in my English class. He was a football player. I sat behind him and stared at the bristly hairs of his military cut, the only marker of where his head ended and his neck began. When there were football games after school, Becca insisted that I sit with her on the rickety bleachers instead of going to Boo's. She promised that football, cold autumn sunshine, and hot chocolate in Styrofoam cups were somehow critical to our survival at Quimby High. But more often than not we wound up sitting with the football players' mothers, a high-strung and husky-voiced lot who patrolled the bleachers like angry bees. The Quimby girls circled the track on the periphery of the football field, their movements as choreographed as the players. Becca and I had not yet learned this dance, so we sat with the football moms.

Roxanne was the queen bee. Her hair was the swirled colors of vanilla and caramel ice cream, but she smelled like booze and cigarettes. She kept a flask inside her bright blue parka vest, sipping at it seductively between drags. She winked at me once; I never trusted her. Her eyes were set far apart, and her face looked like an old glove. Jake had the same wide-set eyes, giving him the look of an overgrown infant, or an alien. In English class, I studied the back of his neck. Flaky patches of dandruff made snow on his shoulders. He wore sweaters without T-shirts underneath, and their ribbed collars were stretched taut, synthetic fibers threatening to tear or to strangle. I felt sorry for him then. He didn't know his mother was sleeping with my father.

If autumn here were made of colored glass, this is the way the light would shine through the autumn when my father met Roxanne: neon red turned upside down inside the green glass of a beer bottle. Sunlight catching dust, making triangles in the air and on the wooden dance floor of the Lodge, where Roxanne got drunk while Daddy poured liquid sunlight into chipped pint glasses. And later, dawn through ruffled curtains hanging over her bed, when he realized he'd forgotten to come home again.

At night, when it was just me and Quinn, we watched TV, eating from cardboard boxes he brought home from the Shop-N-Save's deli. I can still taste the pasty dough of batter-dipped chicken swimming in bright pink duck sauce. Potato salad with too much mayonnaise. Later, he would disappear into his room and shut the door. I don't know what he did in there, but he did it in silence. Not even the sound of the radio escaped. He came out to use the bathroom and then to get a snack, rubbing his knuckles gently across the top of my head on his way to the kitchen, where he would pour a glass of milk and take three Fig Newtons from the package on top of the fridge. "Night, Piper," he'd say, and disappear again.

I could have been alone in the house on the nights when

Daddy didn't come home. But I'd pretend I'd been sent to my room to study, and would stay up staring at my open textbooks until the air turned cold and almost blue, then fall asleep with the light on.

One Friday night in late autumn when the trees were already bare and the windows were covered with frost, Roxanne came home with Daddy. Through my bedroom window I could see the outline of her sharp shoulders and pointed profile. She'd given him a ride. I figured his truck must have died in town; it was probably sitting in the dirt parking lot outside the Lodge. I stayed in my room when Daddy opened the door and ushered her inside. I feigned sleep when he called out my name.

I pretended that her raspy voice was only the sound of rotten leaves covering the road. Ice in their glasses became the sound of bells, their breathing only wind. But her laughter inevitably exploded into the rumble of a smoker's cough, her insides rattling, and I listened to the unmistakable sound of Daddy cooing at her. To the sound of her fingers touching Daddy's collar, chest, beard. I strained to hear their bare feet move down the hall into my mother's room. But then I heard the front door creak open and the sounds of leaving.

Tears welled up in my eyes, hot and certain, at her departure. I should have known that Daddy couldn't replace my mother just like that. I should have trusted that he would always love her. He would send Roxanne back to where he had found her.

In the morning, I woke up tangled in my sheets. Outside the sun was bright and cold. Winter was only moments away. I pulled on the brown sweater I'd most recently brought home from Boo's, my thumb getting stuck in a mothhole near the cuff. I pushed harder, until it ripped, until my thumb was sticking all the way through. I left my jammie bottoms on and pulled on a pair of wool socks.

Quinn was at the kitchen table, eating a bowl of cereal, making a fist around his spoon. I sat down across from him, listening for the sounds of Daddy's shower.

"You workin' today?" I asked.

Quinn looked up from his cereal and shook his head.

"Feels like snow." I nodded. Quinn was on the ski team at school. He was always happiest in winter.

"He left with her, you know," he said.

"What?" I asked, picking up the cereal box, staring at the nutrition label on the side, looking for an explanation that might appear there. *Sugar, calcium, saturated fat.* But I already knew.

Daddy and Roxanne were both gone, along with all of Daddy's clothes I had washed and folded and set on top of the dryer. Along with his razor and toothbrush and his deodorant. Along with his winter boots, even though there wasn't any snow on the ground yet.

Hope. This is my mother's true and cruel legacy. When I was a child, I hoped she would come back. At thirty, I only hope that I will live. And live and live. This is my inheritance. My endowment, my trust. A handful of sand and broken glass.

When the doctors confirmed what I already knew, I hoped. I listened to their statistics in their cold waiting rooms as my nipples hardened against the rough blue paper dresses. I looked at the charts and diagrams and grim smiles and hoped. We scheduled the surgery and, later, my treatments. I bought beautiful scarves, drank liquid vegetables and fruits. I vomited and imagined cancer nothing more than stomach bile, acidic and expendable. And I hoped.

Even though I've stopped going to the hospital for treatments, Becca still brings home articles she prints off the Internet about experimental procedures, about women who have prevailed despite the illness that has battered them. Each story of success and the accompanying picture of the face that belongs to the body inspires a strange desire. Hope is really just desire disguised, just desperation, aching, dressed up like a prayer. But while hope is elusive, desire is something I can understand. I have wanted and wanted and wanted. I can't even count all of the things I have wanted. To have. To do. To be. It's like the familiar longing for a lover; it resides in my heart *and* in my body. I want to be well again.

Hope has become the same as sunlight. Some days it is warm on my shoulders and back. Some days it's just gone. It doesn't worry me, it's just missing. I know you can no easier lose hope than you can lose sunlight. There is never any doubt hope will return. But I am waiting. There have been too many cloudy days lately.

I've started misplacing things and finding them later. Small surprises. Yesterday, I found a pair of scissors in the refrigerator. This morning I found a pincushion under my pillow. It's making work difficult. I work at home, sewing wedding dresses and prom dresses, making costumes and mending holes. At least the sewing machine is too heavy for me to absentmindedly pick up and move.

I am making a wedding dress for a twenty-nine-year-old widow. Her first husband died of meningitis three weeks after their wedding. It came on suddenly: a fever, then blindness, and then she was alone in a brand-new house with a pile of wedding gifts waiting to be unwrapped. I didn't ask, but she offered this story to me, almost as if she were sorry. As if she had to explain falling in love again.

She wants a dress that makes her look like Juliet. I went to Boston and bought ten yards of silk chiffon, embroidered with golden thread. When I showed her the bolt, she unrolled it on my living room floor, careful to blow away the dust bunnies before she smoothed her hand across the fabric. And after she had rolled it back up, she held the fabric to her face and started to cry.

"Don't think I'm terrible," she said softly.

"I don't," I said.

When someone dies, there always has to be someone left

behind. She doesn't know that I am studying her, that she is teaching me the gestures of survivors.

I stopped working when I first got sick, entertaining romantic notions of dying, mostly that it would be my primary obligation. I thought the world as I knew it would stop for me now that I was sick. But dying isn't the way I imagined it. Credit card companies still want their minimum payments; landlords still want their rent. So my hiatus was short-lived, and I am glad now for the distraction that sewing provides. But even when my hands are busy, my mind is still free. It wanders farther than it used to. I suppose that's why today I found my tape measure wound around Bog's dog dish and the iron propping up a row of books on my mantel.

Sometimes I worry about the other things I stand to lose. My faith, my temper, my way. I have lost weight. My hair. Great portions of my breasts. But unlike my scissors and pins, they don't seem to be coming back. I know that other things will go unless I get better, there is still plenty to lose.

He lost his child. *Felicity.* He was reluctant to tell me how. It wasn't as easy as describing the peace in his wife's face or the way the lights reflected off her seatbelt buckle and the broken windshield, blinding him. *Felicity, happiness.* I still wonder if he was just trying to tell me that after his wife was dead, he lost his happiness.

Becca, who has reappeared after all these years (an auburn-haired angel from some other time), assures me that I have held on to the most important things. Dignity. My sense of humor. And, most important, my voice. She knows, as I know, because she was there when I found it, that if I were ever to lose it again, I would have to let go. That losing my voice would mean losing hope.

My mother said that I always sang myself to sleep, so there was never any need for lullabies. I know now she told me this to make me believe I could take care of myself. To prepare me for her departure.

She said I began humming Brahms's Lullaby as an infant, and that later the music became unidentifiable, my own and strange. She said it was terrifying, holding on to me as I sang myself to sleep. I don't remember singing, but I do remember her arms.

Sometimes I still sing without realizing it. Singing is as unconscious to me as breathing or swallowing or blinking my eyes. Trying to control it is like holding my breath.

After my mother left, I became quiet. For a little while, I thought that maybe she had taken my voice with her, along with the good Phillips-head screwdriver and her only pair of heels. But I must have known she wouldn't take that away from me, no more than she would take my lungs, my tongue, or my eyes.

This is the way it feels when I sing: colors and then nothing but breath. The color I see is one she kept in a bottom drawer of her cabinet of glass. *Holiday.* It was the only color she ever made up. When I asked, she pulled a record from the sleeve and touched the vinyl in small, gentle circles. She made me close my eyes and listen. The color I saw then, the color the woman's voice made, was the same one I felt when I sang. Funny, my mother never found any glass to put inside that drawer. She said the glass would have to be the color of sorrow, and where could you find that?

It was because of Becca. We don't talk about it now, but I'm certain that she remembers. Becca was the one who convinced me to go to the high school auditorium with her after school that day.

"Please?" she whispered as we stood outside the auditorium doors. "Wouldn't it be fun?" But I knew what she was really thinking. I knew she believed that inside costumes we might be able to become something other than the Pond kids we were. Becca became an actress out of necessity.

We stood there for several minutes, staring at the mimeographed audition announcement, until finally her face fell, and she shrugged. "Forget it. It was a stupid idea anyway."

"It's not stupid," I said. "But why do you need me to do it too?"

"I don't want to be alone," she said softly. Her brown eyes were wide and scared. I knew she wouldn't go without me.

"All right," I said, acting more irritated than I actually was.

It was Becca who convinced me. To stand alone on the stage while the Quimby girls sat snickering in the dimly lit aisles below me. Convinced me to close my eyes and share the voice I'd been swallowing since my mother left. I remember the sweater I was wearing, an oversized man's cardigan with chipped wooden buttons and stained cuffs. I remember how cold it was, and the way I let the sleeves cover my hands. I already knew the words to the song. I'd seen the movie a thousand times, so I didn't need sheet music. I remember the *plunk, plunk* of Mrs. Jasper's piano in the wings and the smell of mothballs lingering in my hand-me-down sweater. I also remember the hush that fell like snow when I closed my eyes and opened my mouth and allowed the color of sorrow to escape.

Afterward, I blushed and rushed off the stage, sinking into the chair next to Becca, who was smiling. She squeezed my hand and then went up when her name was called.

After a thousand renditions of "My Favorite Things" and "Do-Re-Mi," Mrs. Jasper stood up from her piano, shielded her eyes, and peered out into the audience. "That's everybody, Mr. Hammer," she said.

"Okay," a voice answered.

"Who's that?" I whispered to Becca.

"Tenth-grade English," she said. "He's going to direct the show."

"Oh," I said.

"If Mr. Hammer calls out your name, please come up to the stage," Mrs. Jasper said.

From the back of the auditorium, Mr. Hammer coughed and then started to read off names. I was nervous despite myself. Suddenly, I wanted this more than anything in the entire world. "Lucy Applebee. Peter Kauffman. Rebecca O'Leary." Becca squeezed my hand hard and fast and then scurried quickly up onto the stage. "Steve Gauthier. Melissa Ball. Krista Monroe, and Howie Kramer." My heart sank. And then he said softly, "Piper Kincaid." I stood up, crossed my arms self-consciously, and walked up the stairs onto the stage.

Mrs. Jasper shuffled us around like mannequins, according to our height. I was the tallest girl. Becca was the shortest.

"You'll be Liesl," she said to me. "Unless . . . Mr. Hammer, have you found a Maria?"

"Yes," he said. "Charlene Applebee will be playing Maria. We'll also be casting some children from the elementary school to play the younger Von Trapp children."

Charlene Applebee was Lucy Applebee's mother. Lucy was a senior, a Quimby girl. Her parents owned the big brick house with the columns on the park in town. Lucy smiled knowingly at Melissa Ball, whose family also lived on the park, and nodded. Mrs. Jasper clapped her hands together and said, "Good, good. Then rehearsals will start tomorrow after last period. On the dot. Don't be late, because the doors will be locked at two-thirty."

At Boo's, Becca tried on a pair of silver stilettos and wobbled across the driveway, turning her ankles and laughing. I watched her through the window and wondered if it was really this easy, becoming someone else.

Boo was sorting through men's suits, donated by a woman whose husband had just died. The cardboard box was tearing with the weight of wool.

"Liesl." Boo nodded. "That's a big part. You'll have to sing that duet . . . what is it? 'I am sixteen, going on seventeen.' I just love that movie."

"I'm just doing it to keep Becca company." I sighed and leaned over to pull out one of the jackets. I slipped the jacket on and buttoned it up. It smelled like a nursing home.

Boo handed me the matching pants. I took off the coat and hung them both on a hanger.

Boo said, "Your mum would be proud of you."

I blinked hard and stared out the window. Becca was sitting on Boo's steps, unwinding herself from the silver straps.

Boo knew where my mother was. The hurt of that had been sharp at first, but now it felt like a fading slap. No matter how many times I asked her, she wouldn't tell, couldn't tell, because she would never betray my mother. Boo kept her promises. She was the only one I knew who did, and though it made me ache inside, made my stomach turn and my eyes burn, I had to respect that.

I am grown now. I have to remind myself sometimes that all of this is inevitable, that if it hadn't been cancer, it would have been something else. Everyone has to leave sometime, everyone dies. But at thirty, this feels like an injustice. I read the obituaries every day, looking for others like me. But almost everyone who dies here is already old. Their numbers glare at me, mocking, from the smudged pages: 93, 76, 81.

This morning Becca brings bagels and the Sunday *Burlington Free Press,* dividing it according to our now familiar routine. While she reads the "Living" section, I scour the lists of the newly deceased.

"I'm buying you a juicer," she says, her finger pointing to a glossy Kmart insert. "You like carrot juice?"

"Yuck."

"Tomato juice?" Her finger presses into the advertisement.

I shake my head, returning to the former Navy officer, 75. The grandmother of twenty-seven, 98. The retired surgeon, 81.

"You can use fruit, too. Oranges, kiwi even." She sounds exasperated.

I look up from the obituaries. She is tapping the ad now, insistent.

"We'll go next weekend," I say.

"The sale ends *today,*" she says. "Then it goes right back to the normal price."

"Fine," I say. "This afternoon."

Satisfied, she smiles and folds the advertisement carefully. "I bet you can even use pineapples. Mangoes."

Never mind I know she hasn't once seen a mango at the Shop-N-Save. I nod and smile anyway.

My instinct in the beginning was to fight. I laced up my gloves, stood in the ring, and imagined cancer cloaked in a tacky satin robe in the other corner. For three years, my hands have been curled into fists. But I'm tired now. I am tired and bloodied and my blows are soft. It's because of Becca, my relentless coach, that I continue. I dream the white towel floating down into the center of the ring, but she clings to it. She is holding on to it with every bit of her strength, and her fists are stronger than mine.

But it is autumn here now, and I know I am no different than the precarious leaves, holding on to the branches of the trees outside my window. I dream myself red and gold and purple. I dream the flight from branch to sky to ground. But every time I begin to fall, Becca is there, demanding to know exactly what I think I am doing.

She believes the underdog can win the fight, that winning is as simple as persistence and faith. In my corner, she rinses my bloodied face with cool water and urges me back into the cold ring. She knows how tired I am, knows that without rest there is no way I will be able to win. She thinks that I am only taking a break, only gathering strength.

Daddy almost never came home anymore. Every night that he worked, he spent at Roxanne's house. That was fine with me. When he was home, he just stared at the things my mother left behind. I found him once in the bathroom, holding one of her razors, the bathtub steaming with hot water and the lilac bubble soap she always used.

Before she left, my mother's baths had been intricate rituals. I actually believed that something magical occurred each time she went into the small bathroom off the kitchen and closed the door behind her. She would leave us after dinner, while we were still cleaning our plates. My father would open another beer, Quinn would scrape whatever was left from the blue-and-white casserole dish onto his plate, and I would wonder what she was doing in there. After the dishes were done and Daddy and Quinn had retired to their respective corners of our small house, my mother would emerge in her giant red bathrobe, turbaned like a woman in a commercial.

I thought I might figure out her secrets by studying the artifacts, but there was little to go on. After she was done, I would lock myself in the bathroom as the water drained. The smell was of lilacs, even in winter. Sometimes I would close my eyes and reach into the steam; I swear I could feel the purple petals in my fingers. Along the edge of the cracked porcelain tub lay mysterious instruments, like the tools of a magician. Silver razor, clippers, tweezers. Once, I took the razor and ran it across the length of my arm. When I looked at the blade, it was full of downy hairs. I blew them off and hoped she wouldn't know what I'd done. I was obsessed with my mother's rituals of hand cream and pumice and perfume, because when she came out of the steamy bathroom each night, she looked like a different person. Even if Daddy had spent the whole day lying on the couch with the cool washcloth pressed against his head and a beer in his hand, after her bath, her skin glowed pink and her face looked calm. I imagined her worries swirling down the drain, like bubble soap or the sawdust that always covered our clothes.

What I loved most, though, were the bottles, the plastic containers shaped like champagne bottles, gold foil at the top, plastic corks. Inside, liquid lilacs. Every now and then I would peel a little piece of the foil off, fold it into a tiny square, and put it in my mouth. It hurt when it touched my fillings, but it was a thrilling kind of pain. I wanted my own magic ritual to take away my worries. I wanted instruments that would rid me of all of my fears. I wanted to make my world smell of lilacs, even in winter.

I would stand on the furry bath mat, still soggy from her wet feet, and look at my reflection in the mirror over the sink. I'd turn from side to side, looking for my mother's features in my face. But I could never find them: not eyes, not nose, not throat. I looked like my father. He was me. He was my birth and my death, rendered simply in his hands and in his eyes. I could see my future in his face and hear my past in his words. Watching him staring at the empty places where my mother used to be was like staring at both the self I'd already lost and the person I would become. I was grateful, in a strange way, for

Roxanne. When Daddy was away, I didn't have to stare my own sadness in the face.

By the time winter descended, touching us at the Pond with its frigid white fingers before moving south toward the lake and on into Quimby, Daddy had stopped sleeping in their old bed. Stopped coming by except to drop off a check and, every now and then, something he thought we needed.

"Let's take a walk," Becca says when she finds me buried under covers on my lumpy couch watching the fourth soap opera in a row.

I grumble and burrow deeper into my nest.

"Come on," she says, gently tugging my hand.

Bog, who has been napping on the rug next to me, stands up and stretches his front legs. He is always ready for a walk. But when I don't budge, he looks at me and then lies back down, covering his long snout with his paw.

"It's sunny out," she says. "It smells like fall."

Reluctantly, I pull myself away from the beautiful couple on TV and stand up. I am dizzy and weak and everything aches today. On days like this I wish it were over with already. On days like this it's hard to think I was ever well.

I groan a little with the pain that accompanies the first few movements after hours of stillness. "I don't think I'm up for it today, Beck. My back is hurting."

"You *need* fresh air," she says, exasperated.

What she doesn't understand is how little I really *do* need.

At first, I listened intently to the doctors as they prescribed everything that would be required to wage this war. It's funny how they always use the language of soldiers. They said that first I would need surgery, but that I did not need to worry. The tumor was large, but did not appear to have spread. It was in situ. Contained. But they were wrong. They would need to extract my lymph nodes. I needed radiation, I needed chemotherapy. Every week, Becca drove me from Quimby to Burlington, where I received the treatment I needed to survive. I needed to keep my appetite up, I needed rest, I needed to fight. But even with every necessity fulfilled, I was losing. New growths blossomed like flowers on soldiers' graves.

Now, I only need something sweet to eat after dinner. Warm pajamas. Music. Becca makes sure I have all these things.

It felt strange at first, when she reappeared. Shortly after my surgery, she moved home from New York, where she'd been since college, trying to make a career as an actress. She had been offered a job at the high school, teaching social studies and coaching drama. When she found out I was sick, she knocked on my door and said, "What can I do?"

I hadn't seen her in so long, she was almost a stranger. So I shrugged and said, "I don't really need much."

Now, she brings me the eclairs I love, and big bags of Snickers bars that the doctors say I definitely do *not* need. Sometimes, she stays with me all night, just the way she did when we were kids, and we'll listen to music until one of us falls asleep. Sometimes, I think the only thing I really need now is Becca.

"Fine," I say, and take the wool sweater she is holding out to me. "Let's go for a walk."

She knows I've been thinking about my mother lately. And I think she knows I've been thinking about him, too.

"I wouldn't want to be Maria, anyway," Becca said.

We were sitting on a small sawdust mountain near the Pond, chucking rocks into the half-frozen water. We'd taken the bus home after the tryouts instead of waiting for Quinn, but I'd forgotten my key.

"Liesl is so much prettier," she said, pulling one long strand of red hair under her nose and sniffing it.

"Maybe my mom went to Austria," I said absently. We'd been playing this game since she disappeared.

"Paris!"

"Italy," I said, halfheartedly. I picked up a heavy rock and threw it toward the center of the Pond. It landed on a frozen patch and sat there.

"Africa?"

I laughed, but my stomach turned a little.

Becca nodded her head and stared at her feet. She'd had the same pair of boots since sixth grade. That was when she'd stopped growing. While the seams of my clothes strained, and the hems of my skirts and pants kept rising, Becca remained small. Sometimes she said she was afraid that she'd never grow another inch. I was afraid I'd never stop.

"Do you think you'll have to kiss Rolf?" she asked.

"What?"

"In the play, does Liesl kiss Rolf? In the movie, they kiss. In the gazebo, remember?"

"I don't know," I said. "I hope not."

At this point, neither one of us had really kissed anyone. I'd come close once, at an eighth-grade party when I was forced into a closet with Melissa Ball's younger brother, Frank. He'd smelled like sour milk when he got close to me, and I'd dodged his lips. The one I'd wanted to be in the closet with was Blue Henderson. He smelled like autumn apples, and once when he tackled me playing keep-away, we'd been pressed together long enough for me to imagine what it might feel like to be older. To be in love. But Blue got chickenpox before Melissa's party, and Frank kept lunging at me all night with his hands and hips and tongue.

"You think Quinn's home yet?" Becca asked, shivering a little in her sweater. She didn't wear a coat until after it started snowing, because the only one she had was bright purple with fur around the hood and she'd had it since fourth grade.

"I dunno. Let's go check," I said. "If not, we could go to your house."

"Nah, my mom's got the kitchen tore up. Remodeling. She says no company."

I'd known Becca since kindergarten, and I knew what her house looked like. Her mother was always coming up with reasons for me not to come over. She didn't like Becca spending time with me. It hurt in the same way the glances and whispers from the Quimby girls did. As if I were dirty. Stained.

Back at the house, my father had been by to visit. Sleep was riled up the way he got only when Daddy came by. He was circling the house, bumping into furniture and walls. I think even he felt betrayed. Quinn was locked in his room, and there was a bag of groceries on the table. Generic macaroni and cheese, motor oil, detergent, and bread. Fifteen dollars and change at the bottom of the bag. A note scribbled on the receipt, "Missed you at home. Working tonight. See you at the game tomorrow? Love, Dad."

I dumped everything onto the kitchen table and scooped the money into my hand. I'd almost forgotten the homecoming game scheduled for that weekend. Even Becca seemed to have forgotten about it with all the excitement of the auditions.

"You still wanna go to the game tomorrow?" I asked.

"Of course," she said. "It's *homecoming.*"

The next day at the football game, I looked everywhere for my father, but I only found Roxanne, sitting high on the bleachers wearing one of Jake's jerseys with a scarf and mittens.

"You seen my dad?" I asked her as I climbed up the steps.

"He's workin'," she said. Her voice crackled like flames. Then she smiled sweetly, looking at her friend, who was busy adjusting her bra strap underneath layers and layers of clothes. "This is Eddie's girl, Piper."

"Hi, honey," the woman said, holding out her hand. It was cold and clammy.

"I'll tell him you were lookin' for him," she said.

"Tell him we need wood, we're almost down to a half-cord and it isn't even December yet," I said.

"Sure," she said, frowning.

I yanked on Becca's hand and pulled her away from the bleachers, where she had started to make herself comfortable. "Let's go."

I walked briskly away from the football field, up the hill past the school, and through the gate into the cemetery. I could hear Becca behind me, struggling to keep up. I kicked the first headstone I saw. It hurt my foot but I kept walking.

"Hey," Becca said. "Wait up."

I got to another headstone and kicked it, hard. It was ancient. Gray and crumbling. And instead of resisting, I felt it give with the force of my kick, watched as it fell slowly backward, pulling up bits of frozen ground with it.

"Shit," I whispered.

"Shit's right," Becca said. "Let's get the hell out of here."

We stopped running when we got to the parking lot behind the school. I collapsed on the grass, breathing cold autumn air into my lungs like smoke.

"I hate that bitch," I said. I lay on my back, staring up at the sky. It was strangely cloudless. The sun was bright and made my eyes ache.

"We've got extra wood at home. I can get my dad to bring some over in his truck," Becca offered, even though she knew it wasn't wood that I needed.

I almost didn't go to the first rehearsal that Monday afternoon. Over the weekend I'd come to believe that it was ridiculous, my pretending to be anyone other than who I was. I was about as far from Liesl as anyone could be. The only similarity was that neither of us had a mother. And the women who had stepped in, Maria and Roxanne, were about as far removed as day from night.

On Sunday I stayed in bed all day, reading the script Mrs. Jasper had given me after the auditions. Quinn had the day off, too, but had decided to hike up Franklin to see if he could find snow. He left at five o'clock in the morning with his skis sticking out of the rear window of my mother's car. Becca called three times to make sure I was still going to do the play with her. By the fourth time, I let the phone ring and ring. The fifth time, I picked up the receiver angrily. "Becca, I told you I'm thinking about it. Let me read the damn thing—"

"Piper?"

My hands started to shake.

"Honey?"

My mother's voice was so far away it could have been coming from someone else's dream.

"Mum?" I said, my throat thick with tears and disbelief.

"It's me, honey. Are you okay? I just was taking a nap and I had a terrible dream, and I . . . I just needed to hear your voice. . . . You're okay, though, right?" Her voice sounded the way it always did in the middle of the night when she woke up from a nightmare and needed me to make everything okay.

"Mum," I said, all of my words gone except for the only one that mattered.

"It was the worst dream. I'm so sorry." As she woke up I could hear her realizing what she had done. The mistake she'd made. "Now, honey, let's not tell anybody I called, okay? Not Daddy. Not even Quinn. I'm so sorry. I was just so worried about you. . . ."

"Wait," I said, trying to find the words that would tether her, the ones that would hold her voice on the line. It felt like the times I had tried to hold water, the times I'd tried to hold sand. "I won't tell. I won't tell anyone," I pleaded.

But she was already gone.

I was still lying in bed with the script to *The Sound of Music* dog-eared on my chest. I laid my head on my pillow and listened to the slow click and the dial tone on the other end of the line. Then I took the heavy receiver and hit my nightstand. The noise startled me, the loudness of resistance. I raised my arm again and pounded the phone against the wood until the varnish chipped. Until it stopped resisting, until the wood split. My voice didn't belong to me. The sounds were primitive, coming from some subterranean place.

When the phone rang again, I answered breathless, exhausted. "Mum?"

"Piper?" Becca sounded confused. "Piper, did your mom call you?"

"I . . . I was sleeping," I said, stumbling, crying. "I was dreaming."

"It's just me," she said. "Are you okay? Do you need me to come over?"

I went because of Becca, I went because watching her pick through the bin of winter coats that someone had just dropped off at Boo's made me feel sad. When she found the long wool coat, the camel-colored one with furry cuffs, her face lit up, and she spun in circles in Boo's driveway while Boo and I passed the cold basketball back and forth. I knew I couldn't say no to her.

So we went together after last period to the auditorium to wait for Mrs. Jasper and Mr. Hammer to let us inside. Lucy Applebee was leaning against the trophy case in the hallway, reading her script intently. She would look up and whisper her lines, and then look back down again. Serious. Important. She was going to be the nun who sings "Climb Ev'ry Mountain" to Maria.

Melissa Ball showed up in her field hockey uniform. "I don't know how I'm going to find the time for this," she said loudly to anyone who would listen. "We've still got two more games and then playoffs." She sighed and bent down to adjust her bleached white tube sock and knee pad. She was slated to be Louisa, the second-oldest girl.

Mr. Hammer arrived then, a tattered leather bag flung over his shoulder, one shoe untied. His hair was mussed, like a boy's. He smiled nervously at us. I felt shy suddenly, his embarrassment rubbing off on me. He fumbled with a ring of keys, trying three different ones before the door finally relented. He smiled weakly at us and held the door open, ushering us into the dark auditorium.

He sat on the edge of the stage, and we all sat in the first row.

"Today, I just want to read through the script. I just want to go through it once, to hear your voices. We won't do the songs yet: we'll get started on that next week."

Becca hadn't taken her coat off, but she was perched at the edge of her seat, looking intently at Mr. Hammer. He was younger than a lot of our teachers. Most of them had been teaching at Quimby High for twenty years or more.

"Mr. Hammer?" Melissa said, waving her hand frantically. "I have a game on Wednesday. I *have* to be there."

"Nick," he said. "Please, after school you can all call me Nick."

Melissa looked confused. "But, Mr. Hammer, about the game?"

"If you don't feel that you have the time for rehearsals, we should talk later."

"But, *Nick,*" she said.

"Later, please. Thank you."

It took only about an hour to read through the script, and then Mr. Hammer sent us home. When Becca and I left the auditorium, Melissa was talking to him quietly at the edge of the stage.

We went outside to wait for Quinn, and Melissa came running up behind us.

"Nice coat," she said.

Becca looked around first to see who Melissa was talking to and when she realized it was her, she smiled brightly, looking down at the coat. Her freckles were dark against her pink cheeks.

"It's *exactly* like one of mine that my mom just donated to charity," Melissa said. "Funny. Just like it."

Becca's smile faded.

Melissa grinned wickedly and swung her duffle bag over her shoulder.

"Fuck you," I whispered.

Becca hit me in the arm.

"Excuse me?" Melissa said, her jaw dropping.

"You heard me." I felt my voice rising again, to the surface from the darkest places inside. "I said, *fuck you.*"

"Girls?" Mr. Hammer said, emerging from the auditorium. "What's going on here?"

I felt my skin grow hot.

"Nothing." Melissa smiled. "I was just complimenting Becca on her coat."

Back at my house that night, while Becca and I read through the script again, Becca took off the coat and folded it neatly. She set it next to her on my bed, and as we read, she rubbed the furry cuffs between her fingers.

Becca and I still play dress-up. After the surgery, and later after my hair began to thin and then fall out in my hands like feathers, she brought home bags and bags full of costumes. Loud and garish, but somehow the mountain of clothes and wigs on my bed made everything better.

"Look," she said. "I'm Diana Ross!" In a red dress, her red hair hidden inside a sleek black wig, Becca laughed until she had to run to the bathroom.

I stuffed a bra with rolled-up stockings and became Marilyn Monroe, Dolly Parton, Madonna. The costumes were versatile. I could be anyone I wanted to be. I could be whole.

She still dresses me. When I haven't changed out of my flannel pajamas in a week, she'll force me to get up and put on a pair of jeans, a clean T-shirt, and a necklace or a new barrette. She brushes the hair I have left, muttering under her breath when it fails to yield to her fingers. She helps me to wear the costume of someone who isn't dying.

Last night she brought home a straight blond wig, parted in the middle, and a black beret. "We're going out," she said.

Within minutes, she had me dressed in a black turtleneck sweater and jeans, the blond wig perched on my head, secured with the black beret.

"You look gorgeous!" she said. "Like a beatnik. No, no, like Twiggy!"

And then we were in her car, headed to St. Johnsbury for the Chinese restaurant.

Remarkably, the cancer has not affected my appetite. Especially now that I've stopped the chemo, the familiar waves of crippling nausea are gone. I ordered sweet-and-sour chicken and four egg rolls. The waitress didn't bat an eye at my ensemble. Neither did the two guys who were eating in the booth by the window.

When we left the restaurant Becca said, "Thank you for playing with me," gesturing to the wig and my new beret.

"Let's not go home yet," I said. "Let's get a drink somewhere. Let's go dancing."

"Really?" she asked, her eyes hopeful and sparkling.

"Why not?"

At the Lodge, the doorman took my ID and raised his eyebrows suspiciously. In the photo I was twenty-six years old, with long brown curly hair. I weighed a hundred and thirty-five pounds. "This you?" he asked.

I thought for a second about going into an explanation of how it came to this, about how my hair fell out so quickly I didn't even have time to adjust to the idea of being bald. But before I could open my mouth, Becca said, "She's in disguise." And then softer, "Ex-boyfriend's a stalker."

The doorman ushered us in, looking past us to the parking lot to see if we'd been followed.

The music was loud, and the smoke was thick. Becca motioned toward the bar and I took one of the stools. Becca sat next to me and spun around to get a better view of the rest of the bar. I stared straight ahead, past the glasses and bottles, at my reflection in the mirror behind the bar. It didn't look anything like me. This girl was pretty. This girl was well.

"I'll have a beer, whatever you've got on special," I said to the bartender.

"Do you really think you should drink?" Becca whispered.

"I'm fine. Let me live a little."

"Sure," she said, shrugging. "Hey, look at those guys over there. They're the ones from the restaurant. They must have followed us here."

I turned around and saw the two men showing their IDs to the bouncer.

The bartender set down my beer. But when I pressed the glass to my lips, I felt suddenly sadder than I had in a long time. The cold condensation on my glass, two cute guys looking at us from the doorway, and the simplicity of the twirling seat beneath me were suddenly overwhelming.

"Do you feel like dancing? 'Cause we could ask them," Becca said.

And I realized she'd forgotten that we were only playing, that this wasn't real. And for a minute I'd almost let myself forget, too. I looked at the blond girl in the mirror and my chest heaved.

"I need to go home," I said.

Becca's face fell, but she nodded. "Okay."

Outside it was snowing. Small white flakes descended in triangles of light beneath the street lamps. Becca twirled around with her tongue stuck out. The snow melted as soon as it touched her skin. It wasn't even October yet; the snow wouldn't last. I knew this, but it made me feel betrayed. It was too early. Winter wasn't supposed to come yet. I wasn't ready.

It began with snow.

The night before we were scheduled to start learning the songs for *The Sound of Music,* it began snowing. Quinn was beside himself. He hurried home from work that night with all the ingredients for lasagna. Neither one of us knew how to cook, but we busied ourselves in the kitchen with our mother's cookbooks, mozzarella, mushrooms, and the unruly noodles. Sleep seemed suspicious. As I browned the ground beef in a skillet, he stared at me, cockeyed, in the kitchen doorway. Even after I tossed a handful of hamburger into his bowl, he looked at me as if I were up to something.

"What, Sleepyhead?" I laughed and stirred the tomato sauce into the pan.

After it came out of the oven, Quinn served up two big plates and we sat at the kitchen table watching the snow come down through the open curtains. He opened two bottles of beer and handed me one. I looked at him suspiciously, feeling the way Sleep must have felt when we offered him something other than his usual Purina, and Quinn shrugged.

I'd never had anything to drink before, except for a glass of wine with Mum one rainy afternoon when nobody was home but us. It had made me feel warm and woozy. The beer did the same.

"I'm going to make States this year," Quinn said, staring

out the window at the falling snow illuminated by the bare
bulb on the porch. "If I get to States and place, I'll get a scholarship to UVM."

Quinn had taught himself to ski. He bought a pair of used
skis at a yard sale when he was twelve years old. Franklin didn't
have a chairlift yet, just a rope tow that went about a thousand
yards up the face of the mountain, so as soon as snow fell, he
would hike up with his skis and poles on his back and then ski
down. Every weekend he hitchhiked to Jay Peak and spent all
his extra money on lift tickets. While half of Vermont hiber-
nated in winter, Quinn came to life.

After dinner and after two beers had made me dizzy and
silly, Quinn made a fire.

"You want to hear something on the radio?" he asked, after
getting nothing but snow on the TV.

"Oh, oh," I said, standing up too fast from the couch. I
steadied myself with the armrest and laughed. "Oopsy."

"Piper," Quinn reprimanded softly.

"I'm fine. Let's find Mum's records," I said. "She has the
best ones."

Quinn looked worried when I started to pull on my jacket
and boots and mittens.

"They're out in the shed. I'll be right back."

The porch light made the fresh snow glow golden in the
driveway. It was almost a shame to step on it. I looked at my
footprints and thought they looked a little like an animal's instead of a girl's. When I got to the shed door I shivered. My
hair was covered with snow, and the realization that I hadn't
been inside the shed since she left hit me like a falling icicle.

I stamped my boots hard on the ground. When I pushed
the heavy door open, I almost expected to see her there, sitting
on the high stool where she worked, all the colors of today's
broken things in front of her. But when I pulled the shoestring

cord attached to the light, the room was empty. The card cata-
logue of glass was covered in a film of sawdust, like everything
else in these parts of the woods, and the area where she
worked was tidy. I took my mittens off and ran my fingers
across the makeshift countertop, hoping for a sliver to pierce
my skin. But she had been careful to get rid of the pieces before she left.

There was a pile of boxes in the corner. The milk crate
where she kept her records was teetering on the top of the
pile. Usually she kept it inside the house, but I remembered
that she'd brought the record player into the shed that summer
and had wanted the records near. When she left us, she left
them there.

I lifted the entire box off the stack, careful not to let any of
the carelessly piled records slip out. I hurried out of the shed
and back into the falling snow, turning off the light and closing
the door behind me.

In the house, I felt sober again. Either the cold or the trip
into the shed had made the fuzzy edges sharp. Quinn was sitting in Daddy's La-Z-Boy, his feet propped up and his arm behind his head. He sat up when I came in. I set the milk crate in
the middle of the floor. There were a couple of records I
wanted to find. I lifted each one carefully out of the box and
shuffled through the stack, looking. Remembering. When I
found the one I'd been looking for, the one with "Stormy
Weather," I held it up and said. "Quinn! Here it is! This is the
one!" And I pulled the cold record out of the sleeve. But as I
was looking to see which side the song was on the record
snapped in my hands. It broke into two, perfect halves, and my
palms stung from the impact.

"Oh no!" I cried.

Quinn got out of the chair and joined me on the floor.
"It's okay."

"God, Quinn, this is her favorite. She'll be so mad." My hand flew to my mouth then, with the understanding of what I'd said.

"It's okay, Piper," Quinn said as I started to shiver. He put an awkward hand on my shoulder, and rubbed it gently. "It's okay."

But it wasn't okay. Nothing was okay. Alone in this house where a family used to live, I felt abandoned. Discarded. A second-hand sweater dropped off at Boo's. Outgrown, old, soiled.

I picked up one half of the shattered record and thought about the ragged edge, about whether it was sharp enough to cut. If it could cut, then there was proof that broken things can harm you. I squeezed my hand tightly, the sharp edge pressing into my palm. But when the skin broke and a small trickle of blood ran down my arm, Quinn grabbed my wrist, prying the record loose. He looked at me, afraid.

"She's not coming back, is she?" I asked him, my eyes blurry with tears.

He shook his head no, let go of my hand, and turned to the window. "No, she's not." It was quiet here. Without music there was only the sound of snow.

I swallowed hard and wiped at my eyes with the back of my hand. "It's okay. I'm fine," I said, shrugging his hand off my shoulder when he reached for me again. "Really."

That night it kept snowing. I watched it through my window until I couldn't tell if it was falling up or down. It looked like bits of white glass, and I thought Mum should have had a drawer for this, a drawer called *Snow*.

In the morning I heard Quinn outside trying to start Mum's car. It wouldn't start, and it wouldn't have mattered. The snowplows wouldn't make it up to the Pond until noon. When Quinn crawled back into bed in his long johns and wool socks, cussing and muttering under his breath, I dressed for a long walk. I figured I could probably walk far enough or hitch a ride into town in time to get to second or third period, and I'd be certain not to miss rehearsals. I felt determined to get to school, as if my life depended on it.

"Where you going?" Quinn's voice came from his room.

"School," I said. "I'll hitch. Wanna come?"

"Nah," he said. "Taking the day off."

"Sure?" I asked again, pulling on my hat with the earflaps.

"Sure."

I heaved my backpack onto my shoulders and headed into the cold morning. It was still snowing; the sky was completely white. When I stepped out onto the road, I could have been stepping into a cloud. It was two miles to Gormlaith and then another six miles to Hudson's, the closest store and gas station. I figured I was bound to find somebody between here and there willing to give me a ride.

I trudged through the new snow, going over my lines in my head. I had already memorized all of my own songs as well as the lyrics to all the others. In my room, when Quinn was still at work, I sang them softly, trying on my voice like someone else's clothes.

By the time I got to Gormlaith, I was covered in snow and numb. Not one car had passed me on the road. My cheeks were hot, and I couldn't feel my toes. I thought about turning around, returning home and crawling into bed like Quinn, but I'd made it this far. I figured if I could walk for another mile there would have to be some traffic. Even if they weren't headed into Quimby, they might be willing to give me a lift to where I was going.

I walked past the McInnes camp with the tree house, past old Magoo Tucker's, the Beans' and the Hadleys', and around the lake to the far end, where I found a cottage with a swing.

The seat was heavy with snow. The stained-glass windows were edged in white. And remarkably, there was a car in the driveway, exhaust rising in white clouds from the tailpipe. I stopped walking and stared at the car in disbelief. I was cold and tired, and I figured I might as well go knock on the door and ask for a ride.

But just as I was about to start up the slippery flagstone path, the screen door swung open and a man emerged, bundled up almost as much I was. He was staring at the ground, watching his feet, careful not to slip, as he walked to the car.

"Excuse me," I said. My voice startled me. I expected it to be as quiet as snow.

His feet spun like wheels beneath him and I reached out to help steady him, but his arms quickly compensated for his loss of balance. Like a tightrope walker, he found his equilibrium again. He looked at me. "That was a close one. You startled me!"

"I'm sorry," I said.

"Quite all right." He smiled and pulled his hood down. It was Mr. Hammer.

"Oh, hi!" I said. "Mr. Hammer, I didn't know you lived here."

He looked confused, and I felt my cheeks growing warm; all of me, in fact, felt like steam.

"It's me, Piper," I said, pulling off my own hat. I could hear the static electricity in the ends of my hair.

"Oh, Piper. I couldn't even see your face! What are you doing here?" He still looked startled.

"I live up at the Pond," I said by way of explanation. "My brother's car wouldn't start."

"So you're walking?"

"I was hoping to hitch a ride," I said, sticking up my mittened thumb.

"Well, hop on in," he said, motioning to the rusty Volvo.

"Are you sure?"

"We're headed in the same direction, aren't we?" He laughed and opened the passenger door for me.

I got into the front seat and snow fell all around me. The vents blew hot air, and the white crystals immediately melted, making everything wet. Mr. Hammer got in the driver's side. "Well, then. Off we go."

It was warm inside the car, and he smelled like coffee and snow. It was the warmest I had felt in a long time. I unzipped my coat and unwrapped my scarf. He turned the radio on to the public radio station out of St. Johnsbury, and tapped his gloved fingers on the dashboard along with the violin concerto.

"Do you plan to study music in college?" he asked, turning to me. His eyes were wide and interested.

I had been thinking about Rolf, and whether I would have to kiss him.

"Music?" I asked.

"Music," he said. "Voice?"

"Oh, I don't know. I haven't thought about college, really. I'm only a freshman." I took off my mittens and put them in my lap. I looked down at my knuckles, at my torn-up cuticles, and put the mittens back on again.

"But your voice . . ." he said, still looking at me instead of the road.

"What?" I said and then gasped despite myself as we caught a bit of ice and fishtailed.

He grabbed the wheel tightly, correcting, and said, "I'm sorry. I'm so sorry. We're okay. There we go." He looked back at me sheepishly. "It's just rare, you know. To have such a mature voice at your age."

I blushed at *mature*. "Thanks," I said, shrugging.

"I would have chosen you to play Maria," he said, looking away from the road again. "But Charlene Applebee's husband,

Mr. Applebee is—how do I say this?—*funding* the production. Please, that's between us, but I wanted you to know that I really believe you have a gift."

"You're kidding," I said, incredulously. "He *bought* them the parts?"

"I shouldn't have said anything," he said, shaking his head. "I always do that. Me and my big mouth."

"I won't say anything," I said. "Don't worry. It's just . . . girls like that. Melissa and Lucy . . ."

"I know." He nodded. "I know. Trust me."

When we pulled into the parking lot at school, I gathered my things and bundled myself back up again. "Hey, thanks," I said and reached out my hand, awkwardly to shake his.

"Any time." He smiled and shook my hand. "What are neighbors for?"

That afternoon as I sang, I thought *mature* and *rare*. I also thought about the smell of snow.

I am conscious of the seasons now as I never used to be. Each season that passes feels like a small miracle. The seasons make me feel as if I am moving in circles instead of forward. I've made almost three circles since I found out I was sick. Three springs, three summers, three autumns, and two winters. It is nearing winter again, and I worry that that will make things complete. My body knows this.

I moved into my apartment in Quimby because of the view from the living room. It's on the top floor of one of the old mansions on the park; the windows in the living room face a careful maze of maples that, in autumn, turn fifty-two shades of red. You can't even see the bandstand in the center of the park for all the crimson. From my sewing table in the window, I watch for the clues that signify a change in the seasons. The mud and puddles of spring, the thick haze and dew of summer, the collage of autumn colors. Now I am waiting for the leaves to fall and leave the cold branches exposed like bones. Every day, I pull back the curtains, turn on the sewing machine, and look to the leaves for evidence that time is passing and that I am moving forward with it.

I can also see Melissa Ball's old house and the house where Lucy Applebee's family used to live. Most of these houses have been turned into apartments now. As single-family houses, they had five, sometimes six bedrooms. No one seems to need

as much space anymore. It's just not efficient. I am grateful for
the divisions made in this house. I have all the space I need in
my attic apartment: a room I painted the color of sun-bleached
bricks to sleep in, a little kitchen with bright yellow linoleum
and a painted tile countertop, a bathroom with a clawfoot tub
deep enough to drown in, and a living room where I can
watch the colors of the seasons in the tops of the trees. My rent
is cheap, and Bog has a warm place to lie in front of the gas
fireplace.

Over the last five years, I have watched the little park,
Quimby's hub, from these windows. It's like watching a clock.
If you look too closely, you won't see time pass, but if you
glance away, when you look back again the hands will have
moved.

Not much changes, except the way the town girls dress. I
watched them all summer during the Wednesday-night band
concerts, huddled in groups of three or four by the stone fountain, their skin white in the glow of the soft street lamps that il-
luminate the park. I watched the boys too, pretending only to
be passing through the park on their way somewhere else.
Hands shoved into their front pockets, long hair hanging in
their eyes. Only the way the town girls dress has changed.
When last summer ended and the leaves turned from green to
gold and red, filling my window with autumnal fire, through
the flames I watched old ladies in pairs walk to and from the
Quimby Atheneum, their shopping bags filled with books. I
watched Casper pick up imaginary bottles from the cold
ground and put them in the shopping cart he stole from the
Shop-N-Save. I watched mothers with their babies, bundled
against the chill of September and then October. I've lived in
this little corner of the world my entire life, and the way the
town girls dress is the only thing that has changed.

I am on the verge of winter. I can smell it through the
cracks in the woodwork around my windows.

Daddy came home one night near the end of November with a black eye and thirteen purple stitches in his cheek. He stood in the doorway like an apparition, holding onto the frame with the transparent hands of a ghost.

"Jesus," Quinn said, looking up from his skis, which he was waxing in the middle of the living room floor. "What happened to you?"

"Got into it with someone down at the Lodge," he said, taking off his cap and tossing it on the kitchen table.

I stared down at my math homework. But the numbers swam across the page. I looked up at Daddy and saw him wince as he leaned into the fridge.

"A customer?" I asked.

"Mmm," Daddy said behind the refrigerator door.

Neither Quinn nor I seemed to know what to do with Daddy in the house. We'd gotten used to his absence by then. Having him home felt wrong, like company you don't really want. But neither one of us asked him what he'd come home for. Not then and not later, not when Daddy made himself a sandwich and not after Quinn had ruined our only iron pressing hot wax onto the bottom of his skis. We just pretended it was perfectly normal for Daddy to disappear into the bathroom and run the water so hot that steam poured out from under the door.

But I didn't sleep that night, not with that stranger in our house. Instead I stayed awake and listened to him whispering into the phone in the kitchen. I sat with my back against my closed door and listened for clues. Maybe I fell asleep sitting there, and maybe it was a dream, but I swear I heard him crying.

Daddy stayed only one more night, and then he started staying in town again with Roxanne.

In English class, I kept staring at the back of Jake's neck. When I couldn't take it anymore, I tapped on his thick shoulder. He turned around and looked at me, confused. We'd never spoken.

"Hey," I said, flushing red.

"Hey."

"I was just wondering . . . you know, my dad and your mom . . ."

"What about 'em?" he asked. His breath smelled like chewing tobacco.

"I was just wondering if you might know what's going on."

"What do you mean?" he asked.

"I don't know," I said, and suddenly I didn't. "Forget it."

"Sure," he said, and turned back around. His best friend, Gopher, leaned over to whisper something into Jake's ear. They both looked back at me and laughed.

Later, Becca and I were sitting on the bleachers after school, waiting for rehearsals to start, and I overheard Gopher telling one of the other football players, "Jake's mom beat the crap out of that guy. Sent him to the hospital. No shit. Now his daughter's got the hots for Jake."

When I was eleven years old, a boy named Monty moved into a house down the road from us. Because we were neighbors and because he was two years older than I, Mum thought it would be a good idea if we walked home from the bus stop together. Monty had a glass eye. I thought that was the most fascinating thing in the world. He told me that his brother shot the real one out with a BB gun. On purpose. I'd met his brother, and I believed it.

Monty and I got to be friends on those long walks back to the Pond from Gormlaith. The school bus didn't go as far as the Pond. The roads were bad; they caused too much wear and tear on the town's only bus. He took out his glass eye and let me hold it in the palm of my hand. I remember thinking that it felt exactly like a cold marble. I showed him the pale scar I had on my stomach from the time my appendix almost burst. We shared stories of gore and horror the way we shared our lunches. He always had Devil Dogs he was willing to give up for my mother's homemade oatmeal cookies.

When it started to get cold and the roads turned black with ice, Monty took to shoving me down. He'd wait until I wasn't expecting it, and then he would run from behind me and push as hard as he could. I split my lip twice and scuffed my chin. Pretty soon he couldn't sneak up on me anymore because I was always waiting for the next attack.

The stories he told me became more and more gruesome. He told me about the time he blew up fifteen toads with his brother's fireworks. About how he threw up in the snow once and then his dog ate the frozen vomit. I made up stories to match his. But mine were always about blood.

One afternoon, instead of walking me home first, he said, "Let's go to my house," and pulled me by the hand until my arm felt as if it might come out of its socket. He dragged me behind the small house to the barn in the back and threw open the door. Hanging from the rafters was a newly killed buck. There was ice around its eyes.

"My brother got him this morning before school."

I swallowed hard and tried not to see the deer's eyes. They looked like glass.

"You ever seen one before?"

" 'Course," I said. But I'd really only seen them thrown in the backs of passing pickups. Daddy didn't hunt.

"Then you probably seen one split down the middle, too, huh?"

"Sure," I said.

He smiled in his crooked way and reached into his pocket, pulling out a Swiss Army knife. I knew he didn't know what he was doing, and that his brother would probably kill him when he saw the damage he'd done, but I didn't stop him as he poked the knife tentatively at the deer's exposed belly. I forced my eyes to stay wide open when he sawed away at the animal's tough skin and didn't hold my nose when the smell of the steaming insides hit me.

Monty beamed at me.

"Big deal." I shrugged.

Then he slipped his hand into the pocket-sized hole he'd made, and it took everything I had not to gag. A few seconds later, stifling his own retches, he pulled something brown and wet out of the deer and held it in front of my nose.

"The heart," he said, though it was probably the liver. And I knew then and there that love was a violent thing.

The next time Daddy came home blue with bruises and anxious with shame, I closed myself in the bathroom and would not come out.

"Piper," he pleaded through the door.

I sat on the toilet and stared out the window at the red plastic hummingbird feeder my mother had hung from one of the birch trees. The sugar water was gone and the red had faded to pink in the sun.

"Come on, honey, please let me in," he said. He sounded pathetic; my throat was thick. I felt sorry for him. I hated him.

Outside, the ground was brown; sun had melted most of that pristine snow from the first storm, leaving only dirty piles of it in the places protected by shade. Sleep was outside, hitched on his run. He paced back and forth, stopping at each end when the chain caught short and choked him. Daddy had made him go outside after he found a pair of his shoes chewed up, even though Sleep had done it over a month earlier.

I tapped my fingers against the window, trying to get Sleep's attention. As soon as Daddy left, I would let him in again.

"Piper, let me in right now."

"Why?" I asked. My voice startled me. I hadn't planned on speaking to him.

"Because," he said, "I'm your father, and I told you to. Now open it." He sounded angry now.

"Fine," I said, standing up and unlocking the door.

He stood in the doorway, his right cheek puffy. Scratches like thin red rivers ran across his neck. He looked at me for consolation, and I felt something like thunder welling up inside me.

"Honey, help Daddy find the Bactine," he said softly.

I thought of skinned knees and bumped elbows, my mother's hands working to open the wrappers of a Band-Aid. I'd sat on the toilet in the bathroom, crying through gravel-riddled palms and bumps on my head. Mum would know what to do about Daddy's scratches and bruises. She'd be able to make Roxanne's handprints disappear from his cheeks. But then again, if she were here, none of this would be happening.

Daddy came into the bathroom and moved toward the medicine cabinet and I lunged into him with every ounce of strength I had. He stumbled back, surprised, and braced himself in the doorway. I pounded my fists against his chest, alarmed by how thin he was. I could feel his ribs, sharp and hard. Tears ran hot down my cheeks.

"Piper, stop it. Stop." He sounded like a boy. It made me want to hit him harder.

I kept hitting him until my shoulders ached and he was holding me up.

He looked at me, confused and sad, and I pulled away from him with one last burst of energy.

"How could you?" I screamed.

He turned to face me, standing in the middle of the kitchen. The floor was cold under my bare feet. "How could you be with her?" I asked.

But instead of defending himself, instead of explaining away the fine scratches that looked like a map from his chin to his chest, he just stood there, his shoulders falling forward. He lowered his head, and I stomped my feet on the kitchen floor the way I used to when I was little and mad and thought that making noise would force people to listen.

But he offered me nothing, not one word.

"Your mother is gone," he said after a long silence. *"She* left me."

"You made her go. You made her leave!" I yelled; my throat was hoarse. I didn't sound like myself. The voice that came out of me was like flames, burning everything it touched. "All of this is your fault. And I'm glad."

He looked up at me, his eyes wide and terrified.

"I'm glad you let her beat the shit out of you. You deserve it."

Daddy slowly took his jacket off the back of the chair at the kitchen table and pulled it on. He reached into the pocket and took out his wallet and opened it up. He pulled out two twenty-dollar bills, all the money he had, and held it out to me.

"You'll be needing to get some new boots."

I crossed my arms and left him standing there with his arm

extended. He set the money down on the table between us and then turned to the door.

After he was gone, after my heart had slowed back down to its normal pace, leaving only an echo of the pounding in my chest, I pulled on my old boots, too small and with bald soles, and went out to the backyard, where Sleep was still pacing. Trying not to slip on the icy ground, I unhooked him from the run and grabbed onto his collar when he tried to bolt. "Come on," I said. "Inside." He wagged his tail, and it slapped against my leg. I scooted him in the house, closing the door and locking it behind us.

I hate my father's cowardice. It haunts me more than my own fears.

After the pathologists confirmed that my body was being attacked, I waited nearly two months to call him. He didn't live in Quimby anymore, so he was easy to avoid. He had moved to Burlington almost three years before, with a woman he met at the bar. I knew he lived in an apartment on Pearl Street near Pearl Street Beverage. It was just down the hill from the hospital where I went for my chemo treatments. There were times when, dizzy and sick from the drugs, my veins sore from the needles, I thought about stopping by. Knocking on the door. Making him look me and my illness in the face. But every time I dream-walked the trip up the broken stairs of the old house to his door, I saw only the traces of Roxanne's anger running red across his face. I imagined the scars as fresh as the needle tracks in my arm.

When I finally told him I was sick, he was so quiet on the other end of the line that he could have been sleeping. He had nothing to offer me when I was fourteen, and he had nothing to offer me now.

"Do you need me to come stay with you?" he started, but he knew I wouldn't accept, or else he would never have offered in the first place.

So I gave him what *he* needed. "No, Daddy. I'm okay. I'm doing okay."

The woman he lives with wants me to love her, though, and she sends thoughtful little cards and gift certificates for things I would never buy myself: massages and facials, manicures and pedicures. Before I got sick, I never had such pretty feet and hands.

I hate my father's cowardice, but I don't fault him for his lack of valor; I come from a family of cowards. I am not brave either, never was.

Becca fell in love with Mr. Hammer the second day of rehearsals. I could see the pain of it in the way she wrung her hands and shuffled her feet. Her longing was tangible. It had a scent, loud and insistent, like drugstore perfume.

I watched her watching Mrs. Applebee, who pressed herself against Mr. Hammer at every possible opportunity. Charlene Applebee had a way of pushing herself into small spaces if it meant being closer to Mr. Hammer. I'd been bumped out of the way myself.

Her singing voice was shrill and wavery, like wind in the tops of trees. She didn't have any control over it; it could get away from her sometimes. I watched Becca wince with each misplaced note, with Charlene's frightening falsetto during "The Sound of Music."

Becca would play Brigitta, the middle girl. Marta and Gretl, the littlest ones, were going to be played by two girls from Quimby Graded. Becca wasn't much bigger than they were. Even wearing the navy blue pumps she'd found at the bottom of a bin at Boo's, she was still under five feet tall. She looked up to Mr. Hammer, eyes wide and hopeful. He rested his hand on her soft strawberry hair, forgot her name, and allowed Mrs. Applebee into those tight spaces. But Becca forgave him this.

We convinced Mr. Hammer to play the part of the Captain. Only three boys tried out for the play, and two of them were cast to play Friedrich and Kurt. The third boy, Howie, was a freshman and his voice was subject to whim, at one moment deep and sonorous and then suddenly as shrill as Mrs. Applebee's. He would play Rolf. Mr. Hammer seemed the natural choice for the Captain; he even looked a little like Christopher Plummer. This thrilled Mrs. Applebee to no end.

By the time we got to rehearsing "Edelweiss," I was aware of how painful all this was for Becca. His words had the power to crush; she was breaking into pieces.

"Edelweiss" was the only song that Mr. Hammer had to sing.

This is the moment in the play in which the Captain softens, when he lets down his guard and allows music to move him backward through time to the painful places. It was the only part of the movie that ever made me cry. I thought it was so strange that you could possibly feel pain and joy at the same time. For me, at fourteen, these feelings had always been mutually exclusive. And when Liesl joins him, the harmony of her own loss intertwined with his, my heart strained as tight as Sleep's collar at the end of his run.

"Edelweiss" was my favorite song in the whole play, even more than my duet with Rolf, which I always thought was sort of pathetic. All that "I'll let you take care of me" business.

Normally when we started working on a new song, Mr. Hammer would have everyone who wasn't in the scene sit in the recesses of the auditorium, but this time he asked everyone but me to leave.

"We'll do the blocking for the other children and Maria tomorrow," he said. And everyone left. Becca pointed toward the door and mouthed, "I'll wait for you outside."

Alone on the stage, I worried for a brief moment that he'd decided against having me play Liesl. I'd been less than enthusiastic about the duet with Rolf. I'd tried to hide my disgust at

Howie's sweaty palms on my back as we danced, and the way he spat right into my face when he sang, but I wasn't a very good actress. I knew this.

Mr. Hammer dragged a chair across the stage and sat on it backward, his chin resting on his hands. He smiled. I stood in the middle of the stage, awkward, and I had never felt so tall. I shrugged and said, "Should I sit down?"

"No, no. Please stand."

I put my hands in my pockets and looked at my feet. Instead of buying new boots with Daddy's money, I'd bought Quinn a pair of ski goggles. My old boots were scuffed and made my feet look huge. I blushed.

After several excruciating moments, he stood up and disappeared into the wings. He came out carrying a guitar. He turned the chair around, sitting down in it the right way, and started to pluck at the strings, tuning it. His fingers were long and narrow.

"My mother used to play the guitar," I said.

"Really?" he asked, his fingers continuing to move across the frets and keys, adjusting.

"Sometimes," I said.

"Did she teach you to sing?" he asked.

I shook my head. "I don't remember." Though I did remember those afternoons, our pockets filled with glass, when she asked me to sing for her. I also remembered the battered guitar without a case that she kept in the shed. She tried to teach me the names of the notes I was making, but I could never connect the colors of my voice with the letters she gave me.

"We should get started," he said, looking at me again, his expression puzzled. It made me feel like a mystery.

"Okay," I smiled. "I know the words already. I think."

"Good, good," he said. "This is my favorite song in the play. I don't care one way or the other about the rest."

"Me neither." I sighed, relieved. Lately, since I'd started rehearsing the scenes between Liesl and Rolf, I hadn't been feeling so fond of any of the songs. Howie was always trying to get next to me. Luckily, he wasn't in most of the scenes.

"Well, then, this is our lucky day," he said, and looked down at his hands, which had already started playing the opening cords.

His voice. His voice felt like wind across a field of small white flowers. I closed my eyes and saw all the colors of edelweiss, like the blankets of Queen Anne's lace that fell softly across the banks of the Pond. It had the fragrance of flowers, but was the color of snow.

My voice. Once, my mother and I borrowed a small rowboat and paddled out lazily to the island in the center of Lake Gormlaith. We took off our shoes and wandered through the trees, looking for glass. She thought we might find something special in this remote place. She was certain there would be some sort of treasure here. But in the middle of the lake, on the perfect island, the shores were empty of broken things. Pristine. Instead, we found blueberries. We might have walked right past them if we hadn't been so attentive to the ground. But my mother's fingers reached into the green below us and plucked one perfect berry. She turned it over in her hand, the same way she inspected the fragments we found, and then held it out to me. This is the way my voice felt. A perfect and small berry that I offered him like a gift.

At the end of the song, he set down the guitar and looked at me inquisitively.

I looked at my hands.

He was quiet for a long time, and then he said softly, "I'm not sure where we go next."

I looked up, scared but strangely thrilled. "What do you mean?"

He smiled and looked at me hard, like a question. "I. . ." he

said, ". . . I only meant that I think we need to get you somewhere to study. That it would be such a waste not to pursue
this talent of yours."

"Oh," I said, feeling the blue turning red, red.

"We'll talk about that more later," he said and picked up
the guitar. "One more time?"

"Sure," I said, and fell into his voice like a field of edelweiss
or snow.

I never told Becca about our conversation or about the
way my voice found its way through the field he made. I
thought it would hurt her feelings; I knew how much he was
crushing her. I didn't tell her because I was a coward. I was just
like my father. I was afraid that to tell would make it real. That
articulation was a dangerous thing.

The words have changed. *Diagnosis, treatment, recovery.* These were the stones I would need to cross this river. Now the words lack certainty; the stones are strewn, confusing my steps. I don't know which direction to go. *Time, possibility, prayer.* These are the slippery ones.

The night after the doctor tells me that the cancer has spread to my lungs, Boo offers to find my mother. Over dinner at her house she says, "She's not far. It wouldn't be hard. For her to come see you."

Boo's house looks exactly as it did when I was growing up. Not a picture on the wall has changed. Sometimes when I visit her, I feel like I'm stepping backward back into my childhood. The smells of meatloaf or tuna casserole or a New England boiled dinner are the same as when I was small. Even Boo has only changed slightly: the color of her hair, the lines around her mouth and eyes. She can still win at HORSE.

"Why didn't you ever offer to find her before?" I ask. "When I needed her then?"

Boo looks down at her plate, rakes her mashed potatoes with her fork. "I couldn't."

I think for a minute what it would be like to see my mother again. When I close my eyes sometimes, I can still see her purple Indian blouse, little mirrors sewn into the fabric, reflecting me as a child, clinging to her knees.

"It has to take me *dying* to get her here?" My hands and voice are shaking. "Isn't it a little too late now?"

Boo sets her fork down and reaches across the table for my hands. Part of me is waiting for her to reassure me, to say, *Piper, you're not dying.* But instead she says, "She wants to see you."

"I don't want to see her," I say, tears rolling hot down my cheeks. I can't even remember her face. "It's too late."

I try to imagine what my mother might have to say to me after all of these years. All she's had to offer me are broken things: envelopes with scattered postmarks, filled with glass. I've wished her back so many times. I think briefly that maybe my prayers are just now reaching God. That they have only been delayed like a letter without a correct zip code. But the thought of seeing her hurts more than the fact that she is gone. Hurts more than never knowing why she left in the first place.

"Boo, I can't see her," I say. "It's too much."

Too late. Metastasized. Futile. These are the ridiculous stones, too far apart to use as a bridge.

Blue Henderson started hanging around after school, waiting for me. It was inexplicable, this new interest of his, in theater. In me.

"How were rehearsals?" he asked, ramming his hands into his pockets, walking quickly to keep up with me.

"Fine," I said, mystified.

Becca was walking on the other side of me, equally confounded.

"Hey, you wanna go grab a cup of coffee at the diner?" he asked, and then motioned to Becca. "You too?"

"My brother's waiting to give us a ride home," I said.

Blue nodded. "That's cool. No big deal. Maybe tomorrow?"

"Sure," Becca said, skipping ahead of us. "We don't have rehearsals tomorrow because Nick has a faculty meeting." Becca and Mrs. Applebee were the only ones who had taken to calling Mr. Hammer by his first name.

"Great," Blue said. "Fantastic!" And he walked away.

"Becca," I said. "Jeez."

"What?" she asked. "He likes you."

I met Blue alone the next afternoon after school; Becca suddenly and conveniently had a terrible headache she couldn't shake and left after fourth period. Blue and I walked to the diner together, kicking rocks and trying to make conversation.

"I heard you singing," he said. His eyes looked like small brown pebbles under water.

"Really?" I asked.

"I snuck into the auditorium last week."

"Oh," I said.

It was cold outside, and I'd forgotten my mittens.

"Are your hands cold?" he asked.

I shrugged.

"Here," he said, pulling off his ski gloves and offering them to me.

"Thanks," I said. They were too big; my hands swam inside.

At the diner, we sat in a booth by the window, and ordered coffee and apple pie. I'd never *ordered* coffee before, never been to a restaurant without my mother or father before.

"So Quinn's your brother?" he asked, tearing three sugar packets at the same time and pouring the sugar into his coffee.

"Yeah," I said.

"He's an awesome skier. My brother's on the team, too. He says Quinn might place at States this year."

I nodded. "He wants to get a scholarship."

"Hey, are you going to the football game on Saturday?"

"No."

"Oh," he said, staring into his coffee cup.

"We're having Saturday rehearsals. 'Cause we missed today. I could meet you after. Maybe we could go see a movie or something?" I couldn't believe the words coming out of my mouth. They didn't seem to belong to me.

Blue's face brightened, and he set his coffee cup down. His hands were huge. "That'd be awesome. Cool."

Saturday afternoon, after rehearsals, Mr. Hammer asked me to stay on to practice our duet. Becca said she could call her mom for a ride, and she whispered, "Have fun on your date," in my ear on her way out.

"I have to be somewhere at six," I said. I was sitting in the front row while Mr. Hammer cleared away the props. I had to keep pretending that I hadn't felt that startling thrill the week before. It was the same kind of feeling you get when you put your tongue to cold metal. Like the pleasant sting of getting my ears pierced.

"That's fine," he said. "We'll be finished by then. I'm actually keeping you here because I wanted to talk to you about something."

"Okay," I said, shrugging.

He sat down at the edge of the stage and wrung his hands together. He was wearing jeans and a heavy sweater. He always smelled clean, like laundry soap.

"I've been thinking that you really should be getting some training. Some formal training. If you're at all interested in going to college for music, we need to start working toward that goal right now, while you have a couple of years left, before you need to get your applications in to the schools. I'd be more than happy to do what I can. My minor in college was musical performance. I've taught voice and piano before. Would you be interested in lessons?"

I didn't know what to say. I thought about singing and it seemed strange that there would be anything to *study* about music. It would be like studying the moon or the stars. Like studying snow.

"Sure," I said, and then my heart sank. "I don't have any money."

"That's fine. I volunteer."

I looked at him suspiciously. "I don't know . . ."

"Please don't feel funny. It's important to me. It really is."

"Thank you," I said. Feeling funny.

"Thank *you*." He smiled. "Now, let's go through the song a couple more times and then I'll let you go."

That night, inside the Star Theater in St. Johnsbury, where Blue's mother had dropped us off, Blue leaned against me and reached for my hand. I let his hand close around my own, let his fingers envelop mine. I couldn't hear a single word the actors said for the buzzing in my ears and the buzzing of my skin. For two hours, I concentrated on the fact that his hand was touching my hand, was holding my hand, was warmer than any ski glove or mitten in wintertime. At the end of the movie, my heart ached when the credits started to roll and everyone wanted to get past us to leave. It was like pulling myself from a dream when our fingers disentangled and we stood up to leave. Outside, Blue's mother was waiting for us with her windows rolled down. She was smoking a long brown cigarette and smiling. I sat in the backseat all the way back to my house, staring at Blue's dark curls.

At home, I thought about Blue sitting in the auditorium listening to me sing. It made me feel strange. Not violated, but like he'd stumbled across my secret. It was the same feeling I had when I sang with Mr. Hammer the first time. No one but my mother had heard me sing before. Now I felt as if every drawer in my mother's wooden box were open and the sunlight were streaming through the window, reflecting in every piece of broken glass. Like my mother, I wasn't accustomed to sharing the things that were broken in my life.

On Quinn's eighteenth birthday, the week after Thanksgiving, Boo brought a package wrapped in brown paper to the house. She had carefully cut out the return address, but the handwriting that spelled out Quinn's name, c/o Beatrice Bradley, was clearly my mother's. Quinn kissed Boo on the cheek and set the package down on the kitchen table.

"Well, are you going to open it, or what?" she asked.

Quinn sat down and stared at it.

Boo and I sat down, too, the package like the cage of a dangerous animal between us.

"Open it," I said, nodding.

He carefully removed the brown paper, folding it into neat squares. Then he slipped his pocketknife out to open the box, which was sealed with packing tape. I reached for the paper, touching it gently.

The box was filled with foam peanuts. He dug his hand in deep and came out holding an envelope. He tore it open, and something plastic fell out: a ski pass. A pass for the entire season at Jay Peak. Quinn's eyes were bright. "There's something else in here," he said, lifting the box and shaking the peanuts all over the table. Something fell out hard. The Phillips-head screwdriver.

"What?" Quinn said, puzzled.

"She's returning it." Maybe I was the only one who had noticed the things that were missing.

Quinn shrugged and ran to the coat closet to get his ski parka out. He clipped the pass onto the breast pocket and stared at it.

I picked up the screwdriver and turned it over in my hands. I wondered what she had used it for. I tried to picture the way her hands would hold it.

"My turn!" Boo said, pulling a gift-wrapped box out from under her chair. Inside was a pair of ski pants that still had the tags attached.

"Boo, these are so expensive. You shouldn't have done this," Quinn said.

"I didn't. Someone dropped them off at the shop. I guess they didn't fit or something. I hope they'll fit you."

"They will. Thank you." He leaned over and hugged her.

"Now me," I said, handing Quinn a box. Inside was a little jade elephant I'd bought at the Chinese restaurant in St. J. where Blue's mother took us one night after the movies. "It's for luck. For your first race," I said.

"Thank you," he said, hugging me hard. "I'll keep it right here." He took his parka, unzipped the little pocket above the pass from Mum, and slipped it inside.

Before work, Daddy had dropped off a honey-baked ham, Quinn's favorite, and the three of us ate until our stomachs hurt. Boo left after dinner. Quinn and I played Monopoly until I went bankrupt. And then Quinn went to bed. While he was sleeping, I took the Phillips-head screwdriver out of the tool-box where he had put it and looked around for something to unscrew. Finally, I took all the knobs off the kitchen cabinets and put them in a pile on the kitchen table. The kitchen looked strange without any knobs or handles, and I put them all back on.

After that day, Boo brought us other packages with more things Mum had taken with her inside: a can of shoe polish, a stapler, four pairs of Daddy's wool socks. Those I took and pulled onto my feet. At Christmas, she sent me candles that smelled like Nilla Wafers and the pair of purple glass earrings I'd all but forgotten.

I wondered where she was, and thought she must be doing well. With each returned item, I knew she was that much closer to being free.

I have started giving things away. Little things, so that no one notices. When Quinn came to visit from Colorado, I sent him back home to his wife with three sweaters I said were too big for me now and a dress I said never fit me at all. His wife, Kayla, is a skier too. She is tall like me, but her muscles are strong. I gave my bonsai tree to my friend Lizzie, explaining that I didn't know how to take care of it. I gave my cookie cutters and a rolling pin as housewarming gifts to my friends Doug and Susan, who just moved in together. I slip things into Becca's pockets when she comes over: a silver cigarette case, paperback books, playing cards with the Empire State Building on them. She never mentions my little gifts; she knows I would deny that they ever belonged to me.

The things I can't give away are the ones no one would want anyway: the old pair of slippers that look like two tired moose, the antique sewing machine from Boo's shop that doesn't work, my empty perfume bottles and my books of lists. I have never kept diaries, but my life is documented in hundreds of spiral notebooks. One notebook for each type of list. *Groceries, Christmas Gifts, Books to Read, Books Read, Bills, Birds, Borrowed Things, Names, News,* and *Movies Seen.* I am compulsive about my lists. Classification helps me understand where I'm going and where I've been. I worry about what will happen to them.

I'm also worried about Bog. He's old, and he smells terrible. He's a hemophiliac, so I can't brush his teeth without endangering his life. But I love him, and I hope that someone will be willing to take him too—along with my collection of butterfly wings, my box of buttons, and all my broken pairs of sunglasses.

Becca wants me to make a recording of my voice, just for her to keep, she says. I don't have my voice on tape. Not even my speaking voice. Becca says it's important to her, but I'm hesitant. It's been a long time since I sang anywhere but in my kitchen over the hum of the dishwasher or in the bathtub while the water is still running. I worry that it's not the way she remembers it. I worry that the cancer may be changing it, turning it like autumn leaves into something brittle.

I went to Mr. Hammer's house on Sunday for my first music lesson. Quinn dropped me off on his way to Jay Peak.

"Why's he doing this?" Quinn asked.

"He says I need lessons," I said.

"Isn't it a little creepy that he wants you to go to his house?" Quinn looked in the rearview mirror at a spot he missed when he was shaving.

"No," I said. "The only day he can do it is Sunday, and the chorus uses the auditorium on Sundays. He has a piano at his house. *Plus,* we live just up the road."

"Well, be careful," he said as we pulled up in front of the little house.

"I *will,*" I said, rolling my eyes.

Mr. Hammer held the door open for me as I stomped the snow off my boots and stepped into his warm house.

"Thanks," I said.

It was bright inside, sunshine streaming through the stained-glass windows, illuminating dust in red and orange and blue. It made me think of Mum. He motioned toward an upright piano against one wall and said, "This is where we'll start."

"Okay."

"Sit down," he said. "Would you like something? Some water? Juice?"

"No, thanks," I said, sitting down on the piano bench. "I'm not going to learn the piano, am I?"

"Not unless you want to," he said, disappearing into the little kitchen off the living room. He came back with two glasses of water. He set them both on the small table near the piano and sat down next to me on the piano bench.

"No thanks. I'll stick to singing, I think," I said, smiling.

He rested his fingers on the piano keys and plunked a couple of notes.

I didn't know what I should be doing.

He played something I didn't recognize, softly, like he was only thinking about playing it for real. It was pretty. His fingers kept moving over the keys, the lightest fingers I have ever seen. It sounded like the music was turned down. Barely audible, but beautiful. When the song was finished, his fingers lingered on the keys, on the silence.

"Should I start singing?" I asked. "I don't know the words to that one."

He picked up his hands and looked at me. When he smiled, I noticed that his bottom teeth were a little crooked. I also noticed the faintest dimple in his left cheek. He could easily have been a boy instead of a man.

"No, you don't need to sing today. I'm just listening to you breathe. It helps me to figure out where to begin."

I thought about breathing, and coughed. He handed me a glass of water, which I accepted.

After I went home, I lay down on my bed, closed my eyes, and listened to myself breathe. I'd never paid attention before, to the rhythms of my breath. It seemed strange to me, that he was sitting there the whole time, listening to something I didn't even know I was doing. It felt as if he'd overheard my dreams.

Blue's breath sounded like small drums. We were sitting on the curb by the theater, waiting for his mother to come get us.

I didn't want him to know I was listening to him breathing, so I said, "What do you want for Christmas?"

He tilted his head to look at me, his eyes the soft brown of melted chocolate. Then he leaned and put his head on my shoulder. "I want you," he whispered, and his breath turned into rain trembling on glass.

"Me?" I said, punching him a little too hard in the arm.

"Mmm-hmm," he said. "Well, you and a motorcycle."

It was cold outside, so cold our breath came out in clouds and mixed together in front of our faces.

"Why are you named Blue?" I asked, as he laid his head back on my shoulder.

"When I was born I almost died. I had a twin brother and we both got tangled up in the umbilical cord. I was blue because I couldn't breathe."

"What happened to your brother?"

"He died," he said.

I looked at him, horrified.

"It's just a nickname." He shrugged. "My real name's Jim."

And then as I watched the air in front of us, each stream of Blue's breath was suddenly miraculous.

Nighttime is the worst time here. Evenings are when I allow myself to be afraid.

I dread sunset, the slow descent of darkness, and the flickering of streetlights outside. As soon as the sun begins to disappear, I fill my rooms with light, even the ones I'm not using. I have begun collecting lamps; there is one on each table, each shelf, each countertop. I have advised Boo to keep her eye out for the stained glass of a Tiffany shade, the sparkle of something beaded, the smooth arch of a brass stand. I am fighting darkness.

Becca used to leave me in the late afternoons. Her house is up on Kinsey Hill, a good long drive from town. She would come to my apartment after school and sit with me, leaving to make it home before dark. She isn't fond of nighttime, either. Now, most nights she just curls up on my couch to sleep. She says it's because she doesn't like to drive at night, but I know she stays to make me feel safe.

Last night Becca fell asleep and I watched her curl into herself, like a cat or a flower. She would have been embarrassed to know I was watching her; she sleeps with her mouth open, and she snores, too. But what she can't understand is how pacifying it is for me to know that someone else besides myself is breathing in this house. When I can't hear my own breath, at least I can hear hers. She brought her favorite pillow from home. During the day, she puts it on the rocking chair by the window, the chair illuminated by a green glass lamp. But on the nights when she does go home, when there are lessons to plan or pipes to keep from freezing, I am alone, with only the orange glow of secondhand lamps to keep me company. Bog does his best to protect me, but most noises fail to wake him, and he seems to have forgotten how to bark.

Last week I woke up in the middle of the night and couldn't breathe. Under covers, I could have been under a collapsed building. Panicked, I reached out to the nightstand and knocked against it, hard, signaling to Becca. And only moments after she came into the room, bleary-eyed, like a sleepwalker, she was on the phone with the hospital. In my nightgown, a wool coat, and boots, I followed her down the narrow stairwell to her car, trying to slow my heart and save my breath. But when the car doors wouldn't open and Becca left me standing in the cold, midnight driveway, to run upstairs for hot water to melt the frozen locks, I almost let my legs buckle beneath me, almost sat down on the gravel driveway. Almost let myself crumble. But within seconds, she was back with a silver pan of hot water, the locks came loose, and she was helping me into the passenger seat, whispering, "Everything's going to be fine, don't worry one bit. Everything's okay."

This midnight trip to the hospital to restore my breath made me realize the power of fear. It can make me weak. It can make me throw up my hands; it can make me lose. If Becca hadn't been with me, hadn't set up camp in my living room, I believe I would have simply sat down in the driveway and waited until the building crushed me.

Becca and I go to the movies every Sunday now. I look forward to the weekends because of this. Quimby just opened a one-screen theater, and they change the movie every week. We'll go see anything. Inside the dark theater, I am able to suspend everything for a couple of hours. Like a magician's assistant, rising above the table at his command. At the movies, I have learned how to defy the laws of nature. At the movies, I am only floating above the world in which I wake up choking at night.

Today we went to see a romantic comedy, one of those ditzy films with a pretty actress and a handsome actor who can't stand each other and then realize that they've been in love all along. There was a scene in which the female character is grocery shopping, trying to decide which cantaloupe to pick from the mountain of cantaloupes in the produce section when she sees her nemesis/true love in the next aisle with his obnoxious current girlfriend. As the couple turns their cart toward the female lead, the cantaloupe slips and then the entire pyramid of melons is falling around her. I laughed out loud despite myself, but Becca, who was sitting next to me with a giant bucket of popcorn between her knees, was silent. When I glanced at her, the light from the screen reflected in her wet eyes, caught in the tears that streaked down her cheeks. She kept staring at the screen, as the fruit kept tumbling, burying the girl, and cried silently. I looked away, felt my own throat grow thick, the muscles in my neck tightening.

One snowy night in December, Roxanne and Daddy got in a fight at the Lodge right after closing time. In the strange glow of the parking lot, Daddy leaned against his car, his arms shielding him from Roxanne's angry fists. I imagined him cowering, crouching as she beat him. I imagined her voice like a crumpled paper bag, scratchy, humiliating him. And then what must have happened, what I know must have happened, was that Daddy finally had enough. On the backs of my eyes when I closed them, I could see her ringed fingers striking his temples and cheekbones, the neon sign in the bar window making everything red. He stood up then; I could see his hands reaching for her shoulders, squeezing her shoulders, restraining her. Keeping her from killing him. And then I heard her voice turn from scratchy to screaming, a horror movie scream, loud enough to wake someone. And then someone called 911. And then Daddy woke us up with a collect call made from the courthouse jail in Quimby.

The next morning, after Daddy was released on bail but didn't come home, Child Protective Services came to visit me and Quinn. Quinn was getting ready to head out the door to hitch a ride to the mountain, when a lady who smelled like vinegar stuck her head into our door and looked around. I guess she was looking for Daddy. Quinn did all the talking, and I sat staring at cartoons on the TV, sitting on the floor cross-legged in my pajamas with a bowl of cereal in my lap like I did when I was little. It seemed like hours before she left. My cereal was too soggy to eat by the time she walked back out our door.

We didn't even talk to Boo about it. We both knew that she'd chosen to live her life alone, that, unlike Mum, she'd made up her mind before it was too late. The last thing she needed was two nearly grown kids moving into her small house. That's how Quinn came to be my legal guardian. *Legal* made me think of papers and file cabinets. *Guardian* made me think of angels.

Roxanne didn't press charges against Daddy; she even *allowed* him back into her home, *after all he'd done,* and Quinn and I were on our own. The following morning, when we got ready for school, I got in the passenger side of Mum's old car. I felt grown. I felt older than the Pond, the rocks, and the trees.

Maybe that's why when Blue Henderson asked me if I wanted to go with him to a party at Kyle Kaplan's house the next weekend, I said yes. Kyle's parents were on vacation. His older sister and he were home alone. We told Blue's mother we were going to dinner at the Miss Quimby Diner and then to a dance at school. I told Quinn I was going to a party at Kyle Kaplan's house, that his parents were gone, but that I'd be safe and that I'd call him if I needed a ride home.

There were only a few people at the party when we got there. Everyone was sitting on the sofas and the chairs in the living room, looking like kids trying to have a party in a grown-up's house. Kyle was searching for the key to unlock the liquor cabinet, and his sister, Ann, was on the phone.

As soon as Kyle found the key and unlocked the doors, unscrewed the caps and poured the drinks, everything changed. The music grew louder, the bass pounding in the floors under our feet. Some of the liquor tasted like candy: peach schnapps, peppermint schnapps, Kahlúa. It felt like Easter or Christmas. I wanted to try a little of every kind. I couldn't get enough of the sweetness. Blue put his arm around my waist as we sat on stools at the island in Kyle's mother's kitchen drinking straight out of the bottles, wiping our mouths with the backs of our hands. Melissa Ball showed up and sat down on the other side of Blue.

"Hi, Blue," she said sweetly, grabbing a bottle of rum from the center of the island and unscrewing the cap. "Piper," she said, raising the bottle in a toast and sipping delicately from it.

I felt the same warm and melty feeling I felt when Quinn gave me that beer, but warmer and meltier. Liquid. My whole body was fluid. I thought for a second that Blue's hand might pass right through me.

"Let's go to the living room," I whispered. I leaned into him, smelling the unfamiliar scent of cologne on his neck. I wrinkled my nose, and he pretended he didn't see me do it.

We left Melissa, who was now sitting on the island and flirting with Kyle, and went to the living room, where the lights were turned down low and someone had built a fire in the fireplace. This was a nice house, maybe the nicest one I'd ever been inside. I felt a twinge of guilt that I hadn't asked Becca to come along. There were pictures of Kyle's family on the walls. In one, they were all wearing red turtlenecks and black pants; in another, blue sweaters with a starched white collar underneath. His mother was pretty, with auburn hair flipped up at the ends. His father looked intelligent: he wore glasses and had a serious face. There were plastercast handprints spray-painted silver: Kyle and Ann's little hands captured in something close to stone.

I sat down on the couch, and Blue sat down next to me. We were only a few feet from the fire, and it was making me warm. I pulled my sweater over my head and blew the hair out of my eyes. He put his arm around me and whispered, "You look pretty."

"Thanks," I said, punching him again in the arm. I didn't know what else to do.

Then he reached across the coffee table where someone had set a six-pack of beer and handed me one. I twisted the cap off and foam started to spill over the top. Blue motioned for me to drink it, and I did. The bubbles made me want to burp, but I held it inside.

We sat looking at the fire, listening to the music, drinking beer, and I felt changed. I crossed and uncrossed my legs, for some reason thinking about the way Mum had sat when the owner of the gallery wrote her a check for her artwork.

Someone turned the music up. It was a slow song, the one that had been on the radio all the time lately.

"We told my mother we were going to a dance. Maybe we should dance," Blue teased. He stood up, and reached for my hand.

"Okay." I set my empty beer bottle on the coffee table. My knees were liquid, my hands liquid. I caught my knee on the edge of the table and winced.

"C'mere," Blue said, pulling me against him gently.

I allowed my body to fall against his. We were warm from the fire: I could feel the heat from his skin through his jeans and his soft cotton shirt. I loved this song. Sometimes something on the radio could move me, and I'd find myself singing along without realizing it. This was one of those songs. I put my arms around Blue's neck like the other girls were doing, and he rested his hands on my hips, around my waist. I liked the way it felt. I liked the smell of cologne on his neck when I buried my head there. I liked how I could feel the music running through me, like water into water.

Blue's breath was warm on my scalp as he breathed into my hair. He whispered into my hair, but the words got tangled up. I could feel him pressing against me, his hips pressing against my hips. I wanted him to be closer. I wanted to hold him so hard he would fall into me, like a ghost, transparent like water. Everything was liquid and buzzing.

When he finally kissed me, I was startled. I'd been so conscious of our bodies that the cold clang of his teeth against mine interrupted the watery dream. His lips were thicker than I expected, his tongue pressing as hard as hips. But soon, the kiss became as liquid as the music, and I wanted it to go on forever.

He looked at me, his eyebrows raised, asking permission, and I nodded.

Gently, he steered me out of the living room and up the stairs. He grabbed two beers from the coffee table on the way and handed me one as we reached the landing. I sat down on one of the steps and struggled to get the cap off.

"Here," he said, taking the bottle and sitting next to me. He unscrewed the cap and handed it back.

"Thanks." I swallowed long and hard, wanting this moment to last forever.

We sat on the steps, watching everyone in the living room, until our beers were gone. He set the empty bottles on the flat part of the banister and helped me up. I followed him up the stairs and down a long hallway that smelled like cedar, into someone's room.

It must have been a guest room. There was nothing personal in there. No photos or books. Nothing that could have belonged to anybody. For some reason this made me sad.

"You okay?" he asked, sitting down on the edge of the bed and taking both of my hands.

I nodded and wanted, needed, to sit down. I sat down next to him on the hard mattress, and he circled me with his arms. The bedspread was red and blue plaid.

He kissed me again and we lay on our sides, pressing into each other until there were no spaces between us anymore. He pushed his knee between my legs, and I liked the way it felt. I liked the way it felt when his hands reached under my shirt and found the skin underneath. I wanted to feel his skin against my skin. I wanted to know.

But under me the bed was beginning to turn. When I closed my eyes I could see the faces of Kyle's family, framed in red turtleneck sweaters, and spinning. I could see Roxanne in her parka, her flask reflecting the sun. I saw my father's bruised face, the colors of red and blue slowly turning into the plaid bedspread beneath my fingers. The water had turned into waves.

"Stop," I whispered into Blue's hands as they found my face.

"It's okay," he said. "I love you."

I love you, love you. And then his skin against my skin. And I was spinning, just a top, just a toy, just a girl spinning with her arms out before falling to the ground. The spinning stopped when I felt his hands pressed against the inside of my knees, pushing them apart. I was almost grateful to him for stopping the reeling. I could feel bile rising in my throat. And then he was on top of me, keeping me still, keeping me grounded, his fingers working hard to pull aside my cotton panties, working hard to open me up. *To open me to open me to open me.* Prying.

Downstairs, the bass pounded so hard I could feel it in my temples and in my eyes. I could feel it in his hips. I could feel it as he found his way inside.

Afterward, he kissed me, furiously, across my sweaty forehead and stomach, across my naked thighs. And then he said, "I'll be right back," and left me in the room that belonged to no one. Opened wide, everything revealed. All of my secrets stolen. In the bathroom I found at the end of the hall, I threw up all over the toilet seat and on the floor. I was completely empty now, and I guessed that meant I was truly grown.

I used to think about having a family, about a husband and the way an infant might feel like a small bird, lying on my chest. I dreamed the same things everyone else dreamed. I wanted the same things.

Over the years, the faces of my boyfriends have been different, but there has always been something similar about them. My choices are predictable, inevitable. I always look for something removed in their eyes. Something distant. I don't search consciously; I am just being careful. I don't need anyone getting too attached. It would bring me too close to those dreams I used to entertain. Maybe I have always known I was dying.

I wish I weren't alone now, though. It makes me sad that I've spent my life keeping men at a careful distance. If I'd lapsed even once and found someone whose eyes didn't have that vague dimensionless quality, then maybe I wouldn't live alone with my aging greyhound now.

Becca believes it's not too late for me. That, as in the movies where the heroine dies, some gentle stranger will find me and love me until it's over. I allow her this hope. I think it keeps her going, gives her a mission. She's looking for him.

The first thing I thought when I pulled the music box out of the closet was that maybe it *wasn't* too late. If anyone would love the fragments I have become it would be he. For a few terrifying moments, I thought about looking again. Since I lost him, this feeling has come over me more times than I will ever admit. In light of the light that is fading, I am thinking about him again.

At the Quimby Atheneum, there is a room filled with computers that can connect you with anyone you've lost. Finding someone is as simple as a few key strokes. Quimby, which was always so remote, is now instantly connected to everything that was mysterious and unknowable before. Nothing is a secret anymore. Nothing is out of reach. But each time the impulse to find him touches me, the way his fingers once touched me (tentative, gentle, and scared), I stop it. I slam the drawer shut. I turn off the light. Like my mother, he would be a stranger to me now.

Becca remains hopeful. She invited her friend Jason from New York to come spend Thanksgiving with her. She has been talking about him incessantly lately. When he accepted, she was beside herself.

"You're going to love him. This is going to be great. I am *so* excited. Do you want to have Thanksgiving dinner here? You've got so much more room. I'll do all the work. It will be fantastic."

He arrived on Wednesday night and she brought him straight from the bus station to my apartment. She opened up a bottle of wine, even poured a forbidden glass for me, and situated him next to me on my couch. She sat across from us in the big wing chair Boo got at a flea market in Maine, smiling. Halfway through the bottle of wine, she said, "I'm going to the store. I forgot to get the sweet potatoes."

"You want me to come with you?" Jason asked.

"That's okay. You guys stay here and chat."

And then she was gone, and we were alone. It was the first time I'd been alone with a guy in a room in a year.

"So, you're a seamstress?"

"Uh-huh," I said.

He looked at me oddly and then reached for another bot-

tle of wine, busying his hands with the foil and corkscrew. I
worried that we'd sit like this in silence until Becca returned if
I didn't say something quickly.

"I *used* to be a singer," I said. "Back in the day."

He set the bottle down on the coffee table. *"Back in the day.
How old are you? You don't look more than twenty-five."*

"Oh, flatter me some more," I said.

What he couldn't know, what I couldn't tell him because I'd
just met him an hour before, was that I thought of my life like
this. *Before illness.* And now. And that everything that happened
before was like ancient history. *Back in the day* before illness.

"Were you in a band?" he asked.

"A couple of bands," I lied. I felt very much like an old
woman, trying to reach back (past senility, into time). But there
was nothing to grab onto. I had stopped singing when I was
still a child.

"Punk rock?" he asked, grinning at my nearly bald head.

"Blues." And I could see what might have been. Smoky bar
and smoky voice and sparkly dress.

"Mmmm," he said, sipping on his wine.

I was grateful when Becca came back fifteen minutes later,
clutching her plastic bag of sweet potatoes.

Thanksgiving morning, I woke up feeling a lot of pain. It
seemed to reside mostly in my tail bone, emanating out to the
other parts of my lower back. It was all I could do to sit up. In
the kitchen, I could hear Becca and Jason preparing the turkey.
The TV was loud with the Macy's parade.

I reached for some painkillers I'd left on my nightstand,
and swallowed them dry. I could feel them as they made their
way down my throat. I lay back down and tried to wish the
pain away.

When Becca came in to check on me at eleven o'clock, I
was starting to feel better.

"Let's pick out something pretty for you to wear," she said, staring into my closet. I hadn't touched most of those clothes in over a month. I'd divided my clothes into two categories: comfortable and uncomfortable. I shoved all of the uncomfortable clothes into my closet and filled my bureau drawers with T-shirts, pajama bottoms, leggings, and soft sweaters.

She pulled out a Chinese print skirt with frogs along the side slit and a scoop-neck black velvet blouse. Black stockings and ankle-strap heels.

I shook my head.

"Come on," she pleaded. She was wearing her favorite black linen sleeveless dress, despite the thermometer's reading of 10 degrees. Silver hoop earrings and heels.

"Fine, but no bra and no stockings."

"How risqué," she said.

I pulled the blouse over my head; it felt tight compared to the loose T-shirts I'd been sporting lately. I slipped the skirt on next and buttoned it. It slipped down to my hips, hesitated, and then slipped down to the floor, making a pile of embroidered red around my feet.

Becca stared at the skirt, which had fit me just six months ago, and said, "That's okay. Let me find something else. Step out of that."

I stared at my feet as she rummaged through my clothes for something that would fit me. Finally, she pulled out a wrap-around rayon skirt, black with little yellow flowers all over it. She wrapped it around me like a bandage, adjusting the ties to my new body. "Perfect," she said, smiling proudly.

"Can we skip the shoes?" I asked. "My back's been hurting this morning."

"Sure," she said. "Want your slippers? The floors are freezing."

I nodded and she reached under the bed where I had kicked my yellow terrycloth slippers. "They match!" she said, holding them against my skirt.

Dinner was beautiful. The turkey was tender and juicy. Becca made twice-baked potatoes with bacon and sour cream. Pumpkin soup and cranberry-raspberry aspic. I almost cried when I saw the table.

Jason entertained us with stories about his auditions for various on- and off-Broadway shows in New York. He was a bit of a showoff, but I liked him anyway. After a couple of glasses of wine, he could do perfect imitations of Marge Simpson and Edith Bunker. He knew all the words to "Those Were the Days," and he could make a playing card appear from behind my ear.

Becca clapped gleefully, like a child, with each of his tricks, begging him to do just one more. We drank coffee, ate pie and ice cream, listened to music and danced. Outside, winter descended around us, covering the park in a thin coat of crystalline white. Anyone looking up into the orange glow of my attic living room windows would have seen the silhouettes of three people. Happy people. Normal people dancing on Thanksgiving evening. But at seven o'clock, the pain returned to my back, spreading around to my hips like lovers' hands. I ignored the deep ache, willing it away, wishing it away. Pretending it was only from the dancing.

Jason and Becca were happily tipsy, finishing another bottle of wine after the dishes were clean and sitting in the cupboard again.

"I'm sleepy." Becca yawned. "I need a nap. You guys mind if I lie down for a bit?"

Jason said, "Nope."

I shook my head. He and I were sitting on my couch, watching the snow fall.

While Becca was sleeping, Jason tried to kiss me. I knew he would; I knew this was all planned. I knew from the way Becca kept nudging him to sit closer to me. From the way he blushed.

In the warm orange glow of the living room, as he pulled a

card out from under my seat cushion, I thought about how easy it would be to rely on the easy gestures I used to use: the inside of my wrist pressed gently to my temples, the familiar tilt of my head to signify interest, the simple scratch of an ankle. He was trying so hard. But the pain in my back was intense now; it would not be ignored. It was all I could do to concentrate on the cards in his hands.

When he put my card back, set the deck on the coffee table, and sat back into the soft cushions of the couch, the pain shot up both sides of my spine and settled in my shoulders. Quietly. Maybe it would let me be tonight. Just let me *be*.

"You're very pretty," he said softly. We'd been whispering since Becca disappeared into my bedroom.

"Thanks," I said. Fingers of pain rubbed my shoulders. I ignored them and looked at him. I'd never seen eyes that shade of green.

He reached for my hand, quietly, without fuss, and I let him hold on.

"I'm glad I came," he smiled, tilting his head, examining me.

"Me too," I said, and the fingers of pain tapped me on the back, reminding me. I winced.

"You okay?"

I nodded, blinking hard.

"It must take a lot of strength . . ." he started. "To do what you're doing."

"And what's that?" I asked.

"Nothing," he said, leaning toward me. "I only meant I admire you."

His face was close to my face and his eyes were closed. I could have let go. I could have let him in. But the pain shot down both of my arms, and I watched my hands reach forward, grabbing his shoulders, pushing him away. His eyes blinked open, but I didn't let go.

"What is it that you admire?" I hissed.

He looked terrified. "My mother—my mother had breast cancer."

"Did she survive?" I demanded, still holding on to him.

"Yes. She's been in remission for ten years."

"Well, I'm dying, Jason. I am dying and I'm scared shitless." The pain was retreating now, out of my wrists. I let go of his shoulders and put my hands in my lap. "Admire your mother. Don't admire me."

Jason looked at me the way you look at a wounded animal, and I whispered, "I'm not feeling well. I think you should go."

He nodded and went into my bedroom, where he woke up Becca and got her keys. I watched him drive away, and the only pain I felt now was the hard lump in my chest. Becca came out into the living room after he was gone, her linen dress wrinkled, makeup smudged under her eyes.

"What happened?" she asked, pulling her hair out of the messy braid.

"He tried to kiss me," I said. "I didn't want to be kissed."

"Why not?" Becca asked. "I thought you liked him."

"I did, I do, I just didn't want that. I don't need a *boyfriend* right now."

Becca sat down in the chair opposite me. Her jaw was set. "It was just a kiss."

"I just don't need that kind of complication in my life."

Becca looked out the window at the fresh snow. And then she said softly, "What life?"

I stared at her face; I hardly recognized her.

"You act like you're already dead," she said, her voice becoming stronger. But she still wouldn't look at me. "You aren't even trying to stay alive anymore. It's like you don't even care."

"Maybe I don't," I said, shrugging the pain out of my shoulders.

After a few moments, Becca turned to me again. "I don't believe you."

TWO

If winter here were made of colored glass, this is the way the light would shine through the winter I was fourteen: the strange blue of icicles hanging like daggers from our roof, the gray of rain gutters heavy with snow that would not melt, the white of snow on brown trees, on brown ground, on the brown sawdust frozen Pond.

The morning after Kyle Kaplan's party, I almost called Mr. Hammer and canceled our lesson. But when I woke up I knew that if I didn't get out of bed I might stay there forever. I wondered if anyone had ever done that before—just refused to get out of bed. It seemed like a strange fairy tale or nursery rhyme. I would be the girl who wouldn't get up, the girl whose hair grew around the bedposts, tethering her there.

So I pulled myself out of bed, out of my pajamas, and stared at myself in the mirror. I didn't look any different. I didn't *look* broken. But in the bathroom, it burned when I peed and I couldn't stop crying even after I had flushed the toilet.

Quinn's first race was today; he was already gone. I was grateful for his absence. He hadn't even known anything was wrong when he picked me up from Kyle's house the night before. He had handed me a toothbrush though, an aspirin, and a glass of water. He must have smelled the vomit on my breath, despite the stale Butter Rum Life Saver I'd found in my coat pocket.

I showered until the hot water was gone and my skin was

flushed red. I put on my red union suit and two other layers of clothes. I pulled my hair back into a tight ponytail, trying to change the features on my face, but it just made me look wide-eyed and strange.

It was a half-hour before my lesson, so I walked through the woods to the Pond before heading down the road to Gormlaith. In wintertime, abandoned things are buried. Rusty car parts, garbage, and glass are sunken treasures, under an ocean of white. Even the sawdust is hidden in winter.

At the Pond, everything was still. Serene. There was no wind that day; everything was utterly motionless. Frozen. I thought that if I stood there long enough, I might freeze, too. Soon, my arms would grow heavy with the weight of new snow, and my legs might turn into roots that would grow deep into the ground. But despite the complete calm, my heart was racing. I rushed quickly down the bank, looking for something to disturb this terrible peace. Finally I found a large rock, almost too heavy to lift, and put my mittened hands around it. It came loose from the frozen ground easily, but I could feel the muscles in my back straining with the weight. Finally, I was able to pick it up, and I ran to the water's edge with it. I looked at the perfect white of new ice and thought about setting the rock down, preserving this perfect quiet. But underneath all those layers of clothes, I could still feel the sting of what Blue had done and what I had failed to do, and I pushed the rock through the air as hard as I could. It hit the ice and immediately broke through. Cracks grew like an icy spiderweb as the rock sank to the bottom of the Pond. I stepped back, out of breath, my back hurting, and swallowed hard. *Sometimes things need to get broken,* she'd said.

Inside Mr. Hammer's house the phone was ringing, the clothes dryer was rumbling, and a small kitten was tearing across the hardwood floor with a crazed look in its eyes. I

stepped in after he opened the door, the phone cradled between his chin and his shoulder, motioning for me to take off
my coat.

"Got it," he said. "See you on Monday afternoon."

He disappeared into the kitchen and I heard him hang up
the phone. I looked at the little calico kitten, who was looking
back with a scary intensity, and took my coat off and hung it
on a peg by the front door.

"Hi, Piper," Mr. Hammer said from the kitchen.

"Hi."

"Make yourself comfortable. I'm just making some coffee."

I sat down on the couch and, noticing the puddle the snow
was making around my feet, I quickly unlaced my boots and
slipped them off. I looked toward the kitchen and leaned over,
trying to get close enough to my feet to make sure they didn't
smell bad. Then I tried to sop up some of the melted snow
with my scarf, but it just sort of pushed the water around. I got
up and carried my boots to the mat by the door.

I could hear and smell the coffee brewing in the kitchen,
the sound of Mr. Hammer's feet shuffling across the floor. I sat
back down on the couch. The kitten had disappeared.

"Can I get you something?" he asked. "Tea? Hot cocoa?"

"I'm fine."

The sun was starting to come out. It had been a week
without sun. I felt myself smiling despite myself. I moved to
the other side of the couch, into a warm pool of sunlight. The
blue upholstery was faded in this spot. I wondered if I sat there
in that little puddle of sun if I might fade, too.

I was about to tell Mr. Hammer that I *would* like some hot
chocolate when I felt a terrible, sharp pain in my ankle. I cried
out, looking down at the kitten attached to my wool socks and
to my skin by its claws.

"Are you okay?" Mr. Hammer said, rushing into the living
room.

I looked up at him, tears in my eyes, as the kitten released me. It didn't retreat, though; it only stood there, hissing at me, the hair on its back raised.

"Jack! What a horrible cat you are," he said, scooping up the kitten, and then, to me, "Are you okay?"

I nodded, but my ankle stung.

"Take your sock off," he said.

Horrified, I shook my head. My feet had smelled okay, but who knows what would happen if I took off my soggy wool sock?

"You really should let me look at it. Cats are pretty dirty little animals. We should at least put some antiseptic on it. Let me go grab some peroxide," he said, disappearing through another doorway.

I stared at my feet and then, reluctantly, peeled the heavy wool sock off my foot. The claws had made four perfect punctures around the back of my ankle. Already, there were puffy red welts. It stung. Everything stung.

Mr. Hammer came back into the room with a bottle of peroxide, two white cotton balls, and some Band-Aids.

"Put your foot up here," he said, tapping on the other end of the couch.

I lifted my leg up and set it there. He tipped the peroxide bottle against the cotton ball and then dabbed gently at the little wounds. The peroxide bubbled and made the room smell like medicine. Then he used his teeth to tear open two of those little Band-Aids you usually use for your pinky finger, knelt down, and pressed one of them against my skin. He repeated this with the other one, cradling my foot in the palm of his hand. He inspected his handiwork and looked up at me.

"Better?" he asked.

I nodded, but he kept holding my foot as if it were broken instead of only wounded. And all of a sudden I felt so grateful that tears welled up in my eyes like snow puddles.

Becca still takes me to my doctor's appointments, even though I stopped treatment almost four months ago *(when the leaves were still green, when the girls still flirted by the fountain, in the moonlight, summer evenings)*. She has been there with me through three rounds of chemo. She's seen that their elixirs are really poisons. But she was also there when the chemo and radiation worked, when everything slowed down for a while, when I could pretend that I might get better.

When my doctor tells me what I already know: that it is in my bones as well as my lungs, and that now it is only a matter of time *(weeks? months?)* unless I'm willing to allow them to harvest my bone marrow and undergo a bone marrow transplant, Becca will not hear my noes.

On Church Street, at the small dark restaurant where we always go for lunch after my appointments, she is buzzing with excitement. We are the only customers. We sit in the window facing the street, unwrap ourselves from our coats and scarves. She repeats all the things the doctors said about the procedure. I stare at the menu, and I can't remember what any of the words mean: *au jus, au gratin.* The words coming out of her mouth could be menu items, they are so foreign: *autologous, stem cells. Marrow, marrow, marrow.*

As she rattles on, excited, I press my hands against my ears to make all the words go away.

She sees me, stops talking mid-sentence, and looks out the window.

Then I ask her if she remembers the nights I spent curled up in the cold bathtub so that I could be closer to the toilet, if she remembers the sores on my knees. I close my eyes, remembering the first time I washed my hair, and the way it floated across the surface of the bathwater like decaying plants on the surface of a pond. I ask her if she remembers the dreams I had right after my surgery, the ones in which a wild dog was attacking me, biting my breasts, my feet, and my hands. But she only stares into her soup.

"Don't you get it?" I ask.

"What?" she says, her face and voice raised to meet mine.

I stare out at the cold street, where people rush in and out of doorways, bundled and cloaked. You can't see anyone's face when it is this cold. When I look back at Becca, she has set her spoon down and her hands are on the edge of the table, as if she might just stand up. As if she might simply walk away. The thought of that terrifies me more than anything. More than the pain in my hips and my legs. More than the idea of suffocating in my sleep.

"I'm *scared,*" I say. "I'm tired and I'm scared and I just want everything to go away. I want to sit here and talk about what movie to see or some new book or . . . sex, for Christ's sake." I hold up my hands, empty, and feel my shoulders falling. Feel everything falling. "But I *can't.*"

Becca puts her hands back in her lap and looks at me. Her eyes are watercolor blue. She reaches across the table and puts both of my hands inside hers.

"You said I act like I'm already dead."

She looks down at the table.

"But Becca, I don't *remember* how to live. I don't remember the last time I even felt close to normal." Then I am crying.

Hard. Through the blur of tears I can see the waitress and the bartender, leaning into each other, trying not to look.

Becca squeezes her hands over mine, makes a cocoon to keep them safe, and I keep crying, sobbing like a child, letting the sadness shake me. I don't even try to stop, not when the waitress puts her hand on Becca's shoulder and asks if everything is okay. Not when she brings more napkins and sets them on the table. And all the while, Becca waits.

"Please don't leave," I say.

And in that moment, with Becca still sitting across from me, after everything I've said and done and put her through, I realize she *won't* leave. She won't leave me, no matter what I say or don't say, no matter what I do or don't do. In my whole life, she is the only person who has ever stayed. And that's why I start to nod and ask her questions, furiously, about the procedure, about the statistics, about what all the words mean. I hadn't been listening; I hadn't heard any of them. This is all I have to offer her.

And when she says *harvest,* I think about the winter garden behind his house, when he showed me where, in the summer, things would grow, plentiful and good. I can smell the dank, wet sweetness of soil and taste the way rain would taste on fresh lettuce or green beans or peppers. And I realize that it is possible that there is something left inside me that can be salvaged. That there is something left still to be saved.

On Sunday afternoon, after my lesson with Mr. Hammer, I walked home feeling lighter. With each breath, with each released note, a little of the pain of what happened with Blue had disappeared. It wasn't something you could see, though; it was more transparent than breath. But it had weight, and now that weight was lifted.

The sun was shining brightly on Gormlaith; the lake was not frozen yet, only very, very cold. Most of the camps on the lake were closed up for the winter, and I felt briefly that I was the only person in the whole world. If the world ended, I thought, it would feel like this. Cold, bright, and desolate. Light.

By the time I got back to our house, the sun was starting to melt behind the trees, liquid sunshine turning cold as the foliage swallowed it. My mother's car was parked in the driveway: Quinn was home.

Sleep met me at the door, winding his way clumsily through my legs as I tried to take off my coat and boots. Quinn was in the living room. There was a trail of ski clothes: from his boots and skis at the door to his goggles on the table to his ski pants strewn across a chair. He was fast asleep on the couch, wearing his long johns and his ski hat. His hands were clutched together between his knees, and his feet were bare. He and I have the same long, bony toes.

I tiptoed into the living room and carefully pulled the afghan off the back of the couch to cover him up, but as I started to cover his feet he woke up.

"Thanks," he said.

I sat down on the floor next to him. "How did the race go?"

"I came in third for slalom. First for giant slalom," he said.

"That's great!"

He sat up, yanking the afghan around his shoulders. "I'm beat. The sun did a number on me." He had owl eyes from his goggles, a bright red forehead and cheeks.

"Did you bring your charm?" I asked.

He gestured to where his parka was lying, empty, on the floor. "I haven't taken it out of the pocket."

"You hungry?" I asked.

"A little," he said, nodding. "Hey, where have you been all day?"

"At my lesson."

"Oh, I forgot. Is he teaching you anything useful yet?"

I thought about the breathing exercises, the scales like little baby steps. I shrugged.

"You want some tuna pea wiggle?" I asked.

"You cookin'?"

"Sure."

Quinn found the remote control between the couch cushions, flipped on the TV, and lay back down.

"You look silly," I said, pointing at his sunburnt face.

"Thanks."

In the kitchen I got two plates out of the cupboard and crushed up a bunch of saltines, making a big pile of broken crackers on each plate. In a saucepan, I stirred milk and butter and tuna until it was hot, adding a little flour to help thicken it up. Then I dumped in the can of peas. When everything was hot, I poured the sauce on the crackers, grabbed two forks, and carefully carried the plates in to Quinn. I loved tuna pea wiggle. It made me think of times when I was sick and stayed home from school with Mum. She always made it for me, and it always made me feel better. Sometimes if I was feeling well enough by the afternoon, we'd do some sort of project. Once we made candles out of my old crayons and paraffin. One time, we made the thick pretzels you usually can only buy in malls. We even made potato chips once from scratch, using real potatoes.

Quinn ate like he hadn't eaten in a month, getting cracker crumbs all over the afghan and couch.

I snorted like a pig.

"Cut it out . . ." he said.

The phone rang.

"I'll get it," I said and set my plate on the coffee table. I ran to the kitchen, almost slipping when I rounded the corner in my stocking feet.

"Hello?"

"Hi, Piper? It's Blue."

All the heaviness returned, throbbing in my hands and in my chest. I could barely breathe.

"Listen, I was thinking you might like to go to the movies or something? My mom said she could take us tomorrow night."

I could hear his voice, but it felt as if I were only listening to the TV or the radio. He was that far away.

"Piper?" he asked again.

"I . . . I can't," I said.

"Oh . . ." the voice said. "Well, maybe we could get some sandwiches or pie or something after school tomorrow?"

"I have rehearsals. I can't."

I wanted him to go away. I wanted him to give up, hang up the phone, to stop. But he kept on talking, trying out plans as if nothing were out of the ordinary. As if he hadn't taken me and shattered me into little pieces the night before, in some stranger's bedroom, on some stranger's bed.

"I don't want you to come by anymore," I said. My words felt as distant as his.

"Piper, is this about last night?" he asked.

And then I was moving the phone away from my ear, gently setting it back on the cradle. My ears were buzzing. I went back into the living room, where the tuna pea wiggle was already cold and soggy on my plate.

"Who was it?" Quinn asked, flipping the channels so fast it looked the way it does when you watch out the side window of a moving car.

"Nobody," I said.

"Nobody who?" he asked.

"Nobody Henderson," I said, trying to smile.

"Oh," he said, looking away from the TV to me. I was pushing the peas around my plate with my finger. "You okay, Pipe?"

I nodded, trying not to feel the weight of Blue in my shoulders and in my legs. Trying not to remember the weight of Blue on my chest.

There are a lot of people who don't know I'm sick. Sometimes, I think about all the people I've ever met or been acquainted with or loved, and it is incredible to me that most of them have no idea about what is happening inside my body. And then I think about all the people I have met or been acquainted with or loved and wonder if they have similar secrets that they are carrying around with them. It makes you realize how many people, out of all the people you know, are actually important to you.

I started a list book once in which I tried to name every person I had ever known. I started with family, and then worked chronologically through my life. Elementary school classmates, family friends, the librarians at the Quimby Atheneum, girls from swimming lessons and the clerks at the Shop-N-Save. When I got to fifth grade, I stopped. I had twenty college-ruled pages of names, and there were only a handful of people with whom I was still in touch. All those pages, all those people; it made me feel terribly alone.

Sometimes I'll bump into someone at the post office or at the bank, someone I haven't seen in a couple of years, and I'll strike up a conversation with them, realizing halfway through that they don't know me anymore. And that, worse yet, I don't know them either.

A couple of days after my doctor's appointment, I was leaving the fabric store in Quimby when I saw Richard, a friend of a friend who swept into my life one weekend four or five years before. It was one of those things, those flings, you know will amount to nothing, but you do it anyway because you're lonely or bored, and then you forget about it after it's all done.

I was wearing the blond wig that Becca had given me. My hair has still not come back. It might take a while, my doctor says. Normally, I just pull on a baseball cap or a bandanna, but it's getting cold now, and I miss the way my hair used to feel around my neck. My real hair, when I had it, was brown. And curly. I always hated my hair, its willful disorder, but now I miss it terribly.

He was walking down the street, blowing warm air into his bare hands. I recognized him from almost a block away. And I considered, for a moment, waving, calling out, "Hey, Richard! It's me, Piper Kincaid. Remember?" But as he got closer, I simply clutched my paper bag of thread and bias tape and buttons, and waited for him to pass. The funny thing was that he slowed down as he reached me, and a slow smile crept across his face. Startled, I opened my mouth to say something, but he had already passed. And I realized that what he saw was simply a blond girl with cheeks flushed pink from a cold early-winter afternoon. I was nobody he remembered in this disguise. I wasn't who I used to be.

I have told some of my old friends, but mostly people have just figured it out. Quimby is a very small town, and if you walk outside to get your mail, forgetting your hat, someone is bound to notice and spread the word for you. Once, after a trip to the Laundromat when my dryer was on the fritz, and my bandanna slipped, my second-grade teacher showed up at my apartment door with two pans of lasagna. After that day, I barely had to cook for the next three months.

But I've been sick for so long now, it's not hot news any-more. Especially not since one of the cooks at the Miss Quimby

Diner blew his own head off and the undertaker from the Holmes and Holmes Mortuary was arrested for stealing jewelry off his customers' dead bodies. My neighbors still bring me casseroles every now and then, but there's only so much sympathy you can send in one direction. Even I have settled into my illness like an old rumor.

Maybe this is why I decide one afternoon to find him. Maybe it's just some sort of attempt to find someone new to startle with my misfortune. But I don't think so. I've been thinking about him lately. He's been invading my dreams. After Becca convinced me to go through with the bone marrow transplant, to allow myself to hope, he started visiting me in my sleep. Not every night. Not every time I fell asleep. But sometimes I wake up breathless, feeling shame. Guilt heavier than the quilts on my shoulders. More violent than pain.

I didn't know that he loved me yet. I only knew that he was careful with me, as if I were more fragile than I was. We didn't know each other yet. It was too soon. Too dangerous.

When Mr. Hammer told me he wanted to take me to Burlington to see a performance, a woman, a jazz singer, Quinn put his foot down.

"This is *weird,* Piper," he said. We were at Boo's having dinner. She had made Shake 'n Bake pork chops.

"Who's the singer?" Boo asked, scooping some homemade applesauce, pink and thick, onto her plate.

"I can't remember," I said.

"Why does he want to take you?" she asked.

"It's *weird.* Teachers aren't supposed to do that kind of shit," Quinn insisted, spearing another pork chop from the pile in the middle of the table.

"He wants me to go," I told Boo, ignoring Quinn, "because she's one of the old-timers. Like Billie Holiday. And Ella Fitzgerald."

"Then what the hell's she doing coming to *Burlington?*" Quinn asked, his mouth full of pork chop.

"I don't know, but he says it may be the only chance I get to see her. She's getting old and she doesn't perform that much anymore. Mr. Hammer says it's a once-in-a-lifetime opportunity. That if I want to be a singer, I need to listen to the great singers."

"Then why doesn't he buy you a record?" Quinn asked.

"Quinn, he's my teacher. He's *teaching* me." I felt my skin growing flushed. I thought about his hands resting on the keys, about his hand resting on my shoulder as I practiced the scales.

"I don't know," Boo said.

"Mum would have let me go," I snuffed.

"And Daddy wouldn't," Quinn said. "But I'm the one in charge. And I don't think it's a good idea."

"Every weekend, you get on a bus and go miles and miles away from home with *your* teacher to go skiing. Why is this any different?" I felt my face getting hot with frustration now. "I want to go to college for music. Anything I can do to help my chances, of getting a scholarship, of getting accepted even . . . I don't see any difference." I set down my fork and folded my arms across my chest. "It's not fair."

Boo said softly, "Quinn, maybe she's right. Nick Hammer's a good guy. My friend Jessie knew his wife before she passed away. He's a good teacher."

"Mr. Hammer's wife died?" I asked.

She nodded. "Car accident."

"That's sad," I said, forgetting all about the concert. I thought about Mr. Hammer's house, tried to imagine what it might have been like with a woman living there. I imagined wildflowers on the tables, soft curtains in the windows. I thought it might not feel so dusty inside. Maybe his kitten wouldn't be so mean.

"Have you met him?" Quinn asked Boo.

"Once. Remember the charity foul-shot contest last spring? He can't shoot a basketball for shit, but he's a decent guy."

Quinn looked hard at me.

"What?" I said.

"This is important to you?" he asked.

I nodded. I couldn't believe he was about to give in.

"I want to know who this *singer* is first. You better find out her name."

Mr. Hammer pulled into our driveway the following Saturday afternoon. He stopped the car and came to the door, while I was trying to get Sleep out the back. Quinn almost skipped his race to make sure Mr. Hammer wasn't planning to kidnap me, but I promised him everything would be okay. He also seemed to feel better after he talked to Mr. Hammer on the phone and after he saw an ad for the concert in the *Burlington Free Press,* which he went all the way to St. Johnsbury to get.

Sleep kept sitting down, so when I pulled on his collar, his butt just skidded across the kitchen floor.

"Come in," I hollered.

Finally, I got Sleep outside and hooked him to his run. He looked at me, sad-eyed, and I said, "Don't pull that puppy-dog stuff on me. Quinn will be home in a few hours."

Back in the house, Mr. Hammer was standing in the kitchen all dressed up. Underneath his coat, he was wearing a black suit, a clean white shirt, and a red paisley tie. He usually wore jeans and sweaters. His hair was combed back instead of falling into his eyes, too. Suddenly I felt self-conscious about the dress I'd gotten from Boo's shop. I'd altered it myself, cinching in the waist and lowering the hem, but it still looked secondhand. Becca had helped me do my hair, blowing the curls straight with a blow dryer and then spraying my whole head with Aqua Net. She told me she'd do anything to trade places with me. She said if Mr. Hammer had asked her to go all the way to Burlington with him to see a concert, she would have dropped to her knees and thanked God right then and there. She said she'd just about die if he even remembered her name.

"You ready?" Mr. Hammer asked.

"I think so," I said, glancing around the kitchen to make sure I hadn't left the coffee machine on or the toaster plugged in.

He opened the passenger door for me, and I got in. Then he walked around to the driver's side. The car was still warm and smelled a little bit like hamburgers. "Sorry," he said, lifting a greasy paper bag away from my feet. "My lunch. Did you eat already?"

"Yeah," I said.

"I figured we could stop somewhere to get dinner before the concert, if we get hungry."

I nodded. I hadn't brought any money. He'd told me not to worry about the tickets, that a friend of his had given them to him. But I didn't know what I would do if we went to a restaurant. Maybe I wouldn't get hungry.

The sun was gone again, and the sky was completely white. Sometimes in winter, it felt as if we were living inside a giant cocoon. As if you got in a car and tried to drive to Canada or New Hampshire or Massachusetts, at the border you would hit a white wall. It made me feel both anxious and safe.

There's no interstate between Quimby and Burlington. You have to take Route 2 West all the way to Montpelier (which is in the middle of the state) and then get on I-89 North up to Burlington. I'd only been there a couple of times before, each time with Boo, who said the yard sales in Burlington had better junk because the people in Burlington had more money than people in Quimby. I'd gone to Montpelier with Daddy a couple of times when he had to renew his driver's license. I'd also been on a field trip, in the sixth grade, to see the State house and the granite quarries in Barre. I still had the pink granite paperweight I got as a souvenir.

But this trip wasn't like driving with Daddy, high up in the truck, or riding the school bus to the capital. This time I was dressed up and on my way to see one of the most famous jazz singers of all times. *Etta James*. Her name even sounded like the name of someone famous. And I'd been picked special by my teacher to see her because he thought I was *gifted*. I sat up straight in the front seat of Mr. Hammer's Volvo and felt, suddenly, very lucky.

"I saw her once before," Mr. Hammer said when we got to Plainfield.

"You did?"

"Uh-huh. In New York, when I was in graduate school. My wife and I were having a drink at this little bar on the Lower East Side. We were just sitting, talking, when all of a sudden we heard this incredible music. I got up to figure out where it was coming from and found this back room where she was singing. There were only about ten people there. I went back to the front to get my wife and she wouldn't believe me. I practically had to drag her back there."

"What was her name?" I asked. It was hard for me to imagine Mrs. Hammer without a name.

He look at me, confused. "It was Etta James."

"No," I said. "Your wife."

"Oh," he said, staring straight at the road. "Hattie." I felt bad for asking.

He didn't say much else until we got to Montpelier.

"You need to stop somewhere to use a restroom?" he asked, slowing down near a gas station.

I shook my head.

The traffic had slowed and the snow on both sides of the road was dirty.

"Are you looking forward to Christmas?" he asked as we

drove past several street lights wound up in red and green garlands.

I shrugged. I hadn't been thinking about Christmas. The whole idea of Christmas without my mother made me feel strange. It was only a couple of weeks now until school let out for the holidays.

"I'm not a big fan of Christmas, either," Mr. Hammer said.

I smiled. And I thought about how Mr. Hammer might spend Christmas. He and his wife probably used to go out to the woods together to find a tree. I could imagine them dragging it back to their house at Gormlaith through the snow. I could hear the sound of Handel's *Messiah* and taste eggnog sweet with rum. But after she was gone, how could he do that anymore? How could he go alone into the woods to look for the perfect tree? How could he listen to the same music, enjoy the sweetness of eggnog?

And then I thought about Christmases before my mother left. There was a box of Christmas things she kept out in the shed: bread-dough ornaments we had made, a battery-operated Santa Claus that shook and laughed, plastic candles with light-bulb flames. She always took a mirror and put it on the coffee table, arranging cotton balls around the edges. The mirror became a lake and the cotton balls turned into snow when she added the miniature village: post office, grocery store, train station. That was my favorite. There was also a candle holder that looked like a carousel of angels. When you lit the candles, the angels started to spin. I wondered what Christmas would be like this year without Mum. She used to make chocolate cookies with powdered sugar and maraschino cherries, coconut bars almost too sweet to eat, and bread that looked like a shiny blond braid.

We were pulling onto the interstate, increasing speed, and Mr. Hammer held the wheel tightly.

"This is the first Christmas without my mother," I said, more to see what it felt like to say it than to tell him.

He nodded and merged into traffic. But instead of asking where she had gone, the way most people would, he just said softly, "You must miss her."

My hands were sweaty and I could feel my throat trembling even though I wasn't saying anything. I nodded once, hard.

Daddy had already tried to convince Quinn and me to spend Christmas with Roxanne and Jake and him. Quinn said that we already had plans, that we wouldn't be able to make it. Daddy didn't put up much of a fight, Quinn said. But then again, he never did.

The drive from Montpelier to Burlington is only about a half-hour long. The interstate is much faster than the winding road that weaves through every village and hamlet between Quimby and Montpelier. We were talking about the production of *The Sound of Music,* which was scheduled for the end of January. Mr. Hammer was saying he hoped nobody forgot their lines over the holiday, that we should maybe try to squeeze in a rehearsal between Christmas and New Year's. And then we were at the exit for South Burlington, and then the one that would take us downtown.

"Well, here we are," Mr. Hammer said, as surprised as I was. "Have you been here before?"

"A couple of times," I said. "My brother's probably going to be on UVM's ski team next year."

"That's great." He gestured out my window. "There's the main campus."

I tried to picture Quinn, a backpack slung over his shoulder, walking across the snow-covered quad.

We drove down Main Street, past the colorful Victorian houses, the lake at the bottom of the hill a great white expanse.

We parked in a parking garage, on a rooftop that looked out over the marketplace on Church Street.

"Are you hungry yet?" he asked.

I was starving, and I was mad at myself for not getting some money from Quinn. Daddy had just dropped off a check, a little bigger than usual for the holidays.

Mr. Hammer must have sensed that I was hedging, and squeezed my shoulder. "My treat?"

I smiled, and we walked out of the dark parking lot into the city.

He took me to a restaurant called Carbur's, where the menus looked like old-fashioned newspapers and all the items had funny names. It was warm and light inside, and through the window as the sun set, little white lights lit up in the trees, like stars appearing in the night sky.

He pulled out my chair for me and helped me with my coat. No one had ever done that before. I felt as if I were on TV. I ordered a sandwich called Name That Tuna, and a lemonade. Mr. Hammer had a Cool Hand Cuke sandwich and a Coke. The restaurant was crowded and loud with music and conversation. Sitting next to us was a family with three kids. The littlest one kept escaping and crawling underneath my chair. The mother scooped her up, apologizing, each time I signaled that she was underneath my feet. "I'm so sorry," she said. *"Terrible twos."*

For dessert, I ordered a hot fudge sundae. I couldn't remember the last time I'd had one, and Mr. Hammer had said, "Order anything you want." He ordered a cup of coffee, and I asked the waiter if I could have one, too.

The mother strapped her two-year-old into a heavy wooden high chair when their food arrived. The hot fudge was so good, so thick and sweet, I felt suddenly incredibly happy. The waiter lit the candle in the center of our table, and Mr. Hammer sipped on his coffee.

"Is it good?" he asked.

"Mmm–hmm," I said, nodding. "Want some?" I held out a spoon full of ice cream and hot fudge.

"No, thanks," he said.

I shrugged and put the spoonful in my mouth.

"You've got some chocolate," he said, motioning toward the corner of my mouth. I felt my cheeks grow red and I dabbed at my face with my napkin.

"Still there," he said, reaching for his own napkin and quickly wiping at the chocolate smudge. It made me remember my mother's gestures, the rough swipe of a paper napkin or the soft edge of her worn T-shirt.

"Thank you," I said, rolling my eyes, embarrassed.

After Mr. Hammer paid the bill, he said, "I've got to run to the bathroom. Wait here for me?"

"Sure," I said.

While he was in the bathroom, the baby, done eating, escaped again and wriggled under my chair, refusing to move. Her mother came over and said softly, "I am so sorry again. I hope she didn't ruin your date."

The words didn't register for a moment, and I started to tell her, *No, no, it wasn't a date.* And then the immensity of what she had said hit me, and I just shook my head. "That's okay." I set my fork down and glanced anxiously around the room.

When Mr. Hammer came back from the bathroom and I stood up, I wondered what everyone else in the restaurant might think. Had the waiter thought we were a couple? I tugged at the skirt of my dress, straightening it, and let Mr. Hammer help me on with my coat. It struck me as both terrifying and wonderful that anyone would believe I was grown, that I wasn't a girl at all, but a woman. I tried tossing my hair back like a woman on our way out of the restaurant. I tried walking like a woman, and when I spoke again, I wondered if my voice was like a woman's.

The concert was on the UVM campus in one of the old buildings that we had driven by earlier. At night the building looked ominous, but inside, it was quiet and much smaller than it had appeared. Like a church. The audience was even whispering, as if they were waiting for God.

I was nervous and excited. My whole body seemed to be trembling; I sat on my hands to keep from shivering. Mr. Hammer had gotten a cup of coffee for himself from the concession stand and a cup of cocoa for me. I held the foam cup between my hands to keep it steady.

"You okay?" he asked, leaning toward me, whispering.

I nodded.

When the lights went down, darkness descending, Mr. Hammer whispered, "Listen."

She came out while it was still dark. We were close enough to hear the sound of her heels on the wooden stage. When the lights came up on her, I closed my eyes. They were too distracting, all the lights and glitter and equipment. When the music started, I only wanted to feel her voice.

I felt myself fragmenting. I felt everything shattering. Everything that was whole was turning into slivers, each of them a different color of sorrow. And when the pieces came together again, I felt rearranged. Whole.

I was aware of Mr. Hammer sitting next to me. I could feel the warmth of his skin, smell the now familiar scent of his detergent, the vague smell of cologne. Of pine maybe, of the woods where we lived. I opened my eyes once and turned to see if he had been reassembled, too. He turned to me, in that exact moment, and I knew that he understood. I didn't need to say a word. He was right there. Inside the music with me. *Edel-weiss.*

Here was the color my mother had saved the bottom drawer for. It was the color of the sky the morning I woke up and discovered that she was already gone. The color of a single, discarded shoe at Boo's. It was the color Daddy must have seen on his migraine days, the color of bruise. It was the color of a room that belonged to no one, the color of sadness, the color of wanting something that was already gone.

For nearly an hour, I let myself be lost inside Etta James's voice. Each note flowing into the next, each song into the next. I kept my eyes closed, resting my head first on the back of the seat, and then on his shoulder. It was different than it had been with Blue at the Star Theater. I was not aware of the touching. I was only aware of the colors of her voice. Of the perfect silence of music.

But then the music ended and the audience was standing. The ridiculous cacophony of applause made my head ache, and it took everything I had not to put my hands over my ears to stop the noise.

Mr. Hammer was still sitting, too, his hands quiet in his lap.

He smiled at me and reached for my hand. "Are you still cold?"

I realized I hadn't taken my coat off the entire time. My hands were inside the cuffs. I felt a distant ache, and, still, the tremble.

I nodded, and he reached toward me again, pressing the soft inside of his wrist against my head.

His smile faded into concern. "You're burning up. I think you have a fever."

It was only then that I connected the vague pain over my eyes with the rivers of cold running down my shoulders. I'd thought it was only the music. When we stood, I was aware of how weak my legs felt. I feared that if I put my hands together to clap, they wouldn't be strong enough to make sound.

Mr. Hammer tugged gently on my sleeve and ushered me out past the noise into the warm lobby. And as we walked out into the cold night again, into freezing rain and ice, I felt something familiar. *Illness. Flu.*

"We need to get you home," Mr. Hammer said. He looked worried as he helped me down the slippery steps onto the sidewalk. "I'm worried about the roads, though."

When we crossed the road to the car, my feet spun underneath me, and he caught me just as I was about to fall. After I regained my balance, he looked out at the icy street illuminated by the streetlights and headlights, his eyebrows furrowed with worry.

"We may need to wait until morning," he said. "It's glare ice."

My heart was pounding hard from the near fall, and I thought immediately of Quinn. "You mean stay *here?*" I asked. Quinn would be furious. He would make me quit my lessons. He might even make me quit the play. "I really need to go home," I said.

"My sister lives in Shelburne. It's just a couple of miles from here. Piper, I'm really worried about driving all the way back. Could you call home?"

Quinn would have to understand. He'd been stuck before. It happens in Vermont.

I called from a pay phone at a gas station. I closed the door so that Mr. Hammer wouldn't have to listen to me arguing with Quinn.

"The roads are terrible," I said.

"It's fine *here,*" he said. He was pacing. I could hear his boots on the linoleum.

"You're ninety miles away," I said. "It's freezing rain, and

I'm sick." I was starting to cry. Part of me wanted to be at the other end of the phone right now. Lying in my own bed.

"Get his sister's name and phone number," Quinn said.

I opened up the door and ran to Mr. Hammer's car, leaving the phone hanging by its cord. I asked him for her name and number, and he scribbled them on the gas receipt.

"Make him buy you some aspirin and some orange juice. I want you home by ten o'clock tomorrow morning. You tell him that. And I'm calling his sister in an hour to make sure you're there."

I nodded, because the pain behind my eyes was growing too strong to argue.

"I love you, Piper. Just be safe." He paused. "Can I talk to him?"

My heart sank. But I motioned for Mr. Hammer to come to the phone, and I went back to the car. From the passenger seat, I could see him nodding and talking. It didn't look as if Quinn was yelling at him.

Mr. Hammer's sister lived in a little white house; a boat covered with a blue tarp was parked in the driveway. The rain and hail bounced off the tarp in strange rhythms. His sister didn't look anything like him. She had soft blond curly hair, and she was little, like Becca.

By the time she had ushered us into her kitchen, I could feel my fever like hot ice. While Mr. Hammer made some tea, she took me into her room and gave me an armload of warm clothes to change into. The lights in the bathroom hurt my eyes, so I changed in the dark, shaking so hard I could barely pull on the wool socks she had given me.

She returned with aspirin and a cup of tea and steered me into a guest room, where she helped me into a tiny bed, covering me with blankets.

"It's okay, honey," she said. "Everything's going to be fine.

Nick will be in the living room if you need him, and my room is right down the hall. We'll get you home tomorrow."

I nodded.

Mr. Hammer was standing in the doorway, his tie loosened. It looked like a red Christmas ribbon, unfurled.

His sister left the room and Mr. Hammer came over to the side of the bed. He crouched down so he was at my level.

"Are you okay?" he asked.

"I'm sorry," I said, and I felt suddenly overcome with guilt and embarrassment. "I didn't mean to get sick." My throat was thick.

"Shhh," he said, leaning forward and kissing my forehead. The kiss was warm and soft. Like a flower, I thought. Like summertime. But he moved away from me as if my fever had blistered his lips. "I'm sorry. Feel better," he mumbled and he hurried out the door. I closed my eyes and thought about summertime, my fever transformed into the simple heat of sun on my face.

I fell asleep to the hushed sounds of their voices rising and falling outside my door. I woke up once in the middle of the night, the music in my head so loud it had crashed through my dreams and into the quiet room. But when I opened my mouth to call out for someone to come, my own voice was gone.

Becca and I went to the Quimby Atheneum to do some Internet research about bone marrow transplant facilities. My oncologist had suggested traveling all the way to Seattle for the procedure, and Becca wanted to see if there might be someplace closer. I wasn't even sure if my insurance company would pay for any of this, but I told her we could look anyway.

It's so hard to imagine going through all of this again. The idea behind the transplant is that if the healthy cells are harvested prior to treatment, even higher doses of chemotherapy can be administered to—the doctors hope—eradicate the cancer, and then the healthy marrow can be put back inside the body. The thought of drugs more potent than the ones that had almost crippled me with nausea three times before is terrifying. I'd taken the antinausea drugs, changed my diet, even bought a half ounce of weed from a shaggy kid outside Quimby High. Nothing had helped.

But I have been having more and more difficulty breathing lately, and the pain in my legs and hips has become so intense, it snubs its nose at my painkillers. And the procedure makes sense logically. It really does. I think at night about a body without cancer. I think about living without pain for a little longer.

It was a brisk day. Becca parked in the library parking lot

and held onto my arm so I wouldn't slip on the ice. I felt like an old lady, so terrified of breaking a hip.

"You know, back when I was a kid, we didn't have books," I said in my best old-lady voice.

"You're crooked," Becca said, reaching to straighten the blond wig. It has become my favorite lately.

Inside the library, Becca dragged one of the comfortable overstuffed chairs over to the computer table and sat me down in it. "You know how to go online?" she asked.

"Back when I was a kid," I started, "a mouse was a little furry thing."

"Oh, hush," she said.

I'd made a list of things I wanted to check. An online wholesale fabric supplier; eBay for antique buttons and lace. I'd told the widow-bride I'd look for something blue to sew into the dress, and I thought a sapphire button might be perfect. While Becca researched transplant facilities in Seattle and Baltimore and Boston, I looked at silks from India and Paris. Asian mail-order brides. Antique toys from my childhood, and gay porn.

"What are you doing?" Becca asked, looking at my screen. Two men in leather thongs embraced glamorously. Amorously. "Jesus, Piper," she said. "Come see."

She was on the home page for the facility in Seattle that my doctor had recommended. Her notepad was covered with scribbled notes.

"I've never been to Seattle," she said. "We could go to the top of the Space Needle! There's a restaurant up there. We could go to the place where they throw those big fish at you."

I'd been afraid of this. I'd known she would try to do too much. "Becca, you've got school."

She looked at me blankly. "I'll take a leave of absence. It would only be for a month or so."

She sat back down at the computer, her eyes glistening in the light from the screen.

"We could become rock stars," I said softly.

"Drink lattes all day." She smiled.

Becca returned to her research, printing out information about lodging for patients' families, street maps, and airfare bargains. While she clicked and scrolled and printed, I found a site that lets you locate anyone. And while she was busy with the Seattle chamber of commerce, I typed, "Nick Hammer."

Christmas morning, I woke up to the smell of French toast, a remote but familiar smell. I went into the kitchen and Quinn was standing over a frying pan with a dripping piece of bread. "French toad!" he said. That was what he called it when he was a little boy. Every time Mum made breakfast, he asked for French toad. Sometimes she'd even put green food coloring in the eggs and milk.

"Merry Christmas," I said, hugging him from behind. I stayed like that, my face pressed to his back as he flipped the sweet-smelling toast. Vanilla and cinnamon. He made me scrambled eggs with cream cheese, and let me have some coffee.

My flu was finally completely gone. The cough had lingered for two weeks but I was finally able to sleep through the night. Quinn still made sure I drank a whole glass of orange juice and swallowed two chalky vitamins every morning.

He had brought home a little tree from the place in the parking lot outside the Shop-N-Save. Together we had strung popcorn and cranberries. Neither one of us wanted to go through Mum's boxes in the shed. Besides, the tree looked pretty without too much junk on it: just some green lights and a silver star I made from straws and tinfoil. I had asked Quinn to bring home some empty boxes, and I wrapped them up like presents, trying to make it look more like Christmas. But this morning there were some new boxes, ones I hadn't wrapped, underneath the tree.

Two were from Daddy, though the labels said, "From: Daddy, Roxanne, and Jake." Boo had also dropped off presents. She put one in the branches of the tree; that one said, "To: Piper / From: Mum." I thought about leaving it there, stuck in the branches, perched like a strange and colorful bird. Maybe after Christmas, when we brought the tree to the dump, the box would take flight, rise out of the branches in a flutter of red and green and gold.

I ran into the bedroom to get the present I'd gotten for Quinn and said, "You first."

He sat down on the couch and tore the paper off. I had been saving a little bit of the money Daddy gave us every week so I could get it for him. It was one of the expensive ski sweaters that everyone else on the team had. He was always embarrassed by his one lumpy gray pullover. I knew that. This one was navy blue, with a red stripe across the chest. He pulled it on over his head and looked down at it.

"I love it. It's perfect." He motioned for me to hug him.

"Can I have your old one?"

"What for?" he asked.

"I like the way it smells."

I unwrapped Quinn's present, and it was really two presents. An Etta James album and the Billie Holiday record of Mum's that I'd broken. "Thank you," I said, feeling grateful and sad at the same time.

Boo gave us each a pair of slippers and some bubble bath for me. It was the same kind Mum used, the kind that looked like a champagne bottle. Daddy sent some long johns and socks for Quinn. He gave me a Whitman's Sampler and a Storybook box of Life Savers. I cracked the cellophane, took out the roll of Butter Rum, and offered Quinn one.

Mum had sent Quinn a ski hat. It even matched his new sweater, as if she had spied on me staring at the rows and rows of choices at the ski shop in Quimby. He paraded across the living room floor in both and then reached into the branches of the tree for Mum's gift to me.

"Here," he said.

I held the box in my hand as if it really were an exotic bird, afraid and fascinated by it at the same time. I unwrapped the paper, thinking of feathers. Inside the little box, underneath a square of cotton, was a necklace, a silver chain so thin it could have been a silver thread. And hanging from the chain, edged in a silver braid, was a perfectly square piece of blue glass.

The first time we went hunting, I was eleven years old. It was spring, and my mother and I were trespassing.

I used to believe that the world was made of mud. That's what Daddy always said in springtime. The road to our house turned into a thick river of it when the last of the snow finally melted. The banks of the Pond were stinky with it. There was no way to stay clean if you were a kid. I had two sets of clothes: school clothes and mud clothes. Even Sleep was perpetually filthy; his coat turned from golden to a dark, sticky brown in the spring.

But there was something else about spring. Something clean. It descended on us like a slow kiss. Winter always threatened permanence. The sun would tease us with brief appearances in March and April, but then the gray skies would inevitably return, and the mercury would drop again. Spring sunshine was honest.

Quinn hated spring. He'd keep hiking up the mountain well into May, looking for patches of snow that had escaped the sun. When everything had melted, he still kept looking. He'd come home tired and frustrated, his boots filthy. All that mud was like a personal insult from God.

Daddy was working at the gas station that year. His job at the dump didn't start until June. He had to work the early shift, and he worked doubles a lot. Sometimes he'd be gone from the time I woke up until the time I fell asleep. Our whole house smelled like gasoline when he came home and peeled off his gray spaceman suit. That smell wound its way into my dreams.

This is the way I remember spring: gasoline and sunshine and mud, mud, mud.

Mum and I loved spring. We'd sit on the back porch with our dirty feet up on the railing, roll up the sleeves of our T-shirts, and let the cold sunshine settle on our shoulders. She'd fill a Tupperware bowl with grapes, the red ones with seeds, and we'd sit out there for hours, sucking the skins off and spitting the seeds into the muddy driveway.

Mum liked to walk to Gormlaith in the spring, even though the roads were muddy. We'd put on our winter boots and set out like explorers. Mum always acted like a tour guide, like the lady who worked at the Planetarium in Quimby, pointing out things along the way. Raspberry bushes and beaver dams could have been Orion and Cassiopeia, for all her wonder. When we got to the lake, she liked to make up stories about the people who lived at the camps. She said that the tree house at the McInnes camp was built especially for one of Gussy and Frank McInnes's granddaughters, the smallest one who looked like a little elf. Her name was Effie, which sounded just like a fairytale name to me. Mum said that everything inside the tree house was made her size. A little bed and little desk. Little books to read and a little teapot. I would have crawled up the rope ladder that was hanging there, but in the spring, the path was thick with mud.

She told me about old Magoo in the next camp down, how he couldn't see anything except at night. That he was blind during the day, bumping into things if he left his familiar house, but that at night his vision was restored. I pictured him wandering around the lake at night, the sky illuminated only by fireflies. I wondered how someone could live backward like that.

As we walked the long way around the lake, she fabricated lives for all the camp's inhabitants. Her favorite cabin, though, was the one with stained-glass windows, the one that looked like the house in "Hansel and Gretel." She didn't even need to make up stories about that one. The first time we went there, I felt I'd stepped into one of my books. I felt *illustrated*. Unreal. I remember her looking at those windows, at the way the spring sunlight caught in all the impossible colors.

At the boat access area, we sat down on two of the boulders that sat in the shallows. The edges of the water were filmy; parts of the lake were still frozen.

"I would love to see the ocean," she said, staring toward the center of the still lake. "I never have."

I nodded.

"I've heard that in California, you can look out at the ocean and on a still day you can see all the way to Japan. What do you think it looks like?" she asked.

"California?"

"No. Japan."

California was as foreign to me as Japan was. I shrugged. It scared me when she started wondering about other places. Once on a hot summer day, she showed me a picture of Alaska. She said that there's a time of year in Alaska when the sun never sets, a time when it's always day.

She slipped off one of her boots and unrolled her sock.

"Mum, the water's still frozen," I said.

But she let her toes touch anyway, slowly the way she'd tested my bathwater for me when I was little. She let them dangle there until I said, "Mum, you'll get frostbite. Hypothermia." I felt panicked.

She pulled her foot out and looked at it. Then she rolled her sock back on and laced up her boot.

"Let's go," she said, hopping off the rock. She pulled my hand and I jumped off my rock, too.

I followed her down the muddy road toward the far side of the lake. When we got to the wooden gate with the "No Trespassing" sign, I reluctantly followed her as she ducked and went through the opening in the split-rail fence.

It was an old logging road, even muddier and ruttier than the road to the Pond. My boots were completely covered with mud.

"We shouldn't be here," I said, nervous. I'd heard stories abour people getting shot for trespassing.

"Come on," she said, and I followed.

The woods were deep and green. We went so far in that it started to seem we were going backward in time, backward through the seasons. It was still winter this deep in the woods. Some of the tree branches were still burdened with snow.

Finally, we came to a clearing, where the sun was touching the cold brown grass. I stepped into the sunlight and let it warm my shoulders, which were stiff with the cold. There was a little wooden shed in the clearing; it looked like an abandoned sugar shack.

Mum smiled and pointed to the building. The wood looked rotten. The door had fallen off the hinges. "Boo and I used to play here when we were little girls," she said. "Come inside."

Inside, the shack was remarkably dry and warm. I swore to her I could smell maple syrup. And instead of telling me that all the trees on this patch of land had been tapped out years before, she said, "I smell it, too."

"Want to see something neat?" she asked, her eyes bright like a kid's.

"Yeah."

She went to one corner of the room and squatted down, inspecting the floor, running her fingers across the floorboards.

Then she pried up a loose board and pulled out a coffee can. It was rusted, but you could still read *Chock Full o'Nuts* on the side.

"What's inside?" I asked, suddenly thrilled.

"Let's see," she said, raising her eyebrows, teasing me.

"Open it!"

"Okay, okay," she said and peeled back the plastic lid.

Then she poured the contents on the wooden counter that ran the length of one wall. Sunlight was streaming through the one window now, and it caught in all the colors in the pile.

"What is it?" I asked, moving toward the counter.

"Just glass," she said. She carefully picked up a small piece of brilliant green glass and set it gently in the palm of my hand. "I found this one at the access area. Luckily, I had shoes on."

"What about this one?" I asked, picking up a circle of amber.

"It was buried under a rock at the Pond. I think someone hid it." It looked to me like the bottom of a beer bottle, but she handled it as if it were a gem.

We went through the entire pile until there was a story attached to each piece. And then she carefully put them back in the coffee can and put the coffee can back under the floor.

"What will you do with them?" I asked.

"I don't know. What do you think I should do with them?"

"I think you should make windows like the ones at that house," I said, clapping my hands together.

"What a good idea."

When we walked back to our house that afternoon, I started to look at things differently. I was looking for something instead of wandering blindly. I felt like Magoo must have felt when the sun finally set. My eyes were open.

I went to the Pond by myself that afternoon while Mum took a nap. I brought a spoon with me, and my own coffee can. I searched for three hours before I finally saw the sun glinting in a broken piece of glass, but that simple shard of cobalt made me cry out, its beauty as sharp as if it had cut the bottom of my foot.

I brought it home to Mum, waking her from her nap, and she examined it like it was a diamond. A ruby. Or an emerald. "This is a good one," she said. "This may be the best one yet."

I still look for glass. It's something I no longer think about. A lot of the wedding dresses I've made have been sprinkled with it. Glass buttons and beads. Not sharp, not able to cut, but faceted to catch the light.

The dress I am making for the widow is full of glass, too. When we got home from the library, while Becca organized her research into files and later made something green and healthy for dinner, I sat in the living room, curled up on the couch, sewing glass beads so small you could barely see them into the edges of the dress. They're a secret. You won't even see them unless she turns the right way in the sunlight. I imagined making a dress completely of glass someday. But not this time. The bride is too fragile herself for a dress of glass.

Quinn came bursting through the door to our house like a storm. Snow swirled around him, and the cold wind blew a pile of bills off the kitchen table.

"Hey," I said, scooping up the papers and setting them back on the table. "Close the door, will you?"

"Guess what?" he said.

"Chicken butt?"

"Piper, I'm serious."

"Okay," I said, making a serious face. Becca and I had been at rehearsals all morning, and I was feeling silly.

"I got approached by two scouts today," he said. "At the mountain."

"What's a scout?" I asked, imagining Girl Scouts, Boy Scouts, Cub Scouts.

"It's someone who recruits athletes for the colleges," he said. He was still out of breath.

"UVM?" I asked, excited. I'd been thinking a lot lately about what would happen when Quinn went to college. The way I figured it, I would go live with him in Burlington, finish high school there, and then after graduation Becca would move to Burlington, too, to go to college with me at UVM. I already had ideas about what an apartment would look like.

"Yep. UVM *and* UC Boulder."

"What's UC Boulder?" I asked.

"Colorado."

"Oh," I said, confused. "I thought you wanted to go to UVM."

"I did. I do. But, the guy from Colorado said I might be able to get a full scholarship to ski for them. Do you realize how many guys on the Olympic team went to school in Colorado?"

I shook my head.

"I don't know exactly, but way more than UVM. Plus, the snow's completely different out there. It's not as cold as it is here. Not so much ice." Quinn was still wearing his ski clothes. He sat down at the kitchen table and untied his boots.

I was starting to feel shaky, like having the flu all over again. "But, if you go to Colorado, then where will I *go?*"

"To live with Boo," he said, as if he'd already thought this through.

As he pulled off his parka and ski pants, I felt my face growing hot.

"But what about Burlington?" I asked.

"What about Burlington?"

"I thought if you went to UVM, I'd come live with you until it's time for me to go to college, too."

"If I got a scholarship, I'd have to live in the dorms," he said. "You'd have to stay here with Boo anyway."

The heat had spread to my ears and fingertips. I didn't want to cry.

"I thought you knew that," Quinn said, his face full of concern.

"Well, I didn't," I said, my voice trembling. And then I couldn't stand it anymore. Everything was about to burst inside of me. "I didn't know you planned to leave me too!"

Quinn reached out for me, but I rushed past him, yanking my coat off the rack and shoving on my boots. I opened up the door and went outside. It had been ten below zero for three days now.

"Where are you going?" Quinn asked. He was standing in the doorway in his long johns.

"To Becca's," I said.

He didn't say anything, but I could feel him standing there watching me as I walked away from the house as fast as I could through the ice and snow.

I thought about going to Becca's. I knew she was at home, going over her lines again. Mr. Hammer had been right; we'd all gotten rusty over the holiday. Becca's mom didn't like me very much. She never had. Becca would never say so, but I think it was because Daddy worked at the dump. Becca's dad's job wasn't much more glamorous (he worked at the John Deere equipment rental store, renting out tractors), but at least he didn't come home stinking of other people's trash. Mrs. O'Leary always wrinkled her nose when I was around, as if I stank simply by association. Becca feigned ignorance, but I knew she just didn't want to hurt my feelings.

So I walked past the turn to Becca's house and continued toward Gormlaith, trying not to think about what would happen if Quinn went to Colorado. Colorado was one of those places like Alaska and Japan. I couldn't even picture it, it was so far away. And I wondered what would happen to our house. If Quinn was in Colorado, and I was at Boo's, then what would happen to Sleep? Boo didn't even like dogs. Maybe with both of us gone, Daddy would move back in. Maybe he'd bring Roxanne and Jake with him. I thought about Roxanne going through my mother's things, throwing everything she had left behind into the back of Daddy's truck and then making him take it to the dump. I thought about my mother's drawers filled with glass, her records, the clothes she'd left hanging in the closet. I thought about the mountains of broken appliances and cardboard boxes and garbage at the dump, Mum's things getting buried. And then I thought about what would happen to me. What would happen if Boo didn't want me? I couldn't even stay with Becca because her mother thought I was trash.

By the time I got to the lake, I was running and crying. The tears were freezing almost as soon as they came out of my eyes. My lungs hurt from breathing such cold air. I bent over to try to catch my breath, and it felt as if I'd swallowed knives. My legs were tired from running. My whole body was tired. I kept walking, but I just wanted to fall asleep. If I could just fall asleep, maybe I would wake up and none of this would be happening. I'd felt relief from a dream upon waking before.

And so I sat. I just let my legs buckle, and I sat down in the middle of the road. The ice was cold through my jeans, but I was too tired to care about the cold anymore. I sat down in the middle of the road and cried. Like a baby. I cried until there was nothing left.

When I heard the car coming, I scrambled to my feet, embarrassed, jerked back into the reality of soaking wet clothes and numb skin. I moved to the side of the road and pulled my hat down farther over my ears. *Don't stop, don't stop, don't stop, I* whispered.

But as the car came up behind me, I knew it would stop. Only crazy people like Casper went out in cold like this. And I wondered whether whoever was in the car would think I was crazy, too.

"Piper?" Mr. Hammer said through the passenger window. He was leaning from the driver's side, rolling down the window closest to me as he spoke. "Quinn's car not starting again?"

At the mention of my brother, my shoulders started to shake again and I couldn't stop them. I turned to look at Mr. Hammer and he was leaning to open the door. "Piper, get inside. It's too cold, and you don't even have mittens on."

I looked down at my hands as if they weren't attached to my body. I must have forgotten to put on mittens. They were red, my knuckles swollen. I held them to my face, and got in the car.

At Mr. Hammer's house, he sat me down at the little table by the kitchen, put a blanket around my shoulders, and handed me a cup of hot tea. I could feel the steam thawing the frozen tears, and they started flowing again. Mr. Hammer didn't try to stop me from crying. He didn't even ask what was wrong. He just sat across from me at his kitchen table and let me cry until there was nothing left inside except for some dry sobs. They made me cough, so he pushed the mug of tea closer and I sipped on it slowly.

After all the tears were gone, the words came. He must have known they would. I showed him the necklace my mother had sent from wherever she was, told him about the coffee can buried in the sugar shack in the woods. I told him about the way the light shined on the pile of broken red glass after she smashed the vase at Gray Wilder's house, and the way I mistook a pile of empty blankets for her at the foot of my bed. I told him about the stitches in Daddy's cheeks, about the wounds shaped like the rings on Roxanne's fingers. I told him about Becca's mother not letting me into the house unless I took my shoes and socks off, because she was afraid I had garbage stuck to my socks. And how even then, she looked at me as if I were filthy. I told him that was no wonder: I'd dug through mud for three hours just to find a broken piece of blue glass.

While I talked, Mr. Hammer sat and listened. And when I told him that Quinn might go to Colorado and that I would finally be completely alone, he lifted my chin with his finger and looked me square in the eyes.

"It's hard to be alone," he said.

I let him hold my head up, thinking that maybe his hand

was the only thing keeping it from falling permanently to my chest in shame.

"It is the hardest thing in the whole world."

I nodded and could feel the bones in his fingers under my chin.

"You have to be very strong to be by yourself. Most people aren't that strong. But I know you, Piper," he said. "I *know* you."

He leaned forward, as if to kiss my forehead again, the way he'd done when I was sick, and I leaned into his kiss, as if my world depended on it. And when his warm lips touched my skin, I felt everything begin to thaw. Even the tea had not been this warm.

I lifted my head, raising my eyes to meet his, and his lips lingered and slid down the bridge of my nose. An accident. He pulled his face away, but he was still touching my chin with his fingers. His eyes were the color of amber glass. He looked terrified. And I wanted him not to be afraid. I wanted to make all that terror go away. So I closed my eyes and pushed my face closer to his, until I could smell his skin and his breath. It stuttered, like a clumsy breeze, and I felt everything quicken. I didn't know what I wanted, but I knew what I was doing. I knew what I wanted, but I didn't know what I was doing. And then his lips were pressed, closed and warm, on my lips. Or maybe it was mine on his.

I knew this wasn't supposed to happen. I knew everything about it was wrong. But my life had turned backward and upside down now, and what I believed I didn't believe anymore. And what I knew, I didn't know anymore. And what I didn't want, I wanted.

In that room, I was transformed. Inside those four walls, I became old. I entered the door a girl and emerged (and emerged, and emerged) a woman, weathered and wise.

I was out of tears and out of words, so I didn't use words. I didn't ask. I only stood up and went to the piano, closing the lid. And I looked at him, the amber glass of his eyes, softer than any music, and reached for his hand, as if he were the fragile one, as if he could break. When I pulled his hand, when I took him into that room, I didn't know if he would follow. I didn't know what I would do if he did.

The room was that of an ascetic, a monk, someone who has committed a crime. There was a single bed, without a headboard or a footboard, only a steel frame to elevate the mattress and box spring from the floor. The sheets were plain. One wool blanket. A plain white chenille spread, pilly and soft. One pillow. Everything smelled clean.

He sat down on the bed and looked at me, waiting. His whole world was in my hands. I stood between his knees and he tentatively put his hands on the sides of my legs, as if only to steady me. And with this gentle gesture, my muscles relaxed, my knees collapsed, and I sat down on his lap, and he cradled me. That's all. He only held me like an infant.

Sing to me? I asked.

And he sang the lullabies my mother had hoarded. The ones she stole.

It would have ended with this strange embrace, if I hadn't insisted. If I hadn't pressed so hard, if I hadn't wanted *(needed)* so badly to be enclosed. But I did. I insisted with my words, pressed with my head and body, wanted. *Needed.* And let him enclose me, under covers, inside arms and legs and breath. Because I was already broken, I knew it wouldn't hurt. I had already felt his fingers, each time they touched the piano keys. I had been listening to his breathing, too.

THREE

Mr. Hammer offered to drive me back home that afternoon, after the sky grew dark outside his bedroom window. He didn't turn on the little lamp on the nightstand, and in the twilight, I could barely see my hands.

His voice came out of the darkness so softly it might have been only the wind. "I can take you home."

I pretended his voice was indeed nothing more than breeze, and gathered my clothes in my arms. "That's okay. I'll walk." My voice was still hoarse from the flu. I didn't recognize it anymore. "Quinn will be worried."

His shadow stiffened.

I pulled on my clothes, grateful for the darkness. If I could mistake my own voice for someone else's, I might not recognize my own body in the light. But despite the safety of almost-night, I had never felt so naked before; with each clumsy attempt to pull on pants and shirt, I felt more vulnerable and ridiculous. I hadn't dressed in front of anyone before except for Mum.

I found my way out of the bedroom and into the kitchen, where my boots were waiting for me, mouths wide open and laces untied. I yanked them on as hard as I could and grabbed my coat.

Mr. Hammer stood in the bedroom doorway, a silhouette. "Piper?"

I zipped my coat and reached into the pocket for my hat. "I better go."

He nodded and then in a whisper, "I'm sorry."

I shrugged and opened the door to the cold. I gasped, the cold startling my lungs. I almost turned around and asked if I could please stay, but I knew that if I didn't leave now, I might never leave.

Outside, the lake was still, frozen. All of the trees were heavy with snow, burdened and melancholy. I shoved my hands in my pockets, wishing I had asked to borrow some mittens, and started the long walk back to our house.

It's incredible how quiet the world can be. It's easy to forget when you're busy with other things. But deep in the woods, in the winter, at night when even the birds are sleeping, there is something close to silence. Near the turnoff to the Pond, I stood still, so that even the sound of my boots on the icy road disappeared and the only sound remaining was my own breath. And then I slowed my breathing down until it was as deep as the lake, and as quiet. But after only a moment the silence started to terrify me. I knew that silence was a dangerous thing. And so I stomped my feet on the ground as I walked the last mile to the house, and sang, "The hills are alive with the sound of music. . . ." as loudly as I could. I sang every verse and arrived at my door winded, exhausted, and laughing so hard tears were starting to freeze in the corners of my eyes.

Quinn was on the phone when I came in and threw my hat on the table.

"Oh, forget it, she just walked in the door," he said.

"Hi," I said.

"Jesus Christ, Piper." He came toward me and grabbed my shoulders. "Where the hell have you been?"

"Ouch," I said. He was still holding on to me, his fingers boring into my skin. "I told you."

"You didn't go to Becca's. I just talked to her mother."

"Let go of me," I said, trying to squirm out of his grasp.

"Where were you? Was it that asshole Henderson? Did you go off with Blue somewhere?" His eyes were frantic.

"No," I said, shaking my head, squeezing my eyes shut against the thought of Blue.

"Where then?"

"I went for a walk, and I stopped at Mr. Hammer's on the way home. No big deal."

His grip loosened on my shoulders, and the veins at his temples stopped pulsing. "You scared the shit out of me," he said. His eyes were softer now, less angry. "Don't do that again."

"I'm sorry," I said, even though I wasn't. That was the first lie I'd ever told my brother.

It did not begin with this. I am older now, and I know it began long before he found me on the side of the road crying. And it didn't end a month later, when it seemed to end. Maybe it hasn't ended yet.

When my fingers begin to ache from sewing, I put away the widow's dress and pull out the printout from my bag. His name is not uncommon. According to the website I checked, he could be living in New Jersey or New Mexico, Alabama or Alaska. I looked for clues in the e-mail addresses, something that would tell me it was he instead of someone borrowing his name. And when I found the listing for a Nick Hammer whose e-mail address was nhfelicity111@aol.com, I knew I had found him. There was no other information. No address. No phone. Just the e-mail address, just a link that could instantaneously connect me to him. My hand shook as I moved the cursor over the link, but I couldn't do it. Instead, I scribbled down the address and shoved it in my purse like an old tissue.

Finding him is not in my schedule. I've learned that when you're sick, there is little room for deviation from the various tasks at hand. Becca would think this a ridiculous waste of precious time and energy. She would see it as a futile expenditure of my heart. But she knows I need to spend at least a little time making amends. She knows as well as I do that even though there's so little of it left, time to make apologies is a necessary expense.

Becca had been on the phone all morning with hotels in Seattle, with the doctors at the transplant center, with my insurance company, which was reluctant to make a decision. The transplant procedure was still considered experimental, as if everything else I've been through could be considered somehow tried and true.

"Can we go for a drive?" I asked.

"Now?" Her face was red with frustration, her hands shaking, when she hung up the phone.

I nodded.

It was snowing softly outside. As we drove through town, Becca pointed to the lights and decorations, talking excitedly about plans for Christmas. The electric nativity scene in front of the Methodist church had avoided vandalism so far; last year, someone kidnapped one of the Wise Men. Red poinsettias, white lights, and sparkly green garlands. Tacky plastic snowmen in shop windows, and cardboard reindeer.

"I love Christmas," Becca said, beaming.

We stopped at the gas station so she could fill up the tank, and she came out of the mini-mart with two candy canes.

I sucked on mine until the red stripe was gone and the tip was sharp.

"Where do you want to go?" she asked. "We could see if there's a matinee. Or we could go to St. J and do some Christmas shopping? How are you feeling?"

"Let's go to the lake," I said.

"Gormlaith?"

I nodded and kept sucking on my candy cane.

"Okay," she said. "I don't know if the car will make it. My studs are pretty dull."

"Let's try," I said.

Becca talked about Seattle, about a special one of the air-lines was having, about a hotel she'd found near the hospital that gave discounts to patients' families. I thought about all the water there. That it probably never freezes like the lakes and ponds around here. I thought about taking a ferry. I thought about rain. She told me about all of the restaurants and cafés and bookstores; we would have some time between the har-vesting of my marrow and the treatments. We could explore the city together. I thought about a city made of water, about bridges and umbrellas. She told me I would have to be in iso-lation after the chemotherapy, because my immune system would no longer exist; she told me about the risk of infection. She told me she would stay with me, though, read to me, play me my favorite music. I thought about rain making everything clean. I thought about drowning.

I took the candy cane and gently pressed the pointed tip to the top of my hand. I tried to remember the pain of a needle, but it was already too far away.

"What do you want to do up there?" Becca asked.

"In Seattle?"

"At Gormlaith."

I looked out the window at the white fields, cows, and evergreens.

"I want to go by his house," I said.

Becca stared straight ahead at the winding white road in front of us, at the snow that hit the windshield as we passed through the tunnel of snow. She didn't ask why, and she didn't say no. She just kept driving, holding on.

"Do you mind if we stop for coffee at Hudson's?" she asked.

I shook my head.

We parked in the dirt lot and went into the store, the sleigh bells jingling. Becca made us two cappuccinos at the self-service machine and asked the girl at the register for two scratch-off lottery tickets. She handed me a foam cup and one of the tickets.

In the car, I peeled back the plastic lid and blew on the coffee.

"Do your ticket!" she said.

I set my cup in the cup holder and used my nail to scratch off the sticky gray stuff.

"I lost," Becca said, crumpling up her ticket and tossing it in the ashtray.

"Two bucks!" I said, excited.

"Really?" she asked, grabbing for my ticket. "You should cash it in and get a couple more."

"I don't think I'll push my luck," I said. "I'll be right back." I hurried back into the store and handed the girl my ticket.

"You want a couple more?" she asked.

"No. Just give me the two dollars."

"You sure?"

"Positive." I held out my hand. I looked at the bills once before I folded them and put them in my pocket. Evidence of my good fortune.

The roads to Gormlaith are still unpaved dirt. In the winter, the washboards freeze into dangerous ruts. We had to drive Becca's car slowly to avoid getting stuck or damaging her muffler.

Becca's folks still live at the Pond, but she doesn't visit them much anymore. They never liked her decision to leave Vermont and pursue her theatrical aspirations in New York, and even now that she has returned, they aren't much more supportive.

We parked at the boat access area, and Becca asked, "Do you want me to come with you?"

I shook my head and got out of the car.

"I'll leave the engine running," she said. "I'll be right here."

I nodded and closed the door and started to walk toward his house. I heard the radio click on in Becca's car, and the vague sound of her singing along.

A long time ago someone bought it and made it into a summer home. For many years, the summer resident was an artist, a man whose little sister had drowned in Gormlaith. He makes shadow boxes, beautiful little worlds of paper and glass. I've seen them for sale at the art gallery in Quimby. A couple of years ago, he and Effie Greer, the little elfin girl who my mother said would never grow, fell in love. Now they both live in the McInnes camp year round. She drives the mobile library for the Atheneum.

I don't know who lives in the house now. I hope it is another artist.

The swing was still standing, though it was weathered now. My heart nearly stopped as I rounded the corner and saw it there, under snow. The driveway had not been shoveled. The shades were drawn; the house was still. The stained-glass windows were frosty. The little studio, the artists's studio, across the yard was sagging with the weight of time and ice. I walked through the snow, knee high and cold, to the steps. I sat down and put my face in my hands.

"Come out?" I asked softly. "Please?"

I went to him again. And again. When the letters from the college in Boulder arrived, when I saw Daddy walking along the side of the road near the high school with fresh cuts on his face, when Mum sent back our missing silver ice cube tray, I went to him. Each time, convincing him that what we were doing was not wrong. That I was not a child, and that he was not a monster.

I became a liar. It was easier than I had thought. Easier than telling the truth, anyway. Lying to Becca was the hardest, because I still had to go to rehearsals every afternoon and listen as she swooned. There were only three weeks left before our performance. Sometimes we stayed in the high school auditorium so late that Mr. Hammer would offer to bring me and Becca back to the Pond so that Quinn wouldn't have to wait around for us after work. On those nights, Becca and I sat in the backseat and she kicked me every time he glanced at us and smiled in the rearview mirror. He would bring her home first and then I would sit in the backseat as he drove the mile more to my house. He would drive with his left hand and reach back with his right to touch me, as if I would disappear if he didn't.

On Sundays, when I went to his house for lessons, I still sang for him. I gave him my voice and for the first time, I think I understood what my mother was doing. It wasn't that she didn't want the things she was returning to us, but that they were all she had to give back. And in return for this peculiar gift, he read to me. Curled up in his lap, I would press my head against his chest, my bare feet dangling to the floor, as he made music out of words.

I knew he was falling in love with me. And I never reminded him that I was only fourteen; I even forgot it myself on those January afternoons when I lay in his bed and he touched my back with his fingers. But I think he knew it wouldn't last. He was a grown man; he had to have known that something this dangerous was necessarily transient, that spring would inevitably come, that all of this was as ephemeral as snow.

What are you doing? I asked as he traced the outline of my body with the soft tips of his fingers.

I'm memorizing you, he said softly.

When we got home from Gormlaith that afternoon, I was exhausted. I used to blame the chemotherapy for making me tired and sick, but now, I know it is just the cancer. I am coming to appreciate its power, more potent even than the poisons sent in to kill it. Some mornings it's all I can do to make myself get out of bed. The fatigue is like an extra blanket, one made of lead.

Becca kept muttering under her breath. I knew she was angry at herself for letting me wear her down, allowing herself to be talked into driving me to his house. I have heard her chastising herself for other similar missteps: allowing me to go into a restaurant where people were smoking at the bar. Letting me eat a bag of Cheetos while we watched a basketball game on TV with Boo. Not stopping me from running around the park when the leaves fell; I twisted my ankle and it swelled up like a fleshy balloon.

She made a nest for me on my couch, gathering blankets and pillows, brewing some hot tea. She turned on the TV, and didn't make me change the channel when I insisted on watching *Sally Jesus Raphael* and her panel of cheating wives.

"Why don't you go home tonight?" I said. "You haven't been home in over a week."

"I just went yesterday. Remember? I picked up that issue of *People* you wanted."

"I don't mean 'stop by.' I mean, why don't you go home and spend the night in your own bed? You must miss it. This couch isn't very comfortable."

Becca looked at me, dipping the teabag in and out of the cup. Her eyes were hurt.

"Besides, if we go to Seattle, you won't be home for a month. Don't you want to spend a little time there before we go?" I thought she would brighten at my mention of Seattle. She usually clings tightly to each shred of enthusiasm I offer. But she only stared into the steam. What she was waiting for was for this: "Becca. I need some time alone. Come by tomorrow. I'll be okay." This way, she wouldn't be the villain.

She nodded, brought me my tea, and kissed my forehead. "Call me. Call me if you need anything. I'll have my cell phone with me all the time. I'm going to call you in a few hours. Let me put the phone right here so you won't have to get up. Do you want me to have Boo come by with some dinner?"

"I'll be fine," I said. "There's the leftover Chinese in the fridge still. Now go."

I had to do this every now and then. She would never do it on her own. She barely lived in her house anymore. And there was a bit of truth to what I'd said. Though I was terrified of it, I did need some time alone.

"C'mere, Bog," I said. "Snuffle?" And he loped over to me, his jaws quivering in the way that only greyhounds' do, and stuck his long nose into the crook of my arm. He stayed like this until I motioned for him to lie on the floor next to me. But he, like Becca, was a worried soul, and kept glancing upward to make sure I was okay.

I fell asleep to the drone of talk shows and soap operas, waking only once, when I dreamed I'd stepped into a puddle that had no bottom.

Two days before the performance of *The Sound of Music,* the cast and Mr. Hammer took a field trip to the Trapp Family Lodge in Stowe. I always thought it was incredible that such a famous family had settled in Vermont. The possibility that anyone would *choose* to live here dumbfounded me. Everyone I knew was always trying to leave, and those were the people who weren't even famous.

Becca was looking forward to the trip because it meant spending an entire day with Mr. Hammer. She agonized for a whole week over what she should wear. At Boo's, she dug through boxes and bins she had already been through a hundred times. "Haven't you got anything new yet?" she asked Boo.

Boo was working on a paint-by-numbers picture of two ballerinas. Someone had dropped off the kit half done. "Nothing new, honey. It's the dead of winter. Nobody's doing their spring cleaning just yet."

Becca sat down, exasperated.

"What's so important that you need to get all dressed up?" she asked.

"Nothing." Becca pouted. "What are *you* wearing?" she asked me.

"I don't know," I said, shrugging. I had only been thinking about how strange this trip would be, how I'd have to concentrate on not touching him. And he on not touching me. "It's just a dumb field trip."

    While an elder Von Trapp took half the cast inside for a music lesson, the other half of us took a sleigh ride around the sprawling grounds on which the lodge sat like a rustic gem. Mr. Hammer rode in the front of the sleigh with Mrs. Applebee, who was dressed from head to toe in a white ski suit with white fur framing her hood and cuffs. White furry mukluks. She looked like the rich French Canadian ladies who came to Quimby to leaf-peep in the fall. She kept trying to sit closer to Mr. Hammer, and I felt my skin grow hot despite the cold air around us. Becca, Lucy Applebee, and I sat behind them. Becca had given up Melissa Ball's hand-me-down coat in favor of a Navy peacoat she'd found in her father's closet. She almost disappeared inside it. Lucy was dressed in an outfit identical to her mother's, only it was pink. I thought she looked exactly like a pile of throw-up.

    The horses were beautiful but smelly; they left steaming piles of manure in a trail behind the sleigh as we crossed over hills and valleys. By the time we got back to the Lodge, I was cold and tired and ready to go inside even if it meant having to endure Mrs. Applebee's showy removal of her white snowsuit.

    Inside, she did, indeed, make a big fuss about her zipper, asking Mr. Hammer to help her. It seemed the zipper had gotten stuck on a bit of the rabbit fur collar. After he had freed her, we all went into a large room with a stone fireplace, and our group was given a music lesson by two women wearing traditional Austrian dress. Mrs. Applebee sat next to Mr. Hammer, looking over his shoulder at the program they had given us at the door. Afterward, we were given fifteen minutes to browse the gift shop before we were supposed to return to the bus.

I saw some things I would have liked to buy for Quinn. He would have loved the pictures of the Austrian Alps, painted on ceramic plates and coffee mugs. But I was still angry with him.

I was holding a music box, with the same picture of the mountains on the wooden lid, when I felt Mr. Hammer standing behind me. I didn't turn around.

I wound up the music box and let it play the first few bars of "Edelweiss" before I slammed the lid shut and moved to a stack of View-Master cards with tiny pictures from the movie. When Mr. Hammer tapped me on the shoulder, I turned toward him, still holding the red plastic View-Master to my eyes. Instead of seeing him, I clicked and saw Maria in the convent. *Click*. Liesl coming in out of the rain. *Click*. The Captain and Maria dancing outside the party. *Click*.

"Piper," he said.

I lowered the View-Master.

"Everybody's getting on the bus now."

I looked at him hard, wanting to be angry for everything Mrs. Applebee had been doing all day, but his eyes were soft and sad. Pleading.

I fell asleep on the bus. And somehow, while Becca and I were both sleeping he managed to find my open backpack and slip the music box inside. When I saw it sitting in there, on top of my English and math books, I softened. I touched my finger to the frosty window of the bus as Becca stirred next to me, and I started to write the letters of his name. But my finger would not move, so I just rested my fingertip there until it grew numb.

Becca returned in the morning before I had even woken up. I hadn't had the strength to pull myself from the couch and into my bedroom the night before, so I woke up to sun streaming through the living room curtains, and sharp pains in my back. It could have been the couch or it could have been the sickness in my bones.

She used her key, quietly turning the knob, and let herself in. I closed my eyes tightly, pretending to still be asleep. She was carrying grocery bags. She never comes here empty-handed. Just once I want her to forget something, to be selfish or cruel. But her generosity is remarkable, consistent. I can always count on her. And funny, now that she was here again, I drifted off to sleep, the winter sun warming my face. When I woke again, she was popping open a little wooden TV tray next to me. She went into the kitchen and returned with a plate of fresh fruit, things that don't grow here in the winter, and whole wheat toast lightly buttered, a soft-boiled egg balanced in a china egg cup that was a gift from Boo last Christmas. She also set a little package next to my plate.

"Why did you do this?" I asked, gesturing to the box.

"It's not from me," she said.

I picked it up and stared at the handwriting that spelled out my name.

"It was in your mailbox yesterday. I only waited because

you were so worn out after the trip to the lake." Becca picked up my egg and cracked it gently on the edge of the egg cup. She scooped the soft egg out of the shell onto my plate and put the empty shell back in the egg cup.

I looked at the package and then at Becca. Her expression was serious.

This time the return address said Hampton Beach, New Hampshire. My hands began to shake, palsied by the fact that my mother was so close. I'd even been to Hampton Beach once before. It was winter, and the entire town was deserted, cold boardwalk and empty Ferris wheels. I tried to imagine the glass she might find there, broken carnival rides and lights. Carousel slivers and broken bottles in the sand. But maybe she didn't live there at all. Maybe she was only passing through. Maybe she was only like the foul-mouthed carnies who ran the rides and ring-toss games. Maybe she was traveling with the sideshow freaks. Fat lady, bearded lady, snake lady. Maybe she had learned how to walk on the bits of broken glass. Maybe she had learned how to sleep on a bed of them. Maybe the next package would be from Atlantic City, Ocean City, Old Orchard Beach.

My hands stopped trembling, and I unwrapped the box. Inside was a piece of jewelry I vaguely remembered from the times when I would sit on her bed with her jewelry box spilled on the sheets like a treasure chest. It was a bracelet made from black glass beads, strung together on a silver chain. She'd told me that they were black pearls, the kind you find inside sad oysters. The loneliest oysters who lived at the bottom of the sea. She never wore the bracelet; it was too big for her small wrists. Now, when Becca helped me to put it on, I had to squeeze my thumb tightly against my palm before the bracelet would slip over my hand.

"It's pretty," she said.

I nodded and touched the black jewels that sadness made.

The night of the performance, I let myself hope that Mum would be sitting out there in the audience. I allowed myself this. I even imagined that when I sang the harmony to Mr. Hammer's "Edelweiss" she would realize how much I needed her. I hoped that she would stay in her seat until the lights in the auditorium went on and we all emerged from backstage. I dreamed the smell of roses, and the way my stage makeup might make a smudged orange stain on her blouse.

In the girls' locker room where we put on our costumes, Becca paced. Her hair was plaited in two braids with ribbons.

"Relax," I said.

"I can't," she said. "Do you think anyone will come?"

"Aren't your parents coming?"

"I don't mean my *parents*," she said. "I mean *other* people." It seemed funny to me, after all the daydreaming I'd done about Mum showing up with roses and hugs, that she could take her own parents for granted.

"Like who?" I asked.

"Like . . . like . . . our teachers. Other kids. I don't know." Becca undid her braid and then rebraided it.

"Don't be nervous. Mr. Hammer said they've sold out half of the house already. And that's just people who bought tickets in advance." It felt strange saying his name. I tried it out throughout the day like this, conjuring him in the strangest places: at the diner, at Hudson's in the aisle with cereal and diapers and motor oil, in the cafeteria. It was easy, because Becca wanted to talk about him all the time. I could say the words and then he was there. Between us like a spirit.

I was nervous, too, but for different reasons. I had run into Blue one afternoon when Becca and I were at the diner. He said he was coming to the show. Stupidly, he looked at me the same way he had before the night at Kyle Kaplan's house, back when he thought I had something to give him. I simply said, "Don't," and immediately knew that he would anyway. I was also worried that Jake might come, and that if he showed up, Roxanne and Daddy would come too. It wasn't the idea of them all coming together, their strange new family, saving each other seats, that bothered me, but that Daddy would hear me sing. I didn't want him to hear me; my voice was one thing I wanted to keep.

But when I went out onstage, I couldn't see anyone at all in the audience, even after my eyes adjusted to the lights. We could have been singing to a theater of ghosts for all I could tell.

We had been rehearsing for months, but nothing quite prepares you for the reality of a performance. Knowing that we couldn't call out, "Line!" when the words escaped us created a sort of panic to each moment. I was alarmed by how quickly the first act went. My heart was pounding in my throat as we made our way offstage and the audience's applause became a distant thunderstorm.

Backstage, Mr. Hammer gathered us together and made us sit. In his makeup and costume, he looked like a wax model of Mr. Hammer. I was almost startled when he spoke, and the voice that came out was a familiar one.

"Great job, you guys," he said. "Very good. Slow it down a bit, though. It's easy to hurry things when you're nervous."

Mrs. Applebee raised her hand in the annoying way she

always did when she wanted his attention to shift to her. "I felt a little crowded in the 'Favorite Things' scene." She looked at us accusingly. Missy Humbolt and Jessica Feldman, the two little girls playing the youngest Von Trapps, were playing cat's cradle with an old shoelace. "I'd like to have a bit more space when I do my solos."

"Okay, keep that in mind, everybody," he said. "Anything else?"

"Liesl was supposed to kiss me," Howie said. I had been kissing the air near his face for so long, I must have forgotten that I was supposed to kiss him for real tonight.

"Sorry," I said, more to Mr. Hammer than to Howie.

"I don't think anybody noticed," Mr. Hammer reassured Howie.

I imagined my mother going to the concession stand set up at every event by the girls' basketball team, which had yet to secure enough money for matching uniforms. I thought she might order a coffee and the sugar cookies they always sold in threes, stuffed inside wax paper envelopes. I pictured her blushing when someone approached her, asking if she was Piper Kincaid's mom. Nodding and saying, *I'm so proud.*

The second act went as quickly as the first, except that Mrs. Applebee forgot her lines when the Baroness convinces Maria to leave the family and return to the convent. In the wings we watched as she turned three or four consecutively more brilliant shades of red and then blurted the lines as if they'd only been stuck inside her. Mr. Hammer stood behind me in the wings, watching. I could feel his anxiety, but I didn't know whether it had to do with me or with Mrs. Applebee's stuttering.

And then we were all onstage, gathered around Mr. Hammer, as he picked up his guitar and started to pluck the first few notes of "Edelweiss." Becca looked at me and smiled. This was her favorite song, too. But when Mr. Hammer looked at me, we were suddenly alone. The other cast members were not there, the audience filled with teachers and students and parents was not there. When I sang, the lyrics now as familiar to me as my own breath, we could have been simply sitting alone together in his living room. The music felt like something warm and glowing inside me, something secret and sacred and scary. I closed my eyes and let my breath weave around his breath, braided like Becca's hair. Intertwined. Voice embracing voice, hovering above us, wings beating.

But afterward, where there was usually silence, was the sound of applause. Every inch of my body was buzzing, currents of electricity making my nerves ache. And when Becca looked at me again, sitting on the stage, empty now, her expression was not of envy or jealousy or heartbreak, but of disbelief and fear. She knew.

I bought an umbrella.

I bundled up and walked to the drugstore by myself while Becca was napping. My legs were aching, but concentrating on the cold helped to make the pain less real. I left a note on the kitchen table, assuring Becca I would be back soon. That I'd only gone out for some fresh air.

Casper was in the park, bent over in his usual task of picking up imaginary bottles. Rather than walking around him the way I (like other Quimby locals) typically did, I approached him.

"Hi," I said.

He looked up at me, his eyes milky with cataracts. "Whatcha want?"

"Oh, nothing," I said, feeling suddenly ashamed for assuming he'd be interested in talking to me.

"Everybody wants sumthin'," he said, blowing on an imaginary bottle and setting it in his shopping cart.

"You're right," I said. "I only meant I didn't need anything from you. That's not why I said hello."

"Well, watcha want then?"

This could go on forever, I feared. I looked across the park at Railroad Street lit up for Christmas, cars covered with mud and snow, Christmas trees tied to their roofs. Even two blocks away, I could smell lunch being prepared at the diner. Roast beef sandwiches, French fries, and gravy. It made my stomach rumble.

"I said, whatcha want?" Casper demanded.

"Everything," I said.

At the drugstore, I found two umbrellas, dusty and faded, on a shelf near the magazines. One was blue and one was hot pink. I opted for the blue one, trusting that it would open rather than risking bad luck by opening it inside. I did blow the dust off, though, and tried the little plastic strap around my wrist. I wondered if people in Seattle even bothered with umbrellas. I also grabbed a box of Christmas cards and a king-size package of Reese's cups for Becca. On my way out, I saw the widow, crossing the street, heading toward the Atheneum.

I watched her walk up the steps, holding the metal railing tightly to keep from slipping. Despite the salt sprinkled everywhere, people were always falling down. I'd come close so many times now, I figured my number would probably come up soon.

I paid the cashier and went across the street to the library.

Inside, the fireplace made everything warm. Many of the local transients become avid readers in the winter. Almost every seat in the library was occupied. The computers were all in use. There was even a line at the circulation desk.

I found the widow in one of the musty rows of books, sitting on the floor reading.

"Hi, Olivia," I said.

She looked up at me, startled, slamming her book shut.

"Hi . . . oh, hi . . . You scared me!" Her hair was disheveled, and her coat was buttoned wrong.

The book in her hands was one of those paperback self-help books, splashy colors. *Letting Go, Moving On* or some such thing. She was trying to hide the cover with one of her hands.

"I'm almost done with your dress. I'd like to have you

come over for a fitting before Christmas," I said. "I might be gone in January."

Her face fell; she looked horrified.

"I mean—" I stumbled. "I may be away for the month of January."

"Oh, sure, sure. I can come by next week." She blushed and her hands fluttered around her lap. "Will you be here for the holidays?"

I nodded. "Just a quiet Christmas at home." I tried to smile, but something terrible had passed between us; I could barely look at her anymore. It was like staring my own death in the face: her with her messy hair and her book about letting go.

I left her sitting there, between the shelves of books, returned to the main room of the library, and found a free computer.

The slip of paper was in my pocket, folded into the tiny squares as if by a secretive child. I logged on to my e-mail account, clicked on "Compose," and entered his address. But when I rested my fingers on the keyboard, they wouldn't move. I had nothing to say. There was no way to articulate more than fifteen years of *sorry*.

There are rules to searching. My mother taught me this on the banks of the Pond and at Gormlaith's grassy shore. If you fail to abide by the rules, you're liable to find nothing at all. Or the things you find will be lost to you, even while sitting in the palm of your hand.

Mum was always looking for something. It was her nature to seek. Even when we were only taking a walk or washing the car or shopping for groceries. And because she was always looking past her immediate surroundings, she always seemed slightly dissatisfied. She would never accept that a tree struck by lightning was only a dead tree, that a chrome bumper, forgotten in the woods, was just part of something that used to be a car. The moment she accepted things as they were would be the moment that she started to die.

I think that must be why she left us. I think that Daddy was starting to make her see that mud *was* everywhere, and that broken glass was only something that could cut. I blamed him. He was like the person who reveals how a magic trick works. The one who points out the smoke and mirrors, the one who calls attention to what's hiding inside the magician's sleeve. After she was gone, everything felt exposed.

When I realized she wasn't in the audience that night, I wanted to die. I'd really believed that if only I looked hard enough (across the rows and rows of dull white faces), I'd find her. After the lights went up, and we'd wiped the makeup and cold cream off, after Mr. Hammer had given everyone in the cast an envelope and a single pale flower, I went back on stage and stared out into the bright auditorium, looking for my mother.

Melissa Ball was in a circle of arms, flowers, and voices. Lucy Applebee and her mother were with an old woman in a wheelchair. Even Howie was inside a circle of tall people, each of them looking more like the last. Becca was backstage; her parents had left right after the show. She was going to ride home with me and Quinn. Quinn was sitting by himself in the front row of the auditorium, waiting.

I jumped down off the stage and went to him.

"I didn't bring flowers," he said.

"That's okay. I got one anyway," I said, showing him the one from Mr. Hammer.

"You were so good," he said; he seemed nervous, shy here.

"Thanks," I said, blushing.

"You were the best one up there."

I looked toward the stage, where Becca was talking to Mr. Hammer, looking up at him. She looked like a little girl. For a second, I worried that she might be asking him about me. She kept glancing toward us.

But then she left him and ran across the stage, jumping down to meet us.

"What did you think?" she asked Quinn, excited.

"Awesome," he said. "You were really good, too."

"Not like Piper," she said, shaking her head. "Can you believe she can sing like that?"

"Becca," I said.

"It's true. She's going to be famous someday. I know it."

Quinn put his arm around my shoulder and steered me toward the walkway up to the back of the auditorium. "I'm proud of you."

Becca followed. And in the warm circle of Quinn's arm, I forgot all about Mr. Hammer and Blue whom I had seen with a group of friends in the back row of seats. He'd left when he saw me go to Quinn. And when we drove home that night, my eyes still seeing spots from the lights, I thought that I even imagined the expression that had crossed Becca's face during "Edelweiss."

At home, after Quinn had gone to bed, and I had gone to my room to undress, I remembered the envelope inside my coat pocket. I took it out and examined his handwriting for clues. Inside there was a card with the faces of Comedy and Tragedy on the front, embossed silver on black. The poem was handwritten on a piece of paper I recognized as one torn from the notepad he kept near the phone. I read the words until they swam in strange syllables in front of my eyes. And then I read them again. I read them until there was no connection between the words and the world. Until *secret* meant the same thing as *regret,* purely because they almost sounded the same.

My mother taught me that when you are searching, you are bound to create a disturbance. By nature, looking is a disruptive task. Taking a metal spoon and making holes in the mud, cracking the branches of a bush to get at something glimmering in the leaves, loosening floorboards to find a forgotten coffee can. All of this destroys the order that was there before you went seeking. The first rule is that you must restore the order that preceded you; you must make amends before you leave.

At my doctor's appointment two days before Christmas, I read an article about a garden made of glass. It was in an architectural magazine at my oncologist's office. The photos showed how beer bottles and wine bottles had been transformed from a thousand shades of green and yellow glass into grass. As if things, like words, were mutable. There was an amber path leading to a gate; inside, even the trees were made of broken things. Chrysanthemums and irises, tulips and roses grew impossibly together and never wilted. A cobalt waterfall gave the illusion of movement, but was frozen, still. An indigo pond with glass lily pads and cattails. The artists who grew the garden said that it was most beautiful under moonlight or after rain. This is the way I imagined Seattle. Glistening.

When no one was looking, I carefully tore the pages out of the magazine and put them in my purse. Becca was absorbed in a *New Yorker* article about a new Broadway show.

I knew the moment I saw my doctor's face what he was going to say. I knew because he'd broken bad news to me before. He has a way of tilting his head when the news is bad, a way of blinking too many times. Becca sat perched, expectant at the edge of the uncomfortable orange chair next to me in the examination room. He stood with his clipboard, like a shield, in front of his chest.

"They won't cover it," he said.

Becca made a sound like a balloon losing air. A slow, high-pitched cry. I felt everything deflating. I had brought the umbrella home that afternoon, and we'd tried it out in the park, like Gene Kelly. Singing.

"It's nearly a hundred thousand dollars for the procedure alone. That doesn't include the hospital stay. I told you, insurance companies will rarely cover it, at least not completely."

Becca said, "But what about those foundations that fund research? Maybe they'd put up the money."

He shook his head. "I've tried just about every route I can think of. Nothing turned up. Unless you have a rich and generous relative, I think we may have to try another avenue."

I tried to think of all these choices as avenues, as streets, but when I closed my eyes I saw only the pathway made of broken bottles leading into the glass garden.

"Like what?" Becca said. Her neck and her face were bright red. Tears welled up in her eyes, threatening to drown us all if they were to spill.

"There's still hormonal therapy. Tamoxifen. I think we've talked about this before."

We had. A little pill, taken twice a day. A little pill that would *block the estrogen receptor* in my cancer cells. A little pill that might buy me *twelve to fourteen more months* here on earth. It would not cure me, but it might give me one more spring, summer, and fall. One more season of mud and cold sunshine. One more chance to watch the town girls flirting in the park on summer evenings. One more autumn, one more fire. And the side effects, compared to chemotherapy, were minor. Of course, there was the chance that the little pill would *induce menopause*. But instead of seeming tragic, it seemed funny to me that I would, indeed, get a chance to be an old woman before I died.

At the restaurant on Church Street that afternoon, I pulled the article about the glass garden out of my purse. I asked the waitress if she had an envelope, and she found one for me in the back office. At the table, while Becca stared into her French onion soup, not eating any of it, I addressed the envelope to my mother at the Hampton Beach address, sealed it in the envelope, and put on it a stamp I found loose in the bottom of my purse. On our way out of the restaurant, I dropped it in a mailbox. I would give *her* fragments for a change, offer her slivers of me.

Outside, Becca shivered in the cold. Her skin was pale, her face somber.

"I want to go see my dad," I said.

D addy came home in February, just like he'd only been out grocery shopping or dropping off a letter at the post office. It was Valentine's Day, and he was wearing a fresh new heart-shaped welt on his face.

Boo was at the house, helping me paint my bedroom. I'd been wanting to tear down the awful wallpaper, and Boo said she would help me. I wanted to feel clean. I wanted everything to be new. It was one of those false spring days that exists to help you survive the winter: fifty degrees and sunny. It was a promise that spring was coming, but I was old enough to know that even the sky can be insincere. Boo and I opened my windows anyway, welcoming all the warm lies in. I found an old T-shirt of Quinn's to wear; it was for a football team that didn't exist anymore, so I figured it was safe to get dirty. Boo brought a gallon of sky-blue paint she picked up at the True Value.

The weekend before we had torn down the old wallpaper. Boo had helped me steam it off, and the room smelled sour all week. The remaining shreds of paper clung to the walls like dead skin. But now, after hours of grueling work, the walls were smooth. We dipped our paintbrushes into the bucket and they came out dripping liquid sky. In only an hour, the room was transformed into a bright place. Feeling ambitious, I thought that we could paint the whole house, one room at a time, until every room was new. Until our house was unrecognizable. We could become different people here.

I thought that in this blue room, everything about what Mr. Hammer and I were doing that felt frightening or wrong might disappear. In this blue room, I could be like any other girl.

My afternoons with Mr. Hammer still felt unreal. What happened between us happened in a different world, like one of Mum's stories, a place suspended from the rest of the universe. I went to him, each time searching for something, finding nothing. And during the long walks back to our house on Sunday afternoons (my hair still tangled, my shoulders still longing) I felt no different from the trees stripped bare of their leaves. I held out my arms and they were transformed into white branches heavy with snow; I empathized with the birches.

At school, we had been feigning indifference for so long, I started to believe I really *didn't* know him. He carried his soft leather bag slung over his shoulder and nodded at me, impartial, an acquiantance, when we passed each other in the halls. But I knew that inside his bag was the soft velvet drawstring pouch I had put there on my way out of his house. And inside the velvet bag was a sliver of crimson glass. It was like this. Everything seemed normal from the outside, everything was going according to plan, but inside there was the soft velvet secret, protecting something that could both shatter and cut.

Daddy came into the house without knocking, and Boo grabbed the lamp next to my bed, instinctive, protecting, when he walked through my bedroom door. He shielded his face with his hands and Boo set the lamp down.

"Jesus Christ," she said, her hand spreading across her chest to hold her heart in.

Daddy held out a box of chocolates to me, feebly, apologetically. "I picked this up on the way home."

Home. It was one of the heart-shaped boxes I used to covet. Shiny satin with a plastic rose in the center. Lace and a velvety bow.

"What the hell happened to your face?" Boo asked.

Daddy touched the mark absently but didn't answer.

"The room looks nice," he said and then chuckled. "You can paint the outside next if you want."

The outside of our house had never been painted. It was covered with aluminum siding.

"Where's Quinn?" he asked.

"Mad River. A race," I said, opening the chocolate box. Inside there was no heart-shaped sheet of paper to tell which kind was which. I closed the lid.

"You guys eat lunch yet?" he asked. The blue of the room seemed to change with him here. The calm happiness I'd been feeling was disrupted by his presence. He was *staining* everything. When I squeezed my eyes shut, I saw drops of blood all over the new fresh paint. Suddenly, I felt angry. I wanted him to go away.

"What are you doing here anyway?" I said.

"Piper," Boo said, alarmed.

"He doesn't even *live* here."

"Piper," she tried again.

"This is *my* house," he said, his voice raised to a frightening pitch. "Far as I know, I'm the one who makes the mortgage payments on this place. Pays the taxes."

"You can't just come back here whenever you want! It's not a hotel!" My whole body was trembling. Boo reached out to touch me, and I shook her hand away.

Daddy sat down on my bed and looked up at me, defeated.

"I'm coming back to take care of you," he said. "I'm your father."

"You're coming *back* because you got in a fight with Roxanne, and she smacked you in the face. You'll go back there tomorrow and everything will be better and you'll forget all about us again." I looked at the prissy box of chocolates and realized they were probably ones that Roxanne had rejected. I hurled the box across the room. The chocolates hit the new blue walls. "At least when Mum left she *really* left. She didn't keep coming back, pretending she was going to stay."

At the mention of Mum, Daddy's eyes grew soft and sad. It made me feel sick to my stomach.

Boo put her arm around my shoulders and steered me out of the bedroom, leaving Daddy at the edge of my bed.

"Let me talk to him," she said. "Why don't you go for a walk? Cool your head. It's beautiful out."

I nodded and started to get dressed. I knew how to leave. We were a family who sought havens outside our home. We were all cowards.

I stood at Mr. Hammer's doorstep, defeated. He ushered me in, looking past me at the road. He had started doing this every time I came to visit, making sure there was no one to see me coming and going. He tried to be subtle, but I was aware of his fear.

I thought about Daddy, sitting in my new blue room with his brand-new cuts.

I went straight to Mr. Hammer's bedroom, a habit already, and sat down on his bed. I pulled the chenille spread away from the pillow and pressed it against my cheek. I lay on my side, curled up, like an infant.

Mr. Hammer stood in the doorway.

"There's been an accident," he said.

I sat up. I could only think about Roxanne's fists raining on Daddy, a hailstorm. *Accident.* "What?"

"This afternoon. By the covered bridge. Charlene Applebee lost her brakes at the foot of Kirby Hill and flipped her car into the river." His voice sounded distant and strange. "She's gone."

He had told me about his wife, about the car accident. He had given me the moments of silence afterward, he had given me the blinking headlights and shattered windshield, the smell of gasoline. Everything in that accident was on a loop, repeating itself endlessly. I was beginning to learn that this is the nature of grief.

But I hadn't known Mrs. Hammer. She was a part of someone else's sadness, someone else's memory. I *did* know the way Mrs. Applebee smelled, the heady floral scent of expensive perfume. I could picture the way her pink lipstick cracked, the jewelry she wore on her fingers and around her neck. I knew the way her voice sounded.

Mr. Hammer sat down next to me on the bed.

"Was she alone?" I asked. Necessarily linked to my recollections of Mrs. Applebee were thoughts of Lucy. They were intertwined, identical, Lucy being the smaller, more fragile, replica of her mother.

He nodded.

"What should we do?" I asked, as if there were something we *could* do.

"I don't know."

I lay back down and curled my knees to my chest. He lay down behind me and pressed his chest against my back. Lying like this always made me think of the orange slugs that Quinn and I used to catch and torture with Mum's salt shaker.

Inside his arms and legs and the curve of his chest, I thought about Lucy Applebee without a mother, and how strange it was that we had something in common now. How it didn't matter that I was a *Pond kid,* that I had to wear plastic bread bags over my feet to keep the snow and mud from seeping through the holes in my boots. It didn't matter that Lucy probably had one of those pink ruffly canopies over her bed, or that she had never tasted government cheese. Neither one of us had a mother anymore. We'd both been left behind.

I could feel his breath on my neck. It was warm, slow.

"What happened to your little girl?" I asked.

He was quiet for a long time, and I started to think I hadn't asked. But then he gave me a few more pieces. Glimpses through prisms: the color of her hair in the sun, bright red popsicles, and grass-stained knees. After Hattie's accident, after shattered glass and bones, there was terrible sadness. So much sadness that you could smell it in the little house. He said it was like decay: pungent, rotten. It was so strong that no aerosol canister of fresh air could extinguish it. No flowers or bleach or pine-flavored toxins could cover it. It was seeping into the wooden floors, into the woolen rugs, into his sheets. And so he tried to fight it by rivaling it. He stopped throwing away the banana peels and beans and Tupperware containers of leftovers. He left dishes in the sink, in water that grew skins. He didn't take the trash bags out. He even stopped bathing, thinking that he might be able to fight it with the scent of his own sweat and blood and breath. But still, underneath the smell of garbage, it lingered. It was stronger than anything rotten. And the house, filled with spoiled things, was no place for a little girl. No place for someone small.

"They took her," he said, and enclosed me like a cocoon, like a fist.

He was holding me so hard, I felt a little panicked. I couldn't move my arms or my legs. He could have crushed me, or swallowed me, I was becoming so small inside his arms. I pushed gently, trying to move, but his arms closed tighter. I could feel him sobbing, his chest heaving against my back silently, the tears of a grown man making my hair wet. I tried to straighten out, but his body was holding mine in place, a vise of arms and legs and chin. I felt my heart start to beat hard inside my chest.

I pushed again, with all of my strength, and I felt his grasp loosen.

I sat up and touched my shoulders, which were sore. I looked at him angrily.

His eyes were swollen. His skin was blotchy with tears.

"Don't go," he said, reaching for me. "I'm sorry."

But I had seen his weakness, and it made me want to spit. It made me want to hit him. It made me want to slam doors, to run.

"I have to go," I said, hurrying out of the bed and out of his house, running as fast as I could back to my house, where my father was standing at the stove, as if he always made hot dogs and baked beans for us for dinner.

My father's girlfriend, Ruby, answered the door. Despite the fact that she had been sending me cards and beauty salon gift certificates, there was a moment after she answered the door when her face was blank. I could have been selling magazine subscriptions or candy bars. Finally, a flash of recognition and she said, too loudly, "Piper! Hi!"

It was three in the afternoon, but she was wearing a flannel bathrobe and something silky underneath. Knee socks with dirty heels. There were bags under her eyes, bruised crescents. Behind her, I could see that the house was a mess. There was a laundry basket on the kitchen table, half of the clothes hung over the backs of the chairs. There were dirty dishes, overflowing ashtrays, trash bags spilling bloody foam meat trays. Newspapers and cans. It was not what I expected from someone who gave pedicures as gifts.

"Come in," she said nervously.

"This is my friend Becca," I said.

Becca reached for her hand. "Hi."

We went to the living room, where she had to push an old gray dog off the couch. He limped away, into a dark doorway down the hall. The blanket covering the couch was thick with gray fur.

"Is my dad around?" I asked.

"No. He might be back in a little bit, though."

"Oh," I said. I really didn't know what I had expected, and now didn't know what I was doing here. The shades were all drawn. The TV was on, with the sound turned down.

"Were you up to the hospital?" Ruby asked.

"Yeah," I said. "Checkup. I'm starting a new treatment next week."

"That's great!" she said, again too loud. Too enthusiastic.

Becca fidgeted with her gloves.

The coffee table was filthy with ashes, cellophane cigarette wrappers, and magazines. On it were a rusty razor blade, a broken pen—a makeshift straw—and an empty plastic bag, filmy with white dust. A pile of quarters and a box of dryer sheets.

Ruby saw me looking at the debris. I should have noticed how thin her legs were. I should have noticed the scabs on her face. I'd only seen crystal addicts on TV before, like wiry animals sleeping on bare mattresses, forgetting to brush their teeth, to eat, to sleep.

"Listen, if my dad comes, tell him I stopped by," I said.

"You don't have to go already?" she said, standing up and following Becca and me to the kitchen.

"We want to get on the road before it gets dark," Becca offered, smiling too brightly.

In the kitchen, Ruby searched through a pile of junk on the island. *Disorder. Dismay. Decay.* I wondered whether she and Daddy were only trying to fight the stench of sadness.

"Well, let me give you this," Ruby said. "It's from your dad and me. For Christmas."

She handed me an unwrapped box. Inside was a basket of lavender soaps, bath beads, and a loofah shrink-wrapped in purple cellophane.

"Thanks," I said, accepting the basket. "I'll be sending your gift soon."

In the car, I leaned against the window, staring straight ahead at the road. I didn't cry, though, because I was afraid that this feeling might be greater than sadness, that even tears would not suffice. I closed my eyes and concentrated on the car moving forward through snow and space and time. I held on to Becca's leg the whole way back to Quimby and because I was afraid to let go, she slept next to me that night, letting me hold on.

Daddy stayed only through the weekend. I knew he would leave again and that this time would be the last. He sat in the living room flipping through the channels, drinking beer, and falling in and out of sleep while Roxanne called the house every half-hour, asking me to tell him she was sorry and to please come home. *Home.*

On Sunday, after Daddy left again, I didn't go to Mr. Hammer's house for my lesson. I didn't even call him to tell him I wouldn't be there. I imagined him waiting for me. I thought about the way he'd almost crushed me.

Instead of going to my lesson, I rode with Quinn to his race at Sugar Loaf. He was supposed to ride the bus with the rest of the team, but his coach let him do just about anything these days. He was their star now. He was winning almost every meet.

I had never skied before; the very thought terrified me. But while plummeting down a mountain seemed insane to me, the mountain was the one place where Quinn was completely fearless. On the top of the mountain, in the snow and cold of winter, Quinn was entirely at peace. I envied him this; there was no where I felt safe anymore.

He didn't ask why I wanted to come with him. Ever since our argument about Boulder, we'd avoided talking about anything that had to do with skiing. We moved carefully around each other, gently avoiding the subject.

I watched the race with the other team members' families, at the bottom of the run, behind a makeshift red fence. Each time a skier finished, we were dusted with snow. Quinn was seeded in the top five, so he went early on. It was thrilling to watch him navigate the flagged bamboo poles.

After he'd come to a stop, he skied over to me at the fence and pulled his goggles up onto his forehead. His cheeks were bright pink, his eyes sparkling. I was so proud of him. I felt ashamed that I would ever have thought of keeping him from pursuing this, even if it took him all the way to Colorado.

"That was awesome!" I said.

He was out of breath.

"Your bib's coming undone," I said, reaching for its tie and tying it with my bare fingers.

"Thanks," he said. "I've got an hour until the giant slalom race. Want to get something to eat?"

Inside the ski lodge he clomped over to me in his ski boots, carrying a plastic orange tray with hamburgers and fries and sodas. He unwrapped his burger carefully, peeling off the bun and picking off the pickles. We ate quietly.

I studied him as he ate, watching his hands. He caught me and smiled, a bit of ketchup on his knuckle.

"Quinn, I've been thinking maybe you *should* think about Boulder," I said. I could barely believe I was saying this. "It's not so far away. I could always come see you. I could take a bus or something cheap like that." Suddenly, I wanted him to know that I would be okay. If he believed it, then I could too.

Quinn finished his burger quickly, silently, and crumpled up the foil wrapper.

"Really," I said, my eyes welling up with tears. "I'll be *fine*."

He looked at me, at the tears falling against my will. He handed me a napkin from the dispenser. I looked at him through the warbled lens of tears.

"Really. It's going to be great," I said. "I promise."

Becca invited everyone to come to my apartment for Christmas. Boo and our friends Doug and Susan and Lizzie. Her neighbor, Larry the Lawyer, and Kit, another teacher from the high school. She brought home twelve bags of groceries and wouldn't let me help with anything. On Christmas Eve, I lay bundled up on the couch, watching *Holiday Inn* on TV. Bing Crosby's Vermont was so clean and bright. I imagined him trying to get his sleigh through the muddy roads to the Pond.

Becca made the whole house smell like Christmas. Nutmeg. Cinnamon. She gave me a taste of her homemade eggnog with chocolate jimmies and whipped cream. She was a flurry of activity, anxiously checking her watch every few minutes.

"What are you waiting for?" I asked.

"Nothing, I've just got like fifty-five things in the oven."

She bent down to pick up something and banged her head on the counter when someone knocked on the door. "Coming!" she hollered, and skipped down the hall to the door.

I couldn't imagine who would be stopping by at nine o'clock on Christmas Eve. Carolers, probably.

"Who is it?" I asked, hearing only muffled voices. I turned back to the movie.

Quinn came to the couch and threw his arms around me, hugging me so hard I could feel his heart. Kayla stood next to him, smiling.

"Merry Christmas," Quinn whispered and kissed me hard on my cheek. He needed a shave. I was grateful for the sharpness of his scruff. It made him real.

Becca was in the kitchen fixing hors d'oeuvres: mushrooms stuffed with crabmeat and cheese, baked Brie and pesto, tiny triangles of spanakopita. When everything was ready we made a feast on the coffee table and drank eggnog spiked with rum, forgetting why we were here, forgetting everything but the warmth of the fire, the buttery taste of the pastry, and the way it felt to be together again. Bog lay down next to me on the couch, resting his long snout on my leg. Quinn sat on my other side, with *his* head on my shoulder.

Becca had gotten Kayla and Quinn a room at the Days Inn near the interstate, but only Kayla went back to the motel that night. She gave Quinn a kiss and hugged me. "I'll see you in the morning," she said. "Merry Christmas."

"Thank you so much for coming," I said. "This is the best present."

Becca drove Kayla to the motel on her way home, and Quinn stayed with me. We talked and ate leftover hors d'oeuvres until I couldn't keep my eyes open anymore. And then, as I drifted off to sleep, he told me stories about the kids at the ski school where he teaches. About their little cabin at the foot of a mountain. About the way the snow falls in Colorado, softer than here. Cleaner and brighter. Pristine. He said it looks like white glass, like the color Mum called *opal*. He sat up the whole night, brushing my thin hair with his fingertips. He said he wouldn't fall asleep; he promised he wouldn't leave.

At school the weekend after Mrs. Applebee's accident, everything was strange. Lucy wasn't at school, but her friends were. Melissa Ball and Toby Hunter. Jessica Miller and Annie True. All the town girls whose families lived on the park. They huddled tightly together, even more than usual. In the cafeteria at lunch, Principal Stanton made an announcement that anyone who wished to send sympathy cards to the Applebee family could drop them off at the office, that a care package was being assembled by the secretaries. A small cry rose up from the table where Lucy and her friends usually sat, and Melissa Ball ran out of the cafeteria, clutching her books.

Grief was something private in my family; it was strange to see misery on parade. But everything in the lives of the town girls was amplified, as if their accomplishments and their pain mattered to the rest of us more than our own quiet happiness or despair. Becca and I sat at our table, silently watching this display, and I envied the small explosions, the acceptable tears. For the rest of us, sorrow was something to be hoarded. It was the only thing some of us really owned.

It would be easier to avoid Mr. Hammer now that the play was done. I had planned to use the other stairwell so that I wouldn't walk past his classroom, and to catch a ride with Quinn right after school. I thought it would be as easy as that. I thought that if I really believed I'd imagined it, it would disappear. Becca and I would go to Boo's the way we used to. We would play dress-up again, like little girls do.

But he found me. I was coming out of the bathroom after last period when he stopped me.

"Come to my room for a minute?" he asked.

He was holding on to my arm; it was the first time he had touched me at school.

"I can't," I said. "I have to meet Becca." I yanked my arm away from him a little harder than I had intended.

"Please," he said. "I promise, it's not about . . . It's about a summer music program. For high school students. It's in Woodstock."

I looked at him suspiciously. I couldn't shake the way I'd felt, as if he were going to crush me.

His hair was disheveled; there were deep plum circles under his eyes. "I promise," he said.

In his classroom, entire paragraphs were diagrammed on the chalkboard, sentences dissected. Photos of famous writers were push-pinned to the bulletin board. Bookshelves over-flowed with books. His desk was a chaotic pile of papers and books.

He sat down at his desk, riffling anxiously through the mess. Finally, he found a manila envelope in the middle of the pile. He reached into the envelope and pulled out a colorful brochure.

"Piper," he said. The expression in his eyes was familiar. Longing. Want was something I could understand, but now, it only made me feel strangely sorry for him. Pity stabbed my heart like pinpricks.

"Can I take this home?" I asked. I was supposed to meet Becca by the auditorium. I knew she was waiting for me. I knew that Quinn was waiting too, his car running.

Mr. Hammer looked at me, and nodded. His eyes were wide. Pathetic. He walked toward me, holding his arms out to hug me. Careless. I looked toward the open door where I could see students opening and closing their lockers.

I took the brochure and moved away from him toward the open door.

"Thank you," I said, but what I really meant was *Please, let me go.*

He reached for me again. "Piper, please . . ."

I pulled away, hard. *"Stop it.* I can't do this anymore," I said.

Mr. Hammer's face was pale. He looked at his hand, clutching my hand-me-down sweater, and then his fingers let go. I ran out of the room, downstairs, and out the door.

Outside, Quinn was sitting in his car.

I leaned into the window, breathless. "Where's Becca?"

"She took the bus. She said she had to get home to do some homework," he said. "Get in. I'm gonna be late for work."

I waved him away. "Go on ahead. I can walk to Boo's. Pick me up there when you're done."

"You sure? If we hurry I can get you there," he said.

"I'm fine. It's nice out." I thought the fresh cool air might clear the pounding in my head. I thought the breeze might lift the dirty feeling off my skin.

"See you at seven, then," he said and drove away.

I slung my backpack onto both shoulders to distribute the weight. The walk from Quimby High to Boo's is about a mile and a half, not too far. I would have to cross the covered bridge, though, where Mrs. Applebee had fallen in the river. I walked as fast as I could so that Boo wouldn't worry. I kept thinking I probably should have called her from the pay phone at school.

I decided to cut through the cemetery to save time. Some of the snow had melted in the warm weather and I skated between the headstones, skidding across slushy grass. I wondered what they would do with Mrs. Applebee's body. The ground was too cold to dig a grave this time of year. Maybe there was a special place where they kept all the people who were unfortunate enough to die in winter. I wondered if Mr. Hammer's wife was buried here. The idea of being buried in a cemetery was strange to me. I thought that when I died, I would have my ashes tossed into the Pond. They'd probably float on top like sawdust.

When I got to the road again, I could see the covered bridge in the distance. Vermont is famous for its covered bridges. They're always in the calendars and magazines, but most of the bridges are so old and in such bad shape you can't drive over them anymore. A lot of times there's a brand-new functional bridge right next to the covered one. The bridge where Mrs. Applebee died was one of the few still being used. Walking through it was always a little scary because some cars didn't bother to slow down. I walked as close to the side as I could, quickening my pace. A car approached me from behind just as I was out in the open again.

"Hey, Piper," a voice said.

It was Jake, driving a beat-up truck. Gopher was sitting next to him. Both of them had grown beards after football season ended. They looked similar now.

"Hi," I said.

"You need a ride somewhere?"

"I'm just going to my aunt's house up the road," I said.

"Get in. I'll give you a ride. It's no trouble."

My feet were wet, the soles of my boots almost completely worn through, and Boo was probably worried, so I walked around to the other side of the truck and Gopher scooted over to make room for me.

"Hi," I said to Gopher as I got in.

"Hey."

I slammed the door shut and Jake took off. It was a tight

squeeze, and Gopher had to keep moving his legs every time Jake needed to shift.

"It's right up here," I said, pointing to Boo's house.

Jake said, "Do you mind if I just stop by somewhere real quick? It'll only take a minute." Gopher smiled at him.

"It's right *here*," I said. "Just drop me off here."

Jake kept driving, past Boo's, and faster down the street. My hand tightened on the door handle. I could smell cigarettes; the ashtray was overflowing. There were butts on the floor beneath my feet. The smell was making me sick to my stomach.

I remained silent as Jake pulled off onto the road that leads to Gormlaith. *Maybe he's just going to take me home,* I thought. *Maybe, he's only taking me back to the Pond.* Gopher reached behind the seat and pulled out a bottle of something in a brown paper bag. He unscrewed the cap and the smell of liquor filled the cab. He took a swig and handed it to Jake. Jake took a swallow and then handed it to me. I shook my head.

"Come on," he said. "I thought you *liked* to party."

My ears were buzzing with fear. We sped past Hudson's, through the woods to the point where the foliage breaks and you can see Gormlaith through the trees. We drove past Mr. Hammer's cottage, past the McInnes camp and the treehouse, past Becca's, and then Jake turned onto the logging road that led to the Pond.

He and Gopher kept drinking straight out of the bottle. I thought I might vomit from the smell. I rolled down the window and leaned my head out, like a dog.

"Where are we going?" I tried not to sound afraid, but my voice trembled in the wind.

Gopher chuckled and threw back his head for another swig.

Jake parked the truck in a clearing and got out. Gopher slid out the driver's side and shut the door. I tried to figure out how I could escape, how I could get out of the truck and run. But the soles of my boots were worn thin, and the road was sheer ice. It would be like trying to run on an ice rink.

Jake and Gopher sat at the edge of the Pond, drinking, and lighting up a joint Gopher pulled out of the pocket of his Army jacket. Every few minutes, one of them would look up at me. *Maybe if they get drunk enough, they'll forget about me,* I thought. But as soon as I pressed down on the handle and the door of the truck creaked open, Jake was there, pinning me to the truck with his body.

"Where do you think you're going?" he asked. "Don't you want to party with us? Blue says you're quite the little party girl."

I started to cry, silently, only the jerky motions of crying.

"Besides, I thought you liked me." His breath smelled sour. Dank. He struggled with his belt; the buckle was large and silver, a mighty buck protected by silver trees. "Come on," he said. *"Sing to me."*

Gopher came over, stumbling from the ice and the liquor. He swallowed hard and then held the bottle over my face, the last few drops landing on my closed lips. I spat at him.

"Fucking whore," he said, raising the bottle and smashing it against the hood next to my face.

I wonder if she learned to lie on a bed of broken glass. I wonder if she learned how to sleep on shards.

I suppose I could have stayed there after they were done with me and waited for my mother to find me. Just something glimmering in the mud. Just another buried broken thing. But my mother wasn't coming back, so I crawled out of the mud, prehistoric, amphibious. I found my backpack in the ruts left by their tires and put it on my back.

I don't remember the walk home from the Pond. I don't

remember anything but the smell of mud and curling up on the kitchen floor next to Sleep.

When Quinn found me he had already called the police from Boo's. But they had told him they wouldn't start looking until morning. They were busy with the investigation of Charlene Applebee's accident at the bridge. I wasn't "missing" yet. I'd probably only run away.

I remember his hands finding my face first and then the rips in my clothes. I remember how gentle his voice was saying, "Was it Blue?" and his confusion when I shook my head. *Blue* becoming *hyacinth, azure, aquamarine.* I remember thinking about Daddy. If he knew what Jake had done, he would *have* to come home. He would have to leave Roxanne and come home, to take care of me.

To be my father. But what scared me most was what I would do when he *didn't* come home.

And so when Quinn's fingers (only looking for things broken) found the music camp brochure in my coat pocket, I only remember nodding and then saying, "Yes. It was him."

FOUR

Quinn waited for Boo to arrive before he stormed out of our house. As Boo helped me into the bathtub, I could hear the car start up, the engine revving angrily, and the sound of tires struggling against the icy gravel in our driveway.

The water was hot; steam rose up around us in wet clouds. I curled my knees to my chest as Boo washed the mud out of my hair. She used a soft washcloth on the sharp curve of my spine. When the water started to grow cold, she pulled the chain attached to the rubber stopper and ran more hot water into the tub. When she left me alone, after I'd assured her that I was okay, I sank under the water and listened to the sound of water in my ears.

I imagined it this way: Quinn pulled onto Mr. Hammer's lawn, stopping just short of the wooden swing. He got out of the car and went to the door, trying the knob before knocking. When Mr. Hammer opened the door, Quinn pushed into him with all his weight, sending him stumbling backward into the dark living room. I could see the way the dim light fell on the piano keys, the way Quinn's fists fell on Mr. Hammer's chest. I could almost hear his words, trying to explain. But he was not innocent; his fingers had memorized the curve of my spine. And so when Quinn demanded to know if he had touched me, Mr. Hammer told him *yes*. Quinn left him there, hurt but not dead, reminding him that he could have killed him. Should have killed him for hurting a little girl. And I knew that Mr. Hammer thought about Felicity first, about his own little girl, and maybe that was why he nodded. Maybe this was the first time he'd thought of me (the dark-haired orphan who came to him and came to him) as someone's daughter.

That night, after Quinn had come home, sat next to my bed, and asked me what I would like him to do next, Mr. Hammer disappeared. While I pleaded with Quinn not to tell Daddy, not to call the police, Mr. Hammer packed his car with the things he would need to start over somewhere else. But though I knew the way the muscles on the insides of his legs felt, I didn't know what he would take. When I pictured his suitcase, I pictured it empty. I dream-packed it with the books he read, with sheet music, with the glass I had given him.

I didn't go to school for the rest of the week. Every morning, after Quinn left, Becca came and sat with me. She brought PopTarts from home and we sat in my room eating them until the frosting made us sick. She didn't ask questions; she only fed me and talked to me and watched me sleep. She knew. She knew about Mr. Hammer and me, and it made me feel ashamed. Not because of what we'd done, but because I hadn't told her. And the same way she knew about those Sunday afternoons, she also knew that he would never have hurt me. That he wasn't the one who took me to the Pond and left me there, bloodied and muddied and shattered. But she didn't demand answers. She didn't make me tell. She only rubbed my head gently, and waited.

I dreamed that I had breasts again. I dreamed myself whole. I dreamed that I emerged from the Pond that day fully realized. Complete.

Becca keeps trying to get me to do the visualization exercises outlined in the books we've taken out from the Atheneum and endlessly renewed. I've never believed in them before, but on Christmas morning, when I woke up, I felt well. I didn't even need the painkillers that have been a staple of my diet lately. I could breathe and breathe and breathe. I thought it might be one of those miracles you always see on TV this time of year. I thought about being healed. In the bathroom, after I had dressed in a dark red turtleneck sweater and Christmas-colored jammie bottoms (an early gift from Becca), I took the first Tamoxifen, letting it sit on my tongue like communion and then swallowing it with a prayer.

Becca made everything beautiful. Everyone brought food and wine and presents. She had gotten a Christmas album with people like Aretha Franklin and Otis Redding singing the standards. She kept trying to get me to sing along, but I couldn't remember the last time I had used my voice for singing.

Larry the Lawyer argued with everyone, but in his usual lighthearted way. He'd fight with you about *up* and *down* about *black* and *white*. He made Boo so red-faced over who won the 1978 NBA Finals, she finally blurted, "Shut up, Larry! Eat your goddamn pie." Becca and Kit sat next to each other. I kept noticing the way he looked at her, at the way he listened intently to everything she said. I also noticed the pink flush of her cheeks. She couldn't seem to eat with his eyes on her. She fiddled with her fork, laughed nervously when it flipped onto the floor. Doug and Susan brought a bottle of tequila, after some strange tradition in Doug's family, and almost everyone drank shots of it after dessert. Lizzie had made us all mittens. She'd just learned how to knit, and some of them were missing thumbs. When we were finished exchanging gifts, Boo and Larry went outside to shoot hoops in my neighbor's covered driveway.

Later, after everybody had gone home, Quinn whispered, "I have some news."

We were sitting on the couch, eating pumpkin pie with our fingers. Kayla was sitting by the window, sipping tea, and Becca was in the kitchen tying up a trash bag.

"Stop cleaning, Becca," Quinn said. "Come in here."

"What is it?" I asked.

Quinn reached for Kayla's hand, and I knew.

"We're going to have a baby," he said, smiling broadly.

Kayla nodded, her eyes growing wet.

She came to the couch and sat down next to me. I stretched out across her lap, and pressed my ear against her small belly.

"Are you scared?" I asked.

"Of what?" she said.

I realized that this must be why Quinn adores her. She has no fear. She is certain about everything she does: whether she's at the top of a mountain, her head haloed in clouds, or right here on earth. Quinn watched me listening to her belly, and pressed his hand against my exposed ear. It made it easier this way, to hear what was going on inside her.

★　★　★

Kayla and Quinn left at midnight, and Becca and I were alone for the first time in days.

"I felt good today," I said.

"I could tell. How is your back?" She was cleaning the last batch of dishes, plates sticky with mincemeat and coffee cups.

"It doesn't hurt. Not right now, anyway." I got up and found a dish rag to help her.

"Did you take your first pill?" she asked.

"This morning."

Becca nodded and handed me a glass, but her hands were soapy, and it slipped from her fingers. The glass shattered, and when she reached quickly into the mess as if to salvage it, a thin river of red stained the soapy water.

"Come here." I grabbed her wrist with one hand and turned on the cold water with the other. "Stay right here," I said, and went to the bathroom to get a Band-Aid.

When I came out, she was sitting on the couch holding her hand, looking at it with mild disbelief. Her fingers were still wrinkled from the dishwater.

I helped her put the Band-Aid on and said, "Better?"

She nodded, but she was still trembling.

"What's the matter?" I asked. Her lips were quivering, a certain prelude to tears.

She opened her eyes wide. Her hair was coming out of its ponytail, the shorter pieces in front had escaped, making feathery red wings at the sides of her face.

"What is it?" I asked.

She looked at her hands and then back at me. "Last night, when I went home, so you could spend some time with Quinn, I didn't know what to do. I just stood in my kitchen looking around. I must have stood there for a half-hour just trying to figure out what to do next." She patted the Band-Aid on her finger and looked up at me. "I'm scared, too," she said. Her hand flew to her mouth, but the words had already come out.

"You know what?" I asked, smiling.

"What?"

"*I'm* not so scared anymore."

These are the kinds of lies I tell now. Lies that save feelings from being hurt. White lies, the opalescent deceptions that *spare* people pain.

At school, the aftermath of Mr. Hammer's sudden departure was worse than that following Charlene Applebee's accident, more universal. His absence left gaping holes. You could almost see them. You could almost fall into them if you weren't careful.

No one ever found out why he left. There were rumors, of course. It was inevitable. I even heard myself passing them along; I knew that breaking the grapevine could be dangerous. *A better job offer, a family emergency, an unexpected inheritance*—these were the most benign. A *mental breakdown, the illness of his lost daughter, a new lover*—these were the rumors that stung my lips like bee stings. I felt swollen later, even after the buzz and hum had disappeared.

The girls who, like Becca, had also loved him speculated endlessly about who the other woman might be. One girl even ventured that Mrs. Applebee wasn't really dead and that they had run away together. These girls lamented the loss of Mr. Hammer the most. They felt abandoned, betrayed. I nodded when they offered me their unique connections to him: a wink, a kind word, his hand on their shoulder. Becca's bereavement was silent; it wasn't as simple or as easy to endure.

I was aware of other rumors as well. For a time they were overshadowed by the enormity of a teacher's disappearance, but when people grow tired of speculation (as they always will when nothing or everything is confirmed) they have to find something to replicate the thrill.

I waited with patience and tenacity, and indeed, soon enough, at the heart of this new rumor was me. But while those residing in the eye of the storm rarely get a glimpse at the chaos around them, I was fully aware of what the whispers and gestures and stolen glances meant. Of course, Jake and Gopher would never tell the story the way it really happened. That would have implicated them in something bigger than themselves, but for a month or so, I was a certified slut.

I sat behind Jake in English class, staring at the back of his head as I had for the entire school year. I watched every twitch of muscle. Every breath. I thought that if I studied him for long enough I might be able to predict what he would do next. If I understood his gestures, I could save myself from future harm.

We were reading *Great Expectations,* and Mr. Ludwig paced back and forth across the classroom reading passages. His favorites were always about Miss Havisham. He became theatrical when he read the dialogue between her and Pip. Today, Gopher had come into class late, when Mr. Ludwig was already well into his performance. He sat down in his chair, squeezing behind the desk, setting his backpack on the floor. Mr. Ludwig raised one eyebrow and continued reading. Jake leaned over and whispered something to Gopher. I watched Gopher respond, curling his lip, coughing into his hand when he started to laugh. My hands tingled.

Jake sat back up straight in his chair and when Mr. Ludwig was completely absorbed, he turned around to face me. He grinned and slowly stuck his tongue out of his mouth, licking the air in front of his face in slow motion. Then he silently mouthed, *I want to lick your pussy.* He turned around again and kicked Gopher under his chair. Gopher clucked and chuckled, making Mr. Ludwig look over the top of his glasses for the origin of the noise.

I stared at the back of Jake's head, at the tendons and the place where brainstem meets backbone. Watched him and wondered where he might be most vulnerable. I looked at my desk and wondered how a pen, a paperback book, my hands could become a weapon.

When the bell rang, I lingered in the classroom as long as I could, hoping they would just leave. Finally, I followed behind Gopher who turned around and blocked the door. "Hey, Piper," he said.

I tried to duck under his thick arm, but it came down in front of me like the metal arm of a turnstile.

"What do you want?" I asked.

"What do you think I want?"

"Let me through," I hissed.

"Meet me after school," he said. "I'll take you for a *drive.*"

I could see Jake waiting for him in the hallway. I glanced behind me at Mr. Ludwig, who was sitting at his desk, leafing through some papers. He looked up and caught my panicked glance. I turned back to Gopher, who had also seen Mr. Ludwig and was lowering his arm, letting me through as if he were only a toll booth attendant. As if he were just doing his job.

This is how my days went. Guys—sometimes I didn't even know their names—swarmed around me after class, enclosing me in tight cocoons of their bodies and words. Somebody's hands were always touching the edges of me. Hair. Fingers. Hips.

At Boo's house, while Becca looked for dresses that would make her look older, I looked for things that would coincide with how I felt inside. I found a crimson skirt beneath a pile of T-shirts and tank tops. A low-cut blouse that revealed the new curves of my body, the white tops of my new breasts. I pulled the tight skirt over my hips, watched the way secondhand heels made my calves tighten and extend. Becca watched me from behind a rack of dresses. Silently. She must have thought we were still only girls playing dress-up. That we were only pretending still, to be something we weren't.

At school, I fought them by giving them what they wanted. When Jake and Gopher trapped me in doorways and in empty rooms, I slithered past them in tight skirts and high heels. I reeked of perfume. I transformed myself into everything they said they wanted. And it terrified them. I tilted my head at their suggestions and answered back, *Yes, yes.*

In my bedroom at night, I looked at myself in the mirror and saw everything Jake and Gopher had done to me, finger-prints like smudges of blush, the blue and green eyeshadow of bruises.

One afternoon, I got a ride back home from school with some boy, some boy who'd been staring at me from across the cafeteria during lunch. He didn't say a single word to me, he only reached across the seat of his car and opened the door. And even after I slipped inside, we exchanged only glances, not words. I knew who he was (cross-country, Honor Society, all of that) but he had no idea who I was. I was a *Pond* girl, that was all. A girl without money or class and probably without a brain. But I was a girl in a short red skirt, and I had said yes, without even opening my lipsticked mouth.

Inside his car, he reached across the seat and rested his hand on my bare thigh. I watched his fingers as if I were only watching a film, indifferent. Parked in the driveway of my house, in broad daylight, I quietly allowed him in, and then I departed. I remembered the way Mr. Hammer had touched my skin so gently it felt like rain instead of skin. How some-times he was so scared that his hands trembled across me. I re-membered the scent of his gentle fingers, the softness of his hair, the music of his breath. By the time Quinn pulled up be-hind us in the driveway, I was far from this place of wet breath and prying fingers.

I remember hands. Quinn's hands, pulling open the driver's

side door, yanking the back of the boy's collar until his face bloomed red, and he fell onto the gravel driveway. His good-boy khaki pants around his knees, his nakedness repulsive. And then Quinn's hand curled into a fist, striking the boy's face until it blossomed the blue of forget-me-nots. The boy's hands gripping the steering wheel as he peeled out of the driveway, and later Quinn's hands pulling a blanket around me, stroking the hair out of my eyes, and holding me together.

"This is enough," he said. "I don't want this to happen again. I want you to let it go."

What he didn't know was that it wasn't the boys' fault. It was mine. He could never see what was bad in me. That was *his* inheritance from Mum.

But I knew what I was capable of. Quinn didn't know that in exchange for my voice (for hope), I'd destroyed Mr. Hammer's life. That I'd given him my body as easily as any sort of gift, and when he showed his weakness, his sadness, it made me hate him. Quinn didn't know that I'd wanted Mr. Hammer's hands on me, that they made me feel real, alive. Quinn didn't know that I was nothing like our mother. That I could break things as well as mend them.

Quinn came over the night after Christmas to say good-bye. He and Kayla had an early morning flight from Burlington to Denver. Becca and I had been playing cards in the living room. Gin rummy, and I was losing.

"You want to go for a walk?" I said as he was taking off his coat. There were things I wanted to say that I didn't want Becca to hear.

"Sure," he said. "It's frigid out there, though. Bundle up."

I pulled on boots and a sweater. Wrapped a scarf around my neck and found my wool mittens and hat.

"We'll be back in a little bit," I said.

Becca smiled, looking up from the pad where she'd been meticulously keeping score.

Quinn held my hand to keep me from slipping on the steps.

"You look good," he said.

I raised my eyebrow at him, pulling my hat down farther over my ears.

"I mean *happy*. You look happy."

"I'm happy for you," I said. "About the baby. Everything." I squeezed his hand. We walked quietly toward the park. "Wanna go to the fountain?"

He nodded, and we cut across the park to the fountain and

sat on the stone edge. The cherub in the center was frozen, holding a cup that spilled nothing but cold winter air.

"Quinn," I said. I'd been practicing this since the night before. "Mum's been writing to me."

"She has?" He looked down at his feet, kicked a rock.

"Well, not exactly writing, but sending me things. Like she used to. I think she's in New Hampshire somewhere. Close."

I shivered, and he put his arm across my shoulders.

"Are you going to see her?" he asked.

I shrugged.

Casper's empty shopping cart was tipped over near a large elm tree. The lights strung in the tree blinked, small heartbeats of light. Quinn looked up at them with me.

"I didn't tell you everything," I said. This was something I hadn't planned to say. The angel above us held still. Quiet as winter. "About Mr. Hammer and me."

Quinn looked at me. Gently. But I couldn't look back at him. I was ashamed.

Quinn took his arm off my shoulder and turned to face me, putting his gloved finger under my chin, forcing me to look at him. His eyes were warm. I wanted to crawl inside them, cover myself in the color of them.

Tears started to blossom in the corners of my eyes.

"You were a *little girl,*" he said. "You weren't even grown yet."

I felt my breath rise up, deep, the cold air making my lungs clear.

"I miss Mum," I said, tears turning into sobs. My breath strong and certain. "I needed her."

The letter from my mother arrived a few days after the new year. Becca separated it from the bills and other nuisances, and offered it to me with my breakfast. "What do you think it is?" she asked, sitting down next to me, looking at the fine blue ink on the envelope.

"A check for a hundred thousand dollars?" I laughed.

Becca's eyes lit up.

"Please," I said.

"Open it," she said and grabbed a piece of banana from my bowl.

I tore it open carefully; the paper was thin. Inside, the words were small and feathery. *Please let me see you.*

My hands were shaking as if I'd heard her whisper in my ear. I'd dreamed these whispers for years. Becca touched my arm gently, and I folded the paper back along the creases my mother had made. I put it in the envelope and set it on the coffee table.

I felt one of the flashes coming on, the ones the medicine made. It was like lightning, followed by tremendous heat. I went to the window and threw it open to the cold afternoon. Becca was trembling and cold behind me.

Outside, Casper was standing inside the empty fountain, searching for bottles. He kept bending down and standing up again, empty-handed. The heat was enormous; I felt combustible. I knew I was only moments from bursting into flames. I pressed my forehead against the window and stared down at Casper in his futile task. His shopping cart was laden with imaginary treasures. It would be heavy to push. The flames started in my stomach and licked outward toward my hands and feet, my head.

"There's nothing there!" I screamed, the explosion of a burning match touching gasoline. "Stop looking! There isn't anything there!"

I felt Becca's cool fingers on my shoulders, pulling me away from the window, pressing a cool palm to my head, making me sit down and be sane. Afterward, I felt like a pile of blackened ashes. Something as simple as a gust of wind could disassemble me now; a breeze could carry me away.

She did come back once.

It was after Mr. Hammer was gone, after he had already disappeared, lingering only as a vague recollection. It was after winter, when almost everything had thawed, the frozen moments in his room in the cottage with the sugarpane windows melted into the colors of a dream. She came in with the warmth and sunshine of genuine spring and left again without saying hello or good-bye. I'm not sure what her reason was; I only knew that she had been in our house.

If spring here were made of colored glass, this is the way the light would shine through the spring my mother returned. Windows spotted with mud, reflecting the new green of new grass and new leaves. Startling sunshine blinding anything still wearing its winter eyes. Melancholy melting into something like bliss. Springtime, and the whole world was the color of clean.

Becca had talked me into trying out for the spring play. But this time Mrs. Linwood, the ancient art teacher, would direct the show. It was another musical, *Peter Pan,* and Becca was already imagining herself suspended, flying. She wanted me to be Wendy. But when I stood on the stage where I had first found my voice, and opened my mouth to sing, it was gone. *Lost,* I thought. Or *stolen.* The sound that came out was nothing more than a feeble whine. I hurried off the stage and looked under the seat where my jacket was, as if my voice had just fallen to the floor.

Becca was cast as Peter Pan, and I was sent home.

"I won't do it," she said. "I don't want to do it without you."

"Please," I insisted. "I'll volunteer to do something else. Lights, or costumes. It's okay."

Reluctantly, torn, she relented. I left her and took the bus home. It dropped me off at Gormlaith, and I trudged through the mud all the way back to the house. It could have been quicksand, it was so thick.

Outside the house, I pulled off my sneakers. I had been optimistic, leaving my boots at home. My sneakers were completely covered with mud. I would have to put them in the washing machine before the mud dried. I could hear Sleep on his run out back, barking and running back and forth. He strained on his chain to see me through the chain-link fence. As soon as he recognized me, he stopped barking and started whining.

"Hold on, Sleepy," I said. "I'm coming."

I pulled my boots on inside and went out the back door, where Sleep was frantic. It looked like a cyclone had hit the backyard. His food and water dishes were upside down, food strewn everywhere. He had knocked over the plywood doghouse that Daddy built, and the bed inside was torn to shreds. The ground was covered with cedar chips and bits of upholstery.

"What did you do?" I asked. Sleep whimpered and retreated at the tone of my voice.

I stood staring at the wreckage with my hands on my hips. The last time Sleep had destroyed anything was when the man from Quimby Gas & Electric came to read the meter, and nobody was home.

"Was somebody here?" I asked Sleep, trying to make him understand he wasn't in trouble. "Sleepy?"

I unhooked him, turned around, and followed him into the house, scared this time of what I might find. I squeezed my eyes shut tight against the thought that Jake and Gopher might be waiting inside for me, then I grabbed a steak knife from the utensil tray.

"Hello?" I said, willing my voice not to fail me now.

I walked into the living room and then down the hall. Sleep ran up and down the hallway. My heart was beating so hard I could barely breathe. I wondered whether I was too young to have a heart attack.

"Who's there?" I demanded, slowly opening doors. Quinn's room, my room. At the end of the hall, I stood outside Mum and Daddy's room and held the knife with both hands. I pushed the door with my toe and looked quickly around the room.

Then I noticed the footprints on the dusty floor. My throat throbbed. I knelt down, and touched one of the little puddles, the wet shape of her foot.

I followed the prints backward through the kitchen into the bathroom. They started there, at the edge of her bathtub. Outside, it was too soon for lilacs (they wouldn't start blooming until May), but in here their wet perfume filled the air. She'd been here so recently, her footprints were still wet and everything smelled of her. I ran back to the bedroom and reached for the towel that was draped across the back of a chair. I picked it up and pressed it to my face. It was still damp.

Through the fading steam in the bathroom, I looked at my face, at the makeup streaked in carnival colors, at the freckles on my exposed skin, at the way the fabric of my blouse clung to my breasts, and I cried. She wasn't looking back at me from the mirror. I had become everything she wasn't. I took the damp towel I'd been clutching and wiped at my face until it burned, until everything was clean. I soaked it in hot water and made the face in the mirror melt away.

Later I looked for other mementoes, other things she might have left behind, but there was nothing. And soon, the footprints evaporated, and I wasn't sure it had really happened at all. The only evidence of her intrusion was the torn-up backyard.

Olivia, the widow, stood in my living room in the dress I had finally finished. She was balancing on a milk crate so that I could adjust the hem. With pins in my mouth, I asked her, "Well?"

She looked at her reflection in the full-length mirror I had purchased for this purpose and nodded gravely. She is pretty in a very standard way: a homecoming-queen, catalog-model way. Blond hair, eternally coiffed. Brown eyes that might seem too small if not articulated by chocolate eyeliner and mascara. She is one of those girls who knows how to make the best of what she's been given. She'll probably grow old fighting, believing in the power of cosmetic potions. I'd started noticing things like this lately. I couldn't help trying to imagine my friends (as well as strangers) as elderly.

"Where is the wedding again?" I asked her.

"At St. Mary's. The reception's at Dunphy's Pub. He's Catholic. *Irish.*" She held her arms away from her body, awkwardly.

"Relax," I said. "Let your shoulders drop."

"Sorry." She laughed uncomfortably. "I'm so tense."

"A wedding's a big deal," I said. I'm familiar with the posture of brides.

"I'm afraid I won't be able to do it," she said, turning her head to look at me. I was inspecting a little snag in the hem.

"Sure you will. You just need to breathe. Besides, look at you." I gestured to her reflection in the mirror. "You look perfect."

She smiled sadly. She kept looking at me, tentative and puzzled. "Do you think he knows I'm getting married?"

I knew she meant her dead husband.

"I don't know," I said. "I'd like to think so."

She looked back at her reflection and shook her head. "He'd hate John. I know he would. He'd think he was arrogant."

I kept pinning the bottom of her dress, trying to keep my fingers from trembling. The silk was slippery.

"And I keep imagining him sitting in the church, watching all of this, this *display*. He wasn't religious. We had our wedding up at his folks' camp on Gormlaith. He'd think this was silly." The hem lifted as her shoulders tensed.

"Breathe," I said.

"Sorry," she said, the hem falling again. "I don't know what the matter is with me."

I knew though, what she meant. I worried about the decisions people would make after I was gone. I was afraid to leave Becca alone. Afraid of the consequences of my departure.

I finished the hem, and Olivia stepped off the milk crate. She slipped out of the dress, carefully, and I noticed that she was slimmer than the last fitting. I've seen this before. I usually wait until the week before the wedding to sew the buttons on wedding dresses. A body under stress can change incredibly over even a short time.

After she left and I had put the dress back in its plastic garment bag and hung it in the closet, I closed the curtains in the window, took all my clothes off, and looked in the full-length mirror. I hadn't looked at myself in months, except for glimpses of my face in the steamy bathroom mirror. I didn't know what my body looked like anymore.

I stepped onto the milk crate for a better view, the plastic grid pressing painfully into the soles of my bare feet. *Ravaged.* That was the word. I remembered it from a book he read to me all those years ago. About a girl and her older lover. She had said that after a certain point in time, her face changed. She had grown old in an instant. The face she wore after that moment was ravaged, and for the rest of her life she would have to grow into that old face.

I wonder if he knew what he was doing to me. I wonder if he ever feels bad for the part he played. All of this time I have felt guilty for ruining his life, but I wonder if he ever thinks about how he ruined mine. He took something with him that night. Something that belonged to me. It wasn't something as simple as a disposable razor or a rubber band ball. It wasn't something he could return in the mail when he was done using it.

O *nce. Upon a time that did not exist except inside his walls, in-side the light of a winter afternoon, I chose between them. And I chose him over my mother.*

Under covers, under fingers, I told him the secrets she had taught me. The ones about glass. The ones about light. And the ones about why she left us and never came back. I still hear the melody of this story, the true one that I have always known, but never wanted to be-lieve. In gossamer whispers, I gave him a spectrum of explanations that she never gave to me. Poppy, mandarin, maize. When she left, she took everything with her, except for her children. Avocado, jade and blue, blue, blue. It had little to do with Daddy, and everything to do with growing old as only somebody's mother. She knew she was more than that, and she gave us up to prove it. Plum. Violet. Wine. The truth was that she never loved us enough to stay.

And when he told me to let go of her, said it was time to let her go, I gave him bone, silver, snow. I gave him my shoulders. I undressed. I undressed. I undressed until nothing was left. And he made me believe I didn't need her anymore. Inside his walls, inside that light, I grew old.

But I told him, through colors, that I would leave, too. That one day, I would be the one to pack a bag filled with broken things, and leave. I warned him.

Once. Upon a time that did not exist except for inside his walls, inside the light of a winter afternoon, I chose between them. And I chose him.

FIVE

Becca is directing a production of *My Fair Lady* at the high school, and I have agreed to do the costumes. Now that the widow's dress is done, this is a slow time of year for me. I won't get the rush of prom dress orders until April, and this year there will be fewer June weddings than usual. The black flies last June were so bad that a lot of girls who have always dreamed of outdoor weddings have decided to wait until later in the summer.

Getting kids involved in theater these days is next to impossible. Becca cast everyone who tried out, and she was still short. As a result, she will play Eliza Doolittle and Kit, the teacher she brought to Christmas, will be the professor. She's secretly coveted this role for years. She's happier than she has been in months.

"I promise I'll still be here every day, it's just a couple of hours in the afternoon," she said nervously when she told me.

"That's great," I said. *"Please* do it. I'll be fine. You know how much better I've been feeling lately."

She looked at me, dubious, but soon a smile spread across her face. "Oi think I'll do it, then, me lady," she said, dipping into a curtsy.

"Good," I said.

She won't admit it, but I think Kit and she have been flirting.

On the weekends we scour Boo's for clothes we can turn into costumes. We go to the fabric store and wander through the rows and rows of bolts until we're dizzy. I have transformed the living room into a costume shop. I lay out the old clothes and the new fabric on my floor, shoeing Bog away. He's been sleeping a lot lately, and he always wants to nap where I am working.

I'm still tired. The doctor assured me that it's a perfectly normal side effect of the tamoxifen, that a small percentage of patients become lethargic, but I'm skeptical. It's the same fatigue I've been feeling all along. When I first got sick and started treatment, I fought sleep. I'd stay up late at night watching movies. I'd scrub my kitchen floor just to prove that I could. I'm not so proud anymore. I give in. Every afternoon while Becca is at rehearsals, I put away the fabric and half-made costumes and take a long, long nap. I allow myself to sink into the deep sleeps that scared me only months ago. It feels good to let go. To fall. I sleep until Becca comes and wakes me, usually two or three hours later. It's a luxury, all this sleep. I have been feeling more and more like Bog, who naps with me as well as throughout the day.

Today, I try to read before I fall asleep, but my eyes start to cross and then close only a few minutes after I lay down. I close my book and let myself go. I wake up when Becca curls up next to me on the bed. She is facing the opposite wall. I touch her shoulder, and it is shaking. She is crying.

"Becca?"

She rolls over, facing me, and says, "I think Bog is dead."

We put Bog's body in the backseat and drove to Gormlaith. The water was still cold, but no longer frozen, and we borrowed a boat from one of the year-round inhabitants.

"Where you going?" the old man asked, peering out at the car.

"Just out to the island. We'll have it back to you in a couple of hours." Becca'd said she would do all of the talking. My throat was too thick.

He looked at us, skeptical, and then reached into a little wooden cabinet by the door and took a silver key off the hook. "Here's the key to the lock. It's the second dock there."

"Thank you," Becca said. "We'll be back in just a little bit." And when he crossed his arms, still suspicious, she shoved her hands into her pocket and pulled out her wallet. She pressed it into his hands and said, "Here. Collateral."

He nodded and closed the door behind us.

We put Bog's body and a snow shovel in the boat and pushed away from the shore, toward the cold center of Gormlaith. I touched his fur, familiar and fine, ran my fingers across his barrel chest, down his skinny legs. I adopted him almost seven years ago. He would have been killed; at two years old, his racing days were over. When I brought him home, he didn't know how to navigate stairs, and he was afraid of loud noises. I tried to crate train him, on the advice of a friend, but inside the giant cage, he must have thought he was back in his pen at the racetrack, because he started to drool and cry, and pee made a hot puddle around his feet. When I looked at his wet brown eyes, I knew we would be friends. I brought the crate back and let him sleep with me on my bed for the next seven years.

Becca rowed the whole way out to the island, pulling the boat heavy with me and Bog's body up onto the shore so I wouldn't have to step into the icy water. She offered to carry Bog, but I shook my head and lifted him into my arms.

While she dug into the still slightly frozen ground, I sat under a tree and touched Bog's belly. It took almost an hour to make a hole big enough to put him in, and Becca's hands were raw from the shovel's metal handle.

She rested her foot on the shovel and her chin on the handle when she was done.

"Ready, sweetie?" she asked me softly.

I lay down and hugged Bog's smelly old body and blinked away my tears.

"'Bye, friend," I said, kissing his snout.

Becca looked out toward the water as I picked him up and set him gently in the shallow grave. Then she covered him. And we got back in the boat and headed back to the shore.

The sun was struggling to break through one heavy cloud. Each time it succeeded, the water sparkled like glass beneath us. I stuck my fingers into the cold water, letting them become numb.

"I want to be cremated," I said, staring down into the murky water. "And I want you to come out here, on the sunniest day in summer, and put my ashes in the water."

Becca's arms were shaking from the effort of digging and rowing. She took her hands off the oars and let them rest in the oar locks.

"Will you do that for me?" I asked.

Becca stared past me at the island becoming smaller in the distance.

I reached for her hands, forcing her to look at me.

"Of course," she said, wiping at tears with the back of one freckled arm. "On the sunniest day."

"Thank you," I whispered. I stood up and motioned for her to switch places with me. But after only a few strokes, my left arm was so tired, the boat just started to move in a futile circle.

"Let me," she said, and I did.

Mr. Hammer did not come back. A "For Sale" sign appeared in the front yard as soon as the ground was thawed enough to hammer the post in. The summer caretaker came early, to clean out the things he had left behind.

While Becca was at rehearsals for *Peter Pan,* I took the bus back to Gormlaith every day after school and watched his house become empty. I made friends with the caretaker from a distance. While she swept the front walk and removed the storm windows, I sat on the grassy shore with my homework. I watched the ice melt. I watched everything turn green. Soon enough school would be done, and Becca and I would watch the summer people from this same shore. Becca might fall in love with the boy whose parents rented the big blue camp. We might watch him like this, from a distance, all summer. We might lie in the grass with the other Pond girls, the ones who emerged from the woods in the summer in their one-piece bathing suits, with their pale skin glowing in the new sun. But for now, it was just me and the lady who was in charge of removing Mr. Hammer. She waved to me sometimes, and I waved back.

I thought about Daddy, starting his job at the dump again. I knew that some of Mr. Hammer's things would arrive there, bundled neatly into bags. Boxes of stale cereal, bottles of shampoo. All that was nothing but trash. But it was likely that the other things, the salvageable things, would wind up at Boo's. Scuffed wingtips, pot holders, and candlesticks. A kitchen clock, a single sock. Clothespins. I wondered, sometimes, about the kitten.

I watched things arranging themselves around me. It was amazing, I thought, the way the world wants to be an organized place.

The Tamoxifen isn't working. Of course, I don't tell Becca this. She is sure that it will save me, at least for a little while. Even my doctor is optimistic; it sometimes takes several months before any progress is made. I will feel nothing but side effects until then, and I shouldn't mistake this for failure. For futility. But I *know,* the same way I knew that my mother had come home and taken a bath in our house that day. And, as when I knew my mother had returned, there is something pacifying in this understanding. It's something I can hold on to, something that makes sense. I feel finally as if I know where I am going; it's the first time in a long time that I've had this sort of certainty. Now I can go about my business, clean the closets out.

But some things are best kept secret. This is one thing I learned from Mr. Hammer. So I allow Becca to believe. I have so little to offer her, and I've been so selfish. I'm trying to return her kindness, with the gift of innocence. Of hope.

I sat in the auditorium one afternoon in late March, and watched her transformed onstage into Eliza Doolittle, and then again into a fair lady. She's a wonderful actress. I am ashamed that I haven't noticed before. Never mind that she's been rehearsing for this part since we were children. She is just as good as the actresses I've seen in the touring plays that come to Boston and Montreal. As she sang, and danced, a terrible sadness descended over me. I couldn't believe how stupid I had been. I have always just assumed she'd told me the truth: that she returned to Quimby because she couldn't make it in New York. But that night after rehearsals, when I asked her and she answered, I knew she was lying.

"Did you come back here because of me?" I asked. "Because you found out I was sick?"

We were sitting on the edge of the stage eating tuna sandwiches I had made at home.

"What do you mean?" she asked.

"From New York."

She stuffed a handful of salt-and-vinegar potato chips between the bread and crunched down on the sandwich.

"I came for the job," she said, her mouth full.

"To teach *social studies?*"

She nodded, but my heart ached.

"Becca, why would you do that? How could you give everything up for me? For this?" I waved wildly at the high school auditorium.

"I didn't give up anything," she said. "I wanted to come home."

I was accustomed to departures. I wasn't used to people coming home.

We lie to each other to save each other, and we keep some secrets to save ourselves. So when I open up the door of my closet and walk in, through the sleeves of summer dresses and boxes of letters and collected things, I tell her I'm only spring cleaning. That the sunshine and blue sky have inspired me to organize my life.

Boo found an elf costume donated by the elementary school. It would have been too small for anyone else, but Becca still hadn't grown. It needed mending, so I brought it home along with a beat-up sewing machine that Boo had been unable to sell. While Quinn moped around the house, wishing the snow hadn't melted, I made Becca's Peter Pan costume.

Quinn had come in second at the state meet. He and the winner, a boy from Killington, had been competing neck and neck all season. But Quinn had a full scholarship to UC Boulder for the fall. Now that ski season was over, he was home on the weekends, and he didn't know what to do with himself.

While I sat at the kitchen table, repairing the green body-suit and felt cap, Quinn stood on his hands, his feet pressing against the window.

"You'll go right through," I said.

His face was red, gravity pulling all of his features down.

"Your head will explode," I said, biting off a piece of green thread with my teeth.

He kicked his legs down and stood up, the scarlet draining slowly out of his face again. "Let's *do* something," he said. "Let's go somewhere."

"I'm trying to make Becca's costume," I said. "She needs it by Monday. Dress rehearsal."

"Boring," he said.

Quinn had a way of wearing me down. I could have been studying for the bar exam or discovering a new planet. He could still distract me. He must have known I'd follow him anywhere.

In the car I said, "Where are we going?"

"Shhhh."

We stopped at Hudson's for gas and he handed me a paper bag. Inside there were two roast-beef grinders, a bag of Cheetos, and two cans of iced tea. I didn't ask him again, I just waited until we got there.

We took the old toll road that goes to the top of Franklin Mountain. It was icy, but Quinn put chains on the tires before we headed up. I worried a few times that we would get stuck, but Quinn kept moving us forward, up into the clouds. We parked at a clearing near the top of the mountain, where the old fire tower was. A long time ago, before we were born, a man lived up there in the summer. All day long he sat in the tower, looking out over the forests surrounding Quimby, and radioed the fire station in town if he saw smoke or flames threatening the woods below. His one-room cabin was still standing, though the fire tower was falling down. I'd never been all the way up here before.

Quinn got out of the car and motioned for me to follow him. I grabbed the bag with our lunch and got out of the car. It was colder up here at this elevation, but the sun was bright. There was still a bit of snow on the ground and in the branches of the trees, but not enough to ski on anymore. The ground was littered with rusty beer cans, and there were the blackened remnants of a campfire.

He was climbing the steps to the tower before I could stop him. I followed, testing every step before putting my full weight on it. At the top, on the rickety platform, my stomach flip-flopped a couple of times with mild vertigo, and then settled.

It was incredible. I could see for miles and miles. The fire watcher must have felt like God up here, looking out over the whole world, protecting it.

Quinn stood up and held his arms out and whooped, "Wa-hoooo!" His voice echoed once, deep and far away. "Try it!" he said.

I set our lunches down on the floor and held tightly onto Quinn's shoulder.

"Come on!" he said and whooped again.

"Wahoo," I said. No echo.

"Louder!"

"Wahoooo!" I let it come from inside my belly this time. And it came back to me, a smaller, weaker "Wahoo."

Quinn laughed. He reached into the paper bag for his sandwich and tore into it, mustard and mayonnaise and toma-toes running down his chin.

I let go of his shoulder and stood at the edge of the world.

"Wahooooo!" And this time, the valleys below us, the forests and fields, returned the favor. "Wahooooo!" My own voice, a gift from below.

I understand what it is that illuminates you, what can turn listless into the exact shade of glow that is you. I am privy to the nature of your yellow, what renders you indigo, red, or the violet of sometimes.

When I found the music box again, wrapped up in Mum's blue dress, I brought it out into the living room and set it on the coffee table. I opened the lid, half expecting it to start playing "Edelweiss" when I wound it up. But it was still broken, the music trapped inside.

You have allowed me this. You have given me the secrets of fireflies, the intricate filament of your incandescence, the filigree embrace of Day rising from Night's reluctant arms.

I thought about looking harder, using the People Finder on the Internet to find his address. I imagined myself walking up the steps to his door.

You have stolen stars by the handful and used them against sorrow, captured them for days when gray threatens us with its naughty fingers to extinguish. On those days, the blue days, I am grateful for the flicker you provide.

I imagined knocking, handing him the music box. I imagined all the things I wouldn't know how to say. Because this was simply an even exchange. He gave me my voice, *my gift,* and then took it away. It was only fair. I had taken something from him, and he from me.

On the other days, the best days, I am thrilled by all of your impossible hues.

I had read the poem inside so many times now that it was hardly different in my mind from the poems I'd read in Mr. Ludwig's class. The phrases were like mantras now. This poem could have been something I'd learned for an exam at school. They were words not connected to me by anything more than a vague memory of someone I used to be. The person I was at fourteen and the world was comprised of colors and lights. When I really believed that there were colors without names.

(Who else knows how many colors are inside the beating of a monarch's wings?)

After our matinee on Sunday, we rolled down the car windows and stopped for hot fudge sundaes at the drive-in. Becca always gets marshmallow, nuts, and whipped cream. I like mine more streamlined: just ice cream, fudge, and a cherry on top.

"Can we stop by the Atheneum?" I asked.

Becca looked at me over the top of her monstrous sundae and nodded. She ate as we drove, managing to keep her new white pants clean.

"I'll be out in a second," I said, when she parked in the library parking lot. "Finish your ice cream."

I ran up the steps, my arms and legs feeling remarkably energetic. Inside, I logged on to a free computer and tried once again to *compose*. But this time, instead of offering apologies, I offered him his own words. I retyped the poem he'd given me all of those years ago; I returned it. And as I clicked on "Send," I said a little prayer that, in exchange, he might send my voice back to me.

At home, the world seemed empty without Bog. I couldn't bear to get rid of his bed yet. I left it sitting in front of the fireplace as if it were just another piece of furniture. I could still smell him on it. I would have to bring it to the cleaners soon and then give it to Boo to sell in her shop.

Becca made Sunday dinner: stuffed Cornish hens and vegetables for everything that ailed me. She has become an expert of the healing powers of foods. Everything I eat now has a purpose. Heart. Lungs. Bones. And while she busied herself in the kitchen, I dug through the closet for an old shoe box.

Please let me see you, she had said.

For a long time I thought about finding her, about driving along the coast of Maine or New Hampshire, Maryland or Massachusetts, searching. I imagined conversations with strangers, directing me here or there for her. I could see myself finding her apartment or house or motel room. I could even imagine the sea-weathered walls and could almost hear myself knocking on the door. But I also knew that I wouldn't recognize her anymore. She could never be how she lived in my memory. She would only be the fragments of someone I used to know.

Please let me see you.

So, here I was. I wrapped the music box in newspaper and put it inside the shoe box. I covered the box in brown paper and wrote my mother's last address on the front. She always knew what to do with broken things; perhaps she would know what to do with this one.

And that night, as Becca snored softly on the couch, I understood what I'd wanted. I'd only wanted for someone to take care of me. To stay. Someone real. Someone whole. And I understood, finally, she was already here.

On the night of Becca's performance in Peter Pan, I went to the shed to look for something to give her as a gift. To thank her and to apologize, as if gratitude and apologies necessarily go hand in hand. I turned on the lightbulb over Mum's worktable, and looked for something, but everything here was broken. She'd left before she finished mending everything.

Inside my room, I stood on my bed and stared through the red glass heart at the full moon outside. She said that without light, the stained glass was useless, that it was not the glass that was beautiful, but the quality of light behind it. I imagined that the night she left, the sky was without moon or stars. Without light, she might not have been able to see how beautiful everything was that she had made.

I carefully lifted the wire suspending it and laid the pane gently on my bed. I wrapped it in a T-shirt and put it in my backpack. Quinn drove me to the high school auditorium, and we sat together in the middle seats of the middle row.

Becca was perfect as Peter Pan. Like Peter Pan, she still hadn't grown up. Maybe she never would; maybe all it took to stay a child was belief. And I knew that despite the harness and wires holding her off the ground, she *believed* that night that she could fly. And for a moment, I believed, too.

After the show, she came running to us before she went to her parents who were standing in their coats waiting by the door.

"I've got to go see my parents, but I'll be right back," she said, out of breath, flushed.

Quinn squeezed my hand. "She was great."

"She *is* great," I said.

I gave the glass picture to Becca, and she touched all the places where the shattered pieces were joined. She held it up to the streetlight outside the school and looked through each color, changing the color of the world.

It was almost summer. Soon, the sun would shine and shine. I knew the way that dawn looked through the red. I knew the colors of sunset it had made on my walls.

My mother taught me how to find grace in wreckage. She taught me not how to reassemble, but how to rearrange. The stained-glass pictures she made were certain evidence that things can be broken and put back together, and that the mended thing will be more beautiful than the original. That true beauty is in the cracks, in the places where the pieces have once been shattered and then mended.

Years later, I am sitting in the same auditorium watching Becca become someone else on stage. She still hasn't grown up; she still believes in the possibility of flight. But tonight the gift I have brought for her is something she won't be able to use until after I'm gone.

I felt silly making it. I sat at the kitchen table, staring at the tape recorder for almost an hour before I hit "Record." I'd practiced a few times, but I was self-conscious. I closed my windows and waited until all the little old ladies had left the park, as if their hearing aids would pick up my voice from this far away.

Then I closed my eyes and waited for the colors to come. The color my mother called *holiday*. The color of sadness, of sorrow. And then slowly the color of sunshine. On water on the sunniest summer day.

SIX

If summer here were made of colored glass, this is the way the light would shine through this summer. Sparklers reflecting in the water of the fountain, lights sparkling in the gazebo in the park. The pink of cotton candy, orange snow cones, and the color of breeze.

From my window I watch Kit and Becca holding hands, walking across the park. They spread a blanket near the fountain and rest there, listening to the band, listening to each other's stories about what came before. Becca has started wearing her hair a different way, down around her shoulders, like liquid fire. The light catches this and holds it, saves it for later.

She will come home after the concert, after she and Kit have stood on the front porch each trying to figure out whether or not the other wants to be kissed, for what might seem to them like hours. And then she'll come up the stairs quietly, so as not to wake me up. I sleep in the living room now, because dawn comes through these windows first. We moved my bed out here three weeks ago. Becca says we're allowed to break these kinds of rules.

I'll open my eyes when I hear the teakettle starting to whistle. She'll try to pull it from the heat in time, but it will already be breathing steam. I think a little part of her hopes that I'll wake up and keep her company on nights like these. Help her to figure the night out. But tonight, I'm very tired. I feel sleep descending like quiet thieves.

I look out the window at the park below and she looks up and sees me. She smiles, waving, and I wave back.

Summer here is made of colored glass. I walk barefoot along the amber path that leads to the gate, put my hand on the amethyst knob, and step carefully into the garden. Moon reflects in cobalt pools: slivers of grass are wet with dew. Emerald blades. Topaz stepping-stones beneath my feet, and wings of tangerine. And in this evening glass garden, I remember the song I've forgotten, the one I used to hum in my mother's arms. The one I made up to keep myself safe, to make myself sleep. I remember the color of sorrow, of sorcery, of sorry. And I sing it softly, so that nothing breaks.

UNDRESSING THE MOON

T. Greenwood

ABOUT THIS GUIDE

The following discussion questions and author interview
are included to enhance your group's reading of
UNDRESSING THE MOON.

Discussion Questions

1. Early in *Undressing the Moon,* Piper calls herself "a thirty-year-old girl." What caused her to see herself that way? Did she ever become a woman?

2. Piper's mother left when Piper was fourteen years old, but in a way, so did her father. Do you think she was affected more or less by his absence than her mother's? Discuss Piper's relationship with her father before and after her mother left as well as in the present.

3. Discuss Piper's relationships with all of the men in her life: her father, Quinn, Mr. Hammer, Blue Henderson, Jake. How has each of them shaped her as a woman, sexually, physically, and emotionally? Are any or all of them the reason she's single now?

4. In a sense, Piper's mother didn't fully leave; she remained attached with phone calls and gifts. Do you think that made it harder for Piper to deal with her abandonment? Would it have been different if her mother completely disappeared from her life?

5. Piper's mother and father also walked out on Quinn. Talk about how he handled the situation, the role he played as a guardian to Piper, and how his new responsibilities affected his school, work, and skiing.

6. Aunt Boo knew where Piper's mother went but wouldn't share that information. Do you feel that was fair to Piper? Considering what she knew, what role did Boo play in Piper's upbringing? Was she more of a substitute mother

or an accomplice? How do you think she felt about her position? How did Piper feel about it?

7. How does Piper cope with her breast cancer? Do you think it's a healthy way to handle her illness? Do you agree with Becca when she says that Piper isn't trying to stay alive anymore? Why?

8. Piper relies on Becca for emotional strength throughout the novel, both as a teenager and as an adult. How would she have gotten through both periods of her life without Becca? What does Becca give up by helping Piper? What does she gain?

9. The image of glass—broken glass and the stained glass Piper's mother creates—is prevalent in *Undressing the Moon*. What does it represent, beyond the shattering of Piper's life? How does it relate to her current situation? Are there other images that resonate with you? If so, which ones and why?

10. Colors are also important in the novel. Do any in particular stand out to you as being especially strong? How do you feel about Piper's mother describing her voice as "holiday"?

11. Discuss the use of music in the novel as well.

12. Why do you think Piper blamed Mr. Hammer when Jake was the one who really raped her? In the end, was telling Quinn the truth atonement enough for that lie? Talk about Piper's breast cancer as a symbol or manifestation of the guilt she's carried.

13. What is the significance of the widow for whom Piper is making a wedding dress? What does Piper learn from her?

14. Why do you think Piper didn't ultimately go looking for her mother once she found out where she lived? Would you have sought her out if you were in that position? Should Piper have let her back into her life when she attempted to make contact?

15. What do you think happens to Piper after the book ends?

A Conversation with T. Greenwood

What was your inspiration for writing *Undressing the Moon*? Which idea came first, Piper's mother leaving, or her breast cancer?

I actually wanted to write a contemporary version of "Hansel and Gretel." It was a story that terrified me when I was young. The idea of two children being left alone to fend for themselves in the woods was unnerving. And so that is how it began, but then there was another voice that kept interrupting. It took awhile, but what I realized was that it was Piper, years later. There was an urgency to her voice, and so I listened.

For that matter, all of your books include characters with tragic backstories. Does their past usually influence their present, or do you write their history to inform their current story?

I think that we are all defined, to a certain extent, by our childhoods. My childhood memories are so vivid: the tragedies as well as the happy times. I am who I am because of the sorrows I suffered as a kid as well as the bliss. Fictional characters are no different. I almost never write about adult characters without understanding where it is that they came from. What haunts them.

Why did you choose to make Piper such a young woman dealing with cancer? Did you consider making her older? Was it hard to imagine, as a young woman yourself, what it would be like?

I wrote this novel when I was thirty years old, and I kept imagining what I would do if all of a sudden there was no such thing as a future. I actually experienced a minor health scare at the time, and my own future was, if briefly, uncertain. I was rattled by this, and it made me think about a lot of things that might be going through a young woman's mind as she, essentially, prepares to die.

The mother-daughter relationship is prominent in many of your books, but probably not as much as it is in *Undressing the Moon*. Why do you think that dynamic is such rich fodder for you?

I think that the mother-daughter relationship is one of the most wonderfully complex relationships there is. My mother has been a prominent and positive force in my life, and we have maintained a strong relationship over the course of my entire life. In my fiction I really like to explore what happens when there are breaks or fissures in this relationship. I had not had my daughters when I wrote *Undressing the Moon*. *The Hungry Season* is actually the first novel that examines this relationship from the mother's side of the fence.

Many of your books take place at the fictional Lake Gormlaith. Why do you keep going back there? Is it based on a place you know well? Do you plan to revisit it anytime soon in future novels?

Lake Gormlaith was originally based on a real place in northeastern Vermont where I grew up. My grandfather and his father built a cabin ("camp") on a pond there in the 1940s. It is still in our family, and we spend our summers there. However, over the course of four novels, Lake Gormlaith has taken on a life of its own. It is as real to me as any true geographical location. I'll always go back to our camp on the pond, and I suspect I'll always go back to Lake Gormlaith.

Talk a little about your writing process. Do you have a routine? A specific place you go to write, or a particular time of day that's more productive? Do you listen to music or prefer quiet?

I usually ruminate about an idea for a long time (months, even years) before I begin to write. But I like to write the first draft of a novel rather quickly. *Undressing the Moon* was written in five weeks. *This Glittering World* took six. Then comes the long, slow process of revision.

In terms of where and when . . . because I have two little girls, I write wherever and whenever I can. I like to get up early when the house is quiet and write until someone needs me. Then I leave my document open so I can return to it whenever I get time. I have a lovely little office, and I like it quiet. Now that both of my girls are in school, there's a lot more of that than there used to be.

Undressing the Moon is your third published book, originally released in 2002. How has your writing evolved since then, in your more recent novels *Two Rivers*, *The Hungry Season*, and the upcoming *This Glittering World*?

My first three novels were all written from the first-person point of view of a female narrator. In the subsequent novels I have utilized a male narrator and rotating third-person narrators. I like to give myself a challenge with each novel. I wanted a sweeping historical scope and a complex narrator in *Two Rivers*. I wanted to explore the central theme of hunger in *The Hungry Season*. And in *This Glittering World*, I wanted to write a tragedy. My hope is that I am growing as a writer with each subsequent book, and that I am not some sort of complacent one-trick pony.

Is there a particular book of yours that you enjoyed writing more than the others or that has a subject to which you felt more of a personal connection? Were any of them easier to write? More difficult?

Two Rivers was the most difficult. The male narrator was demanding, the research was extensive, the plot was complicated, and I had two very small children at the time. But I loved writing it, and I am proud of it because of its ambition. But *Undressing the Moon* and *This Glittering World* were both these magical books that almost seemed to write themselves.

Your books tend to deal with serious topics, such as cancer, rape, and Mr. Hammer's inappropriate relationship with Piper in *Undressing the Moon;* Munchausen's by Proxy in *Nearer Than the Sky;* racial tension in *Two Rivers;* and eating disorders in *The Hungry Season*. Yet you deal with them all very sensitively and explore them through the eyes of relatable characters. What spurs you to tackle such profound ideas?

A reviewer once referred to me, somewhat snidely, as "family damage specialist, T. Greenwood." I thought that was funny, like something I could hang on my office door. But if you're writing about people, you are also always writing about families (of some sort or another). And who wants to read about happy families? I don't. I want to read about struggle, about people who both love and hate each other, people who fight and hurt and then embrace each other.

The very nature of narrative is that there needs to be conflict. Problems. Trouble. I simply figure out what my characters' problems are and then see them through them.

If you could go back and do revisions on *Undressing the Moon,* would you change anything? What?

I wouldn't change anything. I *can't* change anything. When you publish, you let go. The last brushstroke was already made. (I actually don't reread my older novels because I'm afraid of this.)

Has having kids changed the way you write or the themes of your books?

Yes and no. I think being a parent has changed my perspective on the world in too many ways to count. And that will naturally affect my writing.

In terms of the way I write . . . I think they have taught me that writing only when I am inspired is a luxury I no longer can afford. They have taught me a work ethic, a perspiration over inspiration mentality. I write around their lives, around their needs. If I want to be a writer, this flexibility is necessary.

Have you ever reread your old books? If so, what do you think of them now?

I have, and it was a mistake. It's like looking at artwork you did in high school. All I can see are the flaws. It's embarrassing.

Who are your favorite authors, past and present? Does reading their work influence yours at all?

Dorothy Allison, Miranda Beverly-Whittemore, Chris Bohjalian, Michael Chabon, Dan Chaon, Marguerite Duras, Louise Erdrich, Mary Gaitskill, Jane Hamilton, Kathryn Harrison, Ursula Hegi, Alice Hoffman, John Irving, Mary Karr, Jim Kokoris, Barbara Kingsolver, Wally Lamb, Toni Morrison, Howard

Frank Mosher, Anaïs Nin, Flannery O'Connor, Tom Perrotta, Richard Russo, J. D. Salinger, Scott Spencer, Virginia Woolf . . . just a handful of the many, many writers who have influenced me as a writer (and a person) over the years.

What are you working on now?

This Glittering World, my next book, comes out in January 2011. Beyond that, I have a few projects simmering on various back burners, but I am most compelled right now by a sort of contemporary Isaac and Abraham story. I've only written the climactic scene. I don't know what leads up to it, or what will happen after.